W

W9-BGG-445

Contents

Three Yuletide Poems

S. Omar Barker

"Draggin' In the Tree"
"Bunkhouse Christmas"
"A Cowboy's Christmas Prayer"

S. Omar Barker (1894–1985) has been called "the poet laureate of the Old West." For more than fifty years he published hundreds of colorfully authentic Western poems and verses in both slick-paper and pulp magazines and in other publications; the best of these can be found in such collections as Buckaroo Ballads *(1928),* Songs of the Saddleman *(1954), and* Rawhide Rhymes *(1968). He was at his most evocative when writing about the various seasons, as in the oft anthologized "Empty Saddles at Christmas," which won a 1966 Spur Award from the Western Writers of America, and the three lesser-known but no less noteworthy yuletide verses which follow.*

Draggin' In the Tree

The cowboy ain't no lumberjack, an' if you want the facks,
One thing he ain't the fondest of is choppin' with an ax.
But when December snow has got the range all wrapped in white,
There is one job of choppin' that he seems to like all right.
A sharp ax on his shoulder, he will ride off up the draw

Until he finds an evergreen without a single flaw.
A spruce, a fir, a juniper that's shaped just to a T
To set up in a corner for the ranchhouse Christmas tree.

As like as not, last summer while a-ridin' after cows,
He noticed just the tree he wants, with green an' graceful boughs
That's stout enough to ornament without no droop nor saggin',
But still a tree that ain't too big to fetch without a wagon.
It may be that he picked it out when August sun was hot,
But he knows where to find it, for his mind has marked the spot.
It ain't no chore to chop it down, an' if the snow is deep,
He drags it in behind his horse. It warms him up a heap
To see them rancher kids run out a-hollerin' with glee
To watch him an' admire him when he's bringin' in the tree.

Them kids may not belong to him, but that don't matter none—
His boss' brood, a nester's brats—it's still a heap of fun
To some ol' lonesome cowpoke, an' it sets his heart aglow
To come a-draggin' in the tree across the Christmas snow.
Sometimes when there's a schoolmarm an' she wants a tree at
    school,
She gets half a dozen, for you'll find that as a rule
At least that many cowboys, in sweet education's cause,
Will somehow get to feelin' that they're kin to Santy Claus!

Sometimes the rangeland's lonesome an' sometimes it's kind o' grim,
But not when every ranchhouse has a Christmas tree to trim.
An' though the wild cowpuncher ain't no hand to swing an ax,
Across the white December snow you'll often find his tracks
A-leadin' to the timber, then back out again once more,
A-draggin' in the Christmas tree—his purt' near favorite chore!

Bunkhouse Christmas

'Twas Christmas Eve out on the ranch, and all the winter crew
  Was settin' round the bunkhouse fire with nothin' else to do
  But let their fancies wander on the thoughts of Christmas chuck,

And what they'd like the best to eat if just they had the luck
To set down to a table where the feast was laid so thick
That all they'd have to do was reach to take their choice and pick.

Young Sleepy Kid, the wrangler, claims he'd love a stummick-ache
From stuffin' steady half a day on choclit-frosted cake.
"A slab of turkey breast," smacks Pete, "and good ol' punkin pie!"
"I'd reach for oyster dressin'!" Lobo Luther heaves a sigh.
"It ain't no Christmas feed for me," says little Charlie Moss,
"Without brown turkey gravy and some red cranberry sauce!"
"Mince pie!" avers ol' Swaller-Fork. "The kind my ma could make.
It beats your punkin forty ways—and also choclit cake!"

So each they named their fancy, till their chops begun to drip,
Then ol' Pop Williams gives a snort and rubs his crippled hip.
He hitches to the window, sorter sizin' up the night.
"Well, boys," he says, "it's Christmas Eve, and if I figger right,
That snow's too deep for travel, so before I hit the hay,
Upon the subject now in hand I'll have my little say.
It ain't what's in your stummick that's the most important part.
It's the feelin's of your gizzard, or in other words, your heart.
A-doin' others kindness is the road to Christmas cheer,
But that, of course, ain't possible, the way we're snowbound here.

It looks like all that we can do for our good Christmas deed
Is hustle all the livestock in and give 'em extry feed.
To hungry cows an extry fork of hay will seem as nice
As when a hungry cowboy finds a raisin in his rice.
And as for favorite Christmas chuck, I'll name mine now, to wit:
It's beef and beans and biskits—*'cause I know that's what we'll git!*"

A Cowboy's Christmas Prayer

I ain't much good at prayin', and You may not know me, Lord.
I ain't much seen in churches where they preach Thy Holy Word,
But You may have observed me out here on the lonely plains,
A-lookin' after cattle, feelin' thankful when it rains,

Admirin' Thy great handiwork, the miracle of grass,
Aware of Thy kind spirit in the way it comes to pass
That hired men on horseback and the livestock that we tend
Can look up at the stars at night and know we've got a Friend.

So here's ol' Christmas comin' on, remindin' us again
Of Him whose comin' brought good will into the hearts of men.
A cowboy ain't no preacher, Lord, but if You'll hear my prayer,
I'll ask as good as *we* have got for all men everywhere.
Don't let no hearts be bitter, Lord, don't let no child be cold;
Make easy beds for them that's sick, and them that's weak and old.
Let kindness bless the trail we ride, no matter what we're after,
And sorter keep us on Your side, in tears as well as laughter.

I've seen old cows a-starvin', and it ain't no happy sight:
Please don't leave no one hungry, Lord, on Thy good Christmas
    night—
No man, no child, no woman, and no critter on four feet.
I'll aim to do my best to help You find 'em chuck to eat.

I'm just a sinful cowpoke, Lord—ain't got no business prayin'—
But still I hope You'll ketch a word or two of what I'm sayin'.
We speak of Merry Christmas, Lord—I reckon You'll agree
There ain't no Merry Christmas for nobody that ain't free.
So one thing more I'll ask You, Lord, just help us what You can
To save some seeds of freedom for the future sons of man!

How Santa Claus Came to Simpson's Bar

Bret Harte

Once the highest-paid short-story writer in America, Bret Harte wrote perhaps the finest fictional accounts of the lusty and sometimes violent way of life in the mining camps and boomtowns of the California Gold Rush. His writings cover some eighteen volumes of prose and poetry, and include such famous stories as "The Luck of Roaring Camp" and "The Outcasts of Poker Flat," and the memorable short novel M'liss: An Idyll of Red Mountain *(1863). "How Santa Claus Came to Simpson's Bar" is another of his best stories—the poignant tale of the eve of Christmas Day, 1862, in a Sierra mining camp that "clung like a swallow's nest to the rocky entablature and splintered capitals of Table Mountain."*

It had been raining in the valley of the Sacramento. The North Fork had overflowed its banks, and Rattlesnake Creek was impassable. The few boulders that had marked the summer ford at Simpson's Crossing were obliterated by a vast sheet of water stretching to the foothills. The upstage was stopped at Granger's; the last mail had been abandoned in the tules, the rider swimming for his life. "An area," remarked the *Sierra Avalanche,* with pensive local pride, "as large as the State of Massachusetts is now under water."

Nor was the weather any better in the foothills. The mud lay deep on the mountain road; wagons that neither physical force nor moral objurgation could move from the evil ways into which they had fallen encumbered the track, and the way to Simpson's Bar was indicated by broken-down teams and hard swearing. And further on, cut off and inaccessible, rained upon and bedraggled, smitten by high winds and threatened by high water, Simpson's Bar, on the eve of Christmas Day, 1862, clung like a swallow's nest to the rocky entablature and splintered capitals of Table Mountain, and shook in the blast.

As night shut down on the settlement, a few lights gleamed through the mist from the windows of cabins on either side of the highway, now crossed and gullied by lawless streams and swept by marauding winds. Happily most of the population were gathered at Thompson's store, clustered around a red-hot stove, at which they silently spat in some accepted sense of social communion that perhaps rendered conversations unnecessary. Indeed, most methods of diversion had long since been exhausted on Simpson's Bar; high water had suspended the regular occupations on gulch and on river, and a consequent lack of money and whiskey had taken the zest from most illegitimate recreation. Even Mr. Hamlin was fain to leave the Bar with fifty dollars in his pocket—the only amount actually realized of the large sums won by him in the successful exercise of his arduous profession. "Ef I was asked," he remarked somewhat later—"ef I was asked to pint out a purty little village where a retired sport as didn't care for money could exercise hisself, frequent and lively, I'd say Simpson's Bar; but for a young man with a large family depending on his exertions, it don't pay." As Mr. Hamlin's family consisted mainly of female adults, this remark is quoted rather to show the breadth of his humor than the exact extent of his responsibilities.

Howbeit, the unconscious objects of this satire sat that evening in the listless apathy begotten of idleness and lack of excitement. Even the sudden splashing of hoofs before the door did not arouse them. Dick Bullen alone paused in the act of scraping out his pipe, and lifted his head, but no other one of the group indicated any interest in, or recognition of, the man who entered.

It was a figure familiar enough to the company, and known in Simpson's Bar as "The Old Man." A man of perhaps fifty years; grizzled and scant of hair, but still fresh and youthful of complexion. A face full of ready but not very powerful sympathy, with a chameleonlike aptitude for taking on the shade and color of contiguous moods and feelings. He had evidently just left some hilarious companions, and did not at first notice the gravity of the group, but clapped the shoulder of the nearest man jocularly, and threw himself into a vacant chair.

"Jest heard the best thing out, boys! Ye know Smiley, over yar—Jim Smiley—funniest man in the Bar? Well, Jim was jest telling the richest yarn about"—

"Smiley's a—fool," interrupted a gloomy voice.

"A particular—skunk," added another in sepulchral accents.

A silence followed these positive statements. The Old Man glanced quickly around the group. Then his face slowly changed. "That's so," he said reflectively, after a pause, "certainly a sort of a skunk and suthin' of a fool. In course." He was silent for a moment, as in painful contemplation of the unsavoriness and folly of the unpopular Smiley. "Dismal weather, ain't it?" he added, now fully embarked on the current of prevailing sentiment. "Mighty rough papers on the boys, and no show for money this season. And tomorrow's Christmas."

There was a movement among the men at this announcement, but whether of satisfaction or disgust was not plain. "Yes," continued the Old Man in the lugubrious tone he had within the last few moments unconsciously adopted,—"yes, Christmas, and tonight's Christmas Eve. Ye see, boys, I kinder thought—that is, I sorter had an idee, jest passin' like, you know—that maybe ye'd all like to come over to my house tonight and have a sort of tear round. But I suppose, now, you wouldn't? Don't feel like it, maybe?" he added with anxious sympathy, peering into the faces of his companions.

"Well, I don't know," responded Tom Flynn with some cheerfulness. "P'r'aps we may. But how about your wife, Old Man? What does *she* say to it?"

The Old Man hesitated. His conjugal experience had not been a happy one, and the fact was known to Simpson's Bar. His first wife, a delicate, pretty little woman, had suffered keenly and secretly from the jealous suspicions of her husband, until one day he invited the whole Bar to his house to expose her infidelity. On arriving, the party found the shy, petite creature quietly engaged in her household duties, and retired abashed and discomfited. But the sensitive woman did not easily recover from the shock of this extraordinary outrage. It was with difficulty she regained her equanimity sufficiently to release her lover from the closet in which he was concealed, and escape with him. She left a boy of three years to comfort her bereaved husband. The Old

Man's present wife had been his cook. She was large, loyal, and aggressive.

Before he could reply, Joe Dimmick suggested with great directness that it was the "Old Man's house," and that, invoking the Divine Power, if the case were his own, he would invite whom he pleased, even if in so doing he imperiled his salvation. The Powers of Evil, he further remarked, should contend against him vainly. All this delivered with a terseness and vigor lost in this necessary translation.

"In course. Certainly. Thet's it," said the Old Man with a sympathetic frown. "Thar's no trouble about thet. It's my own house, built every stick on it myself. Don't you be afeard o' her, boys. She *may* cut up a trifle rough—ez wimmin do—but she'll come round." Secretly the Old Man trusted to the exaltation of liquor and the power of courageous example to sustain him in such an emergency.

As yet, Dick Bullen, the oracle and leader of Simpson's Bar, had not spoken. He now took his pipe from his lips. "Old Man, how's that yer Johnny gettin' on? Seems to me he didn't look so peart last time I seed him on the bluff heavin' rocks at Chinamen. Didn't seem to take much interest in it. Thar was a gang of 'em by yar yesterday—drownded out up the river—and I kinder thought o' Johnny, and how he'd miss 'em! Maybe now, we'd be in the way ef he wus sick?"

The father, evidently touched not only by this pathetic picture of Johnny's deprivation, but by the considerate delicacy of the speaker, hastened to assure him that Johnny was better, and that a "little fun might 'liven him up." Whereupon Dick arose, shook himself, and saying, "I'm ready. Lead the way, Old Man: here goes," himself led the way with a leap, a characteristic howl, and darted out into the night. As he passed through the outer room he caught up a blazing brand from the hearth. The action was repeated by the rest of the party, closely following and elbowing each other, and before the astonished proprietor of Thompson's grocery was aware of the intention of his guests, the room was deserted.

The night was pitchy dark. In the first gust of wind their temporary torches were extinguished, and only the red brands dancing and flitting in the gloom like drunken will-o'-the-wisps indicated their whereabouts. Their way led up Pine Tree Canyon, at the head of which a broad, low, bark-thatched cabin burrowed in the mountainside. It was the home of the Old Man, and the entrance to the tunnel in which he worked when he worked at all. Here the crowd paused for a moment, out of delicate deference to their host, who came up panting in the rear.

"P'r'aps ye'd better hold on a second out yer, whilst I go in and see that things is all right," said the Old Man, with an indifference he was far from feeling. The suggestion was graciously accepted, the door opened and closed on the host, and the crowd, leaning their backs against the wall and cowering under the eaves, waited and listened.

For a few moments there was no sound but the dripping of water from the eaves and the stir and rustle of wrestling boughs above them. Then the men became uneasy, and whispered suggestion and suspicion passed from the one to the other. "Reckon she's caved in his head the first lick!" "Decoyed him inter the tunnel and barred him up, likely." "Got him down and sittin' on him." "Prob'ly biling suthin' to heave on us: stand clear the door, boys!" For just then the latch clicked, the door slowly opened, and a voice said, "Come in out o' the wet."

The voice was neither that of the Old Man nor of his wife. It was the voice of a small boy, its weak treble broken by that preternatural hoarseness which only vagabondage and the habit of premature self-assertion can give. It was the face of a small boy that looked up at theirs—a face that might have been pretty, and even refined, but that it was darkened by evil knowledge from within, and dirt and hard experience from without. He had a blanket around his shoulders, and had evidently just risen from his bed. "Come in," he repeated, "and don't make no noise. The Old Man's in there talking to mar," he continued, pointing to an adjacent room which seemed to be a kitchen, from which the Old Man's voice came in deprecating accents. "Let me be," he added querulously to Dick Bullen, who had caught him up, blanket and all, and was affecting to toss him into the fire, "let go o' me, you d—d old fool, d'ye hear?"

Thus adjured, Dick Bullen lowered Johnny to the ground with a smothered laugh, while the men, entering quietly, ranged themselves around a long table of rough boards which occupied the center of the room. Johnny then gravely proceeded to a cupboard and brought out several articles, which he deposited on the table. "Thar's whiskey. And crackers. And red herons. And cheese." He took a bite of the latter on his way to the table. "And sugar." He scooped up a mouthful en route with a small and very dirty hand. "And terbacker. Thar's dried appils too on the shelf, but I don't admire 'em. Appils is swellin'. Thar," he concluded, "now wade in, and don't be afeard. *I* don't mind the old woman. She don't b'long to *me*. S'long."

He had stepped to the threshold of a small room, scarcely larger than a closet, partitioned off from the main apartment, and holding in its dim recess a small bed. He stood there a moment looking at the company, his bare feet peeping from the blanket, and nodded.

"Hello, Johnny! You ain't goin' to turn in agin, are ye?" said Dick.

"Yes, I are," responded Johnny decidedly.

"Why, wot's up, old fellow?"

"I'm sick."

"How sick?"

"I've got a fevier. And childblains. And roomatiz," returned Johnny, and vanished within. After a moment's pause, he added in the dark, apparently from under the bedclothes—"And biles!"

There was an embarrassing silence. The men looked at each other and at the fire. Even with the appetizing banquet before them, it seemed as if they might again fall into the despondency of Thompson's grocery, when the voice of the Old Man, incautiously lifted, came deprecatingly from the kitchen.

"Certainly! Thet's so. In course they is. A gang o' lazy, drunken loafers, and that ar Dick Bullen's the ornariest of all. Didn't hev no more *sabe* than to come round yar with sickness in the house and no provision. Thet's what I said: 'Bullen,' sez I, 'it's crazy drunk you are, or a fool,' sez I, 'to think o' such a thing.' 'Staples,' I sez, 'be you a man, Staples, and 'spect to raise h—ll under my roof and invalids lyin' round?' But they would come—they would. Thet's wot you must 'spect o' such trash as lays round the Bar."

A burst of laughter from the men followed this unfortunate exposure. Whether it was overheard in the kitchen, or whether the Old Man's irate companion had just then exhausted all other modes of expressing her contemptuous indignation, I cannot say, but a back door was suddenly slammed with great violence. A moment later and the Old Man reappeared, haply unconscious of the cause of the late hilarious outburst, and smiled blandly.

"The old woman thought she'd jest run over to Mrs. MacFadden's for a sociable call," he explained with jaunty indifference, as he took a seat at the board.

Oddly enough it needed this untoward incident to relieve the embarrassment that was beginning to be felt by the party, and their natural audacity returned with their host. I do not propose to record the convivialities of that evening. The inquisitive reader will accept the statement that the conversation was characterized by the same intellectual exaltation, the same cautious reverence, the same fastidious delicacy, the same rhetorical precision, and the same logical and coherent discourse somewhat later in the evening, which distinguish similar gatherings of the masculine sex in more civilized localities and under more favorable auspices. No glasses were broken in the absence of any; no liquor was uselessly spilt on the floor or table in the scarcity of that article.

It was nearly midnight when the festivities were interrupted. "Hush," said Dick Bullen, holding up his hand. It was the querulous voice of Johnny from his adjacent closet: "O Dad!"

The Old Man arose hurriedly and disappeared in the closet. Presently he reappeared. "His rheumatiz is coming on agin bad," he explained, "and he wants rubbin'." He lifted the demijohn of whiskey from the table and shook it. It was empty. Dick Bullen put down his tin cup with an embarrassed laugh. So did the others. The Old Man examined their contents and said hopefully, "I reckon that's enough; he don't need much. You hold on all o' you for a spell, and I'll be back," and vanished in the closet with an old flannel shirt and the whiskey. The door closed but imperfectly, and the following dialogue was distinctly audible:

"Now, sonny, whar does she ache worst?"

"Sometimes over yar and sometimes under yer; but it's more powerful from yer to ycr. Rub yer, Dad."

A silence seemed to indicate a brisk rubbing. Then Johnny:

"Hevin' a good time out yer, Dad?"

"Yes, sonny."

"Tomorrer's Chrismiss—ain't it?"

"Yes, sonny. How does she feel now?"

"Better. Rub a little furder down. Wot's Chrismiss, anyway? Wot's it all about?"

"Oh, it's a day."

This exhaustive definition was apparently satisfactory, for there was a silent interval of rubbing. Presently Johnny again:

"Mar sez that everywhere else but yer everybody gives things to everybody Chrismiss, and then she jist waded inter you. She sez thar's a man they call Sandy Claws, not a white man, you know, but a kind o'

Chinemin, comes down the chimbley night afore Chrismiss and gives things to chillern—boys like me. Put 'em in their butes! Thet's what she tried to play upon me. Easy now, Pop, whar are you rubbin' to—thet's a mile from the place. She jest made that up, didn't she, jest to aggrewate me and you? Don't rub thar . . . Why, Dad!"

In the great quiet that seemed to have fallen upon the house the sigh of the near pines and the drip of leaves without was very distinct. Johnny's voice, too, was lowered as he went on, "Don't you take on now, for I'm gettin' all right fast. Wot's the boys doin' out thar?"

The Old Man partly opened the door and peered through. His guests were sitting there sociably enough, and there were a few silver coins and a lean buckskin purse on the table. "Bettin' on suthin'—some little game or 'nother. They're all right," he replied to Johnny, and recommenced his rubbing.

"I'd like to take a hand and win some money," said Johnny reflectively after a pause.

The Old Man glibly repeated what was evidently a familiar formula, that if Johnny would wait until he struck it rich in the tunnel he'd have lots of money, etc., etc.

"Yes," said Johnny, "but you don't. And whether you strike it or I win it, it's about the same. It's all luck. But it's mighty cur'o's about Chrismiss—ain't it? Why do they call it Chrismiss?"

Perhaps from some instinctive deference to the overhearing of his guests, or from some vague sense of incongruity, the Old Man's reply was so low as to be inaudible beyond the room.

"Yes," said Johnny, with some slight abatement of interest, "I've heard o' *him* before. Thar, that'll do, Dad. I don't ache near so bad as I did. Now wrap me tight in this yer blanket. So. Now," he added in a muffled whisper, "sit down yer by me till I go asleep." To assure himself of obedience, he disengaged one hand from the blanket, and grasping his father's sleeve, again composed himself to rest.

For some moments the Old Man waited patiently. Then the unwonted stillness of the house excited his curiosity, and without moving from the bed he cautiously opened the door with his disengaged hand, and looked into the main room. To his infinite surprise it was dark and deserted. But even then a smoldering log on the hearth broke, and by the upspringing blaze he saw the figure of Dick Bullen sitting by the dying embers.

"Hello!"

Dick started, rose, and came somewhat unsteadily toward him.

"Whar's the boys?" said the Old Man.

"Gone up the canyon on a little *pasear*. They're coming back for me in a minit. I'm waitin' round for 'em. What are you starin' at, Old Man?" he added, with a forced laugh; "do you think I'm drunk?"

The Old Man might have been pardoned the supposition, for Dick's eyes were humid and his face flushed. He loitered and lounged back to the chimney, yawned, shook himself, buttoned up his coat, and laughed. "Liquor ain't so plenty as that, Old Man. Now don't you git up," he continued, as the Old Man made a movement to release his sleeve from Johnny's hand. "Don't you mind manners. Sit jest whar you be; I'm goin' in a jiffy. Thar, that's them now."

There was a low tap at the door. Dick Bullen opened it quickly, nodded "good night" to his host, and disappeared. The Old Man would have followed him but for the hand that still unconsciously grasped his sleeve. He could have easily disengaged it: it was small, weak, and emaciated. But perhaps because it *was* small, weak, and emaciated he changed his mind, and drawing his chair closer to the bed, rested his head upon it. In this defenseless attitude the potency of his earlier potations surprised him. The room flickered and faded before his eyes, reappeared, faded again, went out, and left him—asleep.

Meantime Dick Bullen, closing the door, confronted his companions. "Are you ready?" said Staples. "Ready," said Dick; "what's the time?" "Past twelve," was the reply; "can you make it?—it's nigh on fifty miles, the round trip hither and yon." "I reckon," returned Dick shortly. "Whar's the mare?" "Bill and Jack's holdin' her at the crossin'." "Let 'em hold on a minit longer," said Dick.

He turned and re-entered the house softly. By the light of the guttering candle and dying fire he saw that the door of the little room was open. He stepped toward it on tip-toe and looked in. The Old Man had fallen back in his chair, snoring, his helpless feet thrust out in a line with his collapsed shoulders, and his hat pulled over his eyes. Beside him, on a narrow wooden bedstead, lay Johnny, muffled tightly in a blanket that hid all save a strip of forehead and a few curls damp with perspiration. Dick Bullen made a step forward, hesitated, and glanced over his shoulder into the deserted room. Everything was quiet. With a sudden resolution he parted his huge mustaches with both hands and stooped over the sleeping boy. But even as he did so a mischievous blast, lying in wait, swooped down the chimney, rekindled the hearth, and lit up the room with a shameless glow from which Dick fled in bashful terror.

His companions were already waiting for him at the crossing. Two of them were struggling in the darkness with some strange misshapen bulk, which as Dick came nearer took the semblance of a great yellow horse.

It was the mare. She was not a pretty picture. From her Roman nose to her rising haunches, from her arched spine hidden by the stiff *machillas* of a Mexican saddle, to her thick, straight bony legs, there was not a line of equine grace. In her half-blind but wholly vicious white eyes, in her protruding underlip, in her monstrous color, there was nothing but ugliness and vice.

"Now then," said Staples, "stand cl'ar of her heels, boys, and up with you. Don't miss your first holt of her mane, and mind ye get your off stirrup *quick*. Ready!"

There was a leap, a scrambling struggle, a bound, a wild retreat of the crowd, a circle of flying hoofs, two springless leaps that jarred the earth, a rapid play and jingle of spurs, a plunge, and then the voice of Dick somewhere in the darkness. "All right!"

"Don't take the lower road back onless you're hard pushed for time! Don't hold her in downhill! We'll be at the ford at five. G'lang! Hoopa! Mula! GO!"

A splash, a spark struck from the ledge in the road, a clatter in the rocky cut beyond, and Dick was gone.

Sing, O Muse, the ride of Richard Bullen! Sing, O Muse, of chivalrous men! the sacred quest, the doughty deeds, the battery of low churls, the fearsome ride and gruesome perils of the Flower of Simpson's Bar! Alack! she is dainty, this Muse! She will have none of this bucking brute and swaggering, ragged rider, and I must fain follow him in prose, afoot!

It was one o'clock, and yet he had only gained Rattlesnake Hill. For in that time Jovita had rehearsed to him all her imperfections and practiced all her vices. Thrice had she stumbled. Twice had she thrown up her Roman nose in a straight line with the reins, and resisting bit and spur, struck out madly across country. Twice had she reared, and rearing, fallen backward; and twice had the agile Dick, unharmed, regained his seat before she found her vicious legs again.

And a mile beyond them, at the foot of a long hill, was Rattlesnake Creek. Dick knew that here was the crucial test of his ability to perform his enterprise, set his teeth grimly, put his knees well into her flanks, and changed his defensive tactics to brisk aggression. Bullied and maddened, Jovita began the descent of the hill. Here the artful Richard pretended to hold her in with ostentatious objurgation and well-feigned cries of alarm. It is unnecessary to add that Jovita instantly ran away. Nor need I state the time made in the descent; it is written in the chronicles of Simpson's Bar. Enough that in another moment, as it seemed to Dick, she was splashing on the overflowed banks of Rattlesnake Creek. As Dick expected, the momentum she had acquired carried her beyond the point of balking, and holding her well together for a mighty leap, they dashed into the middle of the swiftly flowing current. A few moments of kicking, wading, and swimming, and Dick drew a long breath on the opposite bank.

The road from Rattlesnake Creek to Red Mountain was tolerably level. Either the plunge in Rattlesnake Creek had dampened her baleful fire, or the art which led to it had shown her the superior wickedness of her rider, for Jovita no longer wasted her surplus energy in wanton conceits. Once she bucked, but it was from force of habit; once she shied, but it was from a new, freshly painted meetinghouse at the crossing of the county road. Hollows, ditches, gravelly deposits, patches of freshly springing grasses, flew from beneath her rattling hoofs. She began to smell unpleasantly, once or twice she coughed slightly, but there was no abatement of her strength or speed. By two o'clock he had passed Red Mountain and begun the descent to the plain. Ten minutes later the driver of the fast Pioneer coach was overtaken and passed by a "man on a pinto hoss,"—an event sufficiently notable for remark. At half-past two Dick rose in his stirrups with a great shout. Stars were glittering through the rifted clouds, and beyond him, out of the plain, rose two spires, a flagstaff, and a straggling line of black objects. Dick jingled his spurs and swung his *riata,* Jovita bounded forward, and in another moment they swept into Tuttleville, and drew up before the wooden piazza of "The Hotel of All Nations."

What transpired that night at Tuttleville is not strictly a part of this record. Briefly I may state, however, that after Jovita had been handed over to a sleepy ostler, whom she at once kicked into unpleasant consciousness, Dick sallied out with the barkeeper for a tour of the sleeping town. Lights still gleamed from a few saloons and gambling houses; but avoiding these, they stopped before several closed shops, and by persistent tapping and judicious outcry roused the proprietors from their beds, and made them unbar the doors of their magazines and expose their wares. Sometimes they were met by curses, but oftener by interest and some concern in their needs, and the interview was invariably concluded by a drink. It was three o'clock before this pleasantry was given over, and with a small waterproof bag of India rubber strapped on his shoulders, Dick returned to the hotel. But here he was waylaid by Beauty—Beauty opulent in charms, affluent in dress, persuasive in speech, and Spanish in accent! In vain she repeated the invitation in "Excelsior," happily scorned by all Alpine-climbing youth, and rejected by this child of the Sierras—a rejection softened in this instance by a laugh and his last gold coin. And then he sprang to the saddle and dashed down the lonely street and out into the lonelier plain, where presently the lights, the black line of houses, the spires, and the flagstaff sank into the earth behind him again and were lost in the distance.

The storm had cleared away, the air was brisk and cold, the outlines of adjacent landmarks were distinct, but it was half-past four before Dick reached the meetinghouse and the crossing of the country road. To avoid the rising grade he had taken a longer and more circuitous road, in whose viscid mud Jovita sank fetlock deep at every bound. It was a poor preparation for a steady ascent of five miles more; but Jovita, gathering her legs under her, took it with her usual blind, unreasoning fury, and a half-hour later reached the long level that led to Rattlesnake Creek. Another half-hour would bring him to the creek. He threw the reins lightly upon the neck of the mare, chirruped to her, and began to sing.

Suddenly Jovita shied with a bound that would have unseated a less practiced rider. Hanging to her rein was a figure that had leaped from the bank, and at the same time from the road before her arose a shadowy horse and rider.

"Throw up your hands," commanded the second apparition, with an oath.

Dick felt the mare tremble, quiver, and apparently sink under him. He knew what it meant and was prepared.

"Stand aside, Jack Simpson. I know you, you d—d thief! Let me pass, or—"

He did not finish the sentence. Jovita rose straight in the air with a terrific bound, throwing the figure from her bit with a single shake of her vicious head, and charged with deadly malevolence down on the impediment before her. An oath, a pistol shot, horse and highway rolled over in the road, and the next moment Jovita was a hundred yards away. But the good right arm of her rider, shattered by a bullet, dropped helplessly at his side.

Without slacking his speed he shifted the reins to his left hand. But a few moments later he was obliged to halt and tighten the saddle girths that had slipped in the onset. This in his crippled condition took some time. He had no fear of pursuit, but looking up he saw that the eastern stars were already paling, and that the distant peaks had lost their ghostly whiteness and now stood out blackly against a lighter sky. Day was upon him. Then completely absorbed in a single idea, he forgot the pain of his wound, and mounting again dashed on toward Rattlesnake Creek. But now Jovita's breath came broken by gasps; Dick reeled in his saddle, and brighter and brighter grew the sky.

Ride, Richard; run, Jovita; linger, O day!

For the last few rods there was a roaring in his ears. Was it exhaustion from loss of blood, or what? He was dazed and giddy as he swept down the hill, and did not recognize his surroundings. Had he taken the wrong road, or was this Rattlesnake Creek?

It was. But the brawling creek he had swam a few hours before had risen, more than doubled its volume, and now rolled a swift and resistless river between him and Rattlesnake Hill. For the first time that night Richard's heart sank within him. The river, the mountain, the quickening east, swam before his eyes. He shut them to recover his self-control. In that brief interval, by some fantastic mental process, the little room at Simpson's Bar and the figures of the sleeping father and son rose upon him. He opened his eyes wildly, cast off his coat, pistol, boots, and saddle, bound his precious pack tightly to his shoulders, grasped the bare flanks of Jovita with his bared knees, and with a shout dashed into the yellow water. A cry rose from the opposite bank as the head of a man and horse struggled for a few moments against the battling current, and then were swept away amidst uprooted trees and whirling driftwood.

The Old Man started and woke. The fire on the hearth was dead, the candle in the outer room flickering in its socket, and somebody was rapping at the door. He opened it, but fell back with a cry before the dripping, half-naked figure that reeled against the doorpost.

"Dick?"

"Hush! Is he awake yet?"

"No; but, Dick—"

"Dry up, you old fool! Get me some whiskey, *quick!*" The Old Man flew and returned with—an empty bottle! Dick would have sworn, but his strength was not equal to the occasion. He staggered, caught at the handle of the door, and motioned to the Old Man.

"Thar's suthin' in my pack yer for Johnny. Take it off. I can't."

The Old Man unstrapped the pack and laid it before the exhausted man.

"Open it, quick."

He did so with trembling fingers. It contained only a few poor toys —cheap and barbaric enough, goodness knows, but bright with paint and tinsel. One of them was broken; another, I fear, was irretrievably ruined by water, and on the third—ah me! there was a cruel spot.

"It don't look like much, that's a fact," said Dick ruefully. . . . "But it's the best we could do. . . . Take 'em, Old Man, and put 'em in his stocking, and tell him—tell him, you know—hold me, Old Man—" The Old Man caught at his sinking figure. "Tell him," said Dick, with a weak little laugh—"tell him Sandy Claus has come."

And even so, bedraggled, ragged, unshaven and unshorn, with one arm hanging helplessly at his side, Santa Claus came to Simpson's Bar and fell fainting on the first threshold. The Christmas dawn came slowly after, touching the remoter peaks with the rosy warmth of ineffable love. And it looked so tenderly on Simpson's Bar that the whole mountain, as if caught in a generous action, blushed to the skies.

A Journey
in Search
of Christmas

Owen Wister

The first great novel of the Old West, and the one that shaped the cowboy mystique, was Owen Wister's The Virginian *(1902), a bestseller for more than ten years. Wister (1860–1938) traveled widely throughout the West, and not only wrote other outstanding tales of the Wyoming range but equally fine stories set in Arizona, Texas, California, and the Pacific Northwest; the bulk of these appear in his four celebrated collections:* Red Men and White *(1896),* The Jimmyjohn Boss and Other Stories *(1900),* Members of the Family *(1911), and* When West Was West *(1928). In "A Journey in Search of Christmas," an excerpt from his first novel,* Lin McLean *(1897), Wister's boyish cowboy hero sets out on a quest for the meaning of Christmas—and finds it in a boy's heart.*

The Governor descended the steps of the Capitol slowly, with pauses, lifting a list frequently to his eyes. He had intermittently penciled it between the stages of the forenoon's public business, and his gait grew absent as he recurred now to his jottings in their accumulation, with a slight pain at their number, and the definite fear that they would be more in seasons to come. They were the names of his friends' children to whom his excellent heart moved him to give Christmas presents. He had put off this regenerating evil until the latest day, as was his custom, and now he was setting forth to do the whole thing at a blow, entirely planless among the guns and rocking-horses that would presently surround him.

As he reached the highway he heard himself familiarly addressed from a distance, and, turning, saw four sons of the alkali jogging into town from the plain. One who had shouted to him galloped out from the others, rounded the Capitol's enclosure, and, approaching with radiant countenance, leaned to reach the hand of the Governor, and once again greeted him with a hilarious, "Hello, Doc!"

Governor Barker, M.D., seeing Lin McLean unexpectedly after several years, hailed the horseman with frank and lively pleasure, and, inquiring who might be the other riders behind, was told that they were Shorty, Chalkeye, and Dollar Bill, come for Christmas. "And dandies to hit town with," Mr. McLean added. "Red-hot."

"I am acquainted with them," assented His Excellency.

"We've been ridin' trail for twelve weeks," the cowpuncher continued, "makin' our beds down anywhere, and eatin' the same old chuck every day. So we've shook fried beef and heifer's delight, and we're goin' to feed high."

Then Mr. McLean overflowed with talk and pungent confidences, for the holidays already rioted in his spirit, and his tongue was loosed over their coming rites.

"We've soured on scenery," he finished, in his drastic idiom. "We're sick of moonlight and cow dung, and we're heeled for a big time."

"Call on me," remarked the Governor, cheerily, "when you're ready for bromides and sulphates."

"I ain't box-headed no more," protested Mr. McLean. "I've got maturity, Doc, since I seen you at the rain-making, and I'm a heap older than them hospital days when I bust my leg on you. Three or four glasses and quit. That's my rule."

"That your rule, too?" inquired the Governor of Shorty, Chalkeye, and Dollar Bill. These gentlemen of the saddle were sitting quite expressionless upon their horses.

"We ain't talkin', we're waitin'," observed Chalkeye, and the three cynics smiled amiably.

"Well, Doc, see you again," said Mr. McLean. He turned to accompany his brother cowpunchers, but in that particular moment Fate descended or came up from whatever place she dwells in and entered the body of the unsuspecting Governor.

"What's your hurry?" said Fate, speaking in the official's hearty manner. "Come along with me."

"Can't do it. Where're you goin'?"

"Christmasing," replied Fate.

"Well, I've got to feed my horse. Christmasing, you say?"

"Yes, I'm buying toys."

"Toys! You? What for?"

"Oh, some kids."

"Yourn?" screeched Lin, precipitately.

His Excellency the jovial Governor opened his teeth in pleasure at this, for he was a bachelor, and there were 15 upon his list, which he held up for the edification of the hasty McLean. "Not mine, I'm happy to say. My friends keep marrying and settling, and their kids call me uncle, and climb around and bother, and I forget their names, and think it's a girl, and the mother gets mad. Why, if I didn't remember these little folks at Christmas they'd be wondering—not the kids, they just break your toys and don't notice; but the mother would wonder— 'What's the matter with Dr. Barker? Has Governor Barker gone back on us?—that's where the strain comes!" he broke off, facing Mr. McLean with another spacious laugh.

But the cowpuncher had ceased to smile, and now, while Barker ran on exuberantly, McLean's wide-open eyes rested upon him, singular and intent, and in their hazel depths the last gleam of jocularity went out.

"That's where the strain comes, you see. Two sets of acquaintances. Grateful patients and loyal voters, and I've got to keep solid with both outfits, especially the wives and mothers. They're the people. So it's drums, and dolls, and sheep on wheels, and games, and monkeys on a stick, and the saleslady shows you a mechanical bear, and it costs too much, and you forget whether the Judge's second girl is Nellie or Susie, and—well, I'm just in for my annual circus this afternoon! You're in luck. Christmas don't trouble a chap fixed like you."

Lin McLean prolonged the sentence like a distant echo.

"A chap fixed like you!" the cowpuncher said slowly to himself. "No, sure." He seemed to be watching Shorty, and Chalkeye, and Dollar Bill going down the road. "That's a new idea—Christmas," he murmured, for it was one of his oldest, and he was recalling the Christmas when he wore his first long trousers.

"Comes once a year pretty regular," remarked the prosperous Governor. "Seems often when you pay the bill."

"I haven't made a Christmas gift," pursued the cowpuncher, dreamily, "not for—for—Lord! it's a hundred years, I guess. I don't know anybody that has any right to look for such a thing from me." This was indeed a new idea, and it did not stop the chill that was spreading in his heart.

"Gee whiz!" said Barker, briskly, "there goes twelve o'clock. I've got to make a start. Sorry you can't come and help me. Good-by!"

His Excellency left the rider sitting motionless, and forgot him at once in his own preoccupation. He hastened upon his journey to the shops with the list, not in his pocket, but held firmly, like a plank in the imminence of shipwreck. The Nellies and Susies pervaded his mind, and he struggled with the presentiment that in a day or two he would recall some omitted and wretchedly important child. Quick hoofbeats made him look up, and Mr. McLean passed like a wind. The Governor absently watched him go, and saw the pony hunch and stiffen in the check of his speed when Lin overtook his companions. Down there in the distance they took a side street, and Barker rejoicingly remembered one more name and wrote it as he walked. In a few minutes he had come to the shops, and met face to face with Mr. McLean.

"The boys are seein' after my horse," Lin rapidly began, "and I've got to meet 'em sharp at one. We're twelve weeks shy on a square meal, you see, and this first has been a date from 'way back. I'd like to—" Here Mr. McLean cleared his throat, and his speech went less smoothly. "Doc, I'd like just for a while to watch you gettin'—them monkeys, you know."

The Governor expressed his agreeable surprise at this change of mind, and was glad of McLean's company and judgment during the impending selections. A picture of a cowpuncher and himself discussing a couple of dolls rose nimbly in Barker's mental eye, and it was with an imperfect honesty that he said, "You'll help me a heap."

And Lin, quite sincere, replied, "Thank you."

So together these two went Christmasing in the throng. Wyoming's chief executive knocked elbows with the spurred and jingling waif, one man as good as another in that raw, hopeful, full-blooded cattle era, which now the sobered West remembers as the days of its fond youth. For one man has been as good as another in three places—

paradise before the Fall, the Rocky Mountains before the wire fence, and the Declaration of Independence. And then this Governor, besides being young, almost as young as Lin McLean or the Chief Justice (who lately had celebrated his 32nd birthday), had in his doctoring days at Drybone known the cowpuncher with that familiarity which lasts a lifetime without breeding contempt. Accordingly he now laid a hand on Lin's tall shoulder and drew him among the petticoats and toys.

Christmas filled the windows and Christmas stirred in mankind. Cheyenne, not over-zealous in doctrines or litanies, and with the opinion that a world in the hand is worth two in the bush, nevertheless was flocking together, neighbor to think of neighbor, and everyone to remember the children; a sacred assembly, after all, gathered to rehearse unwittingly the articles of its belief, the Creed and Doctrine of the Child.

Lin saw them hurry and smile among the paper fairies; they questioned and hesitated, crowded and made decisions, failed utterly to find the right thing, forgot and hastened back, suffered all the various desperations of the eleventh hour, and turned homeward, dropping their parcels with that undimmed good will that once a year makes gracious the universal human face. This brotherhood swam and beamed before the cowpuncher's brooding eyes, and in his ears the greeting of the season sang. Children escaped from their mothers and ran chirping behind the counters to touch and meddle in places forbidden. Friends dashed against each other with rabbits and magic lanterns, greeted in haste, and were gone, amid the sound of musical boxes.

Through this tinkle and bleating of little machinery the murmur of the human heart drifted in and out of McLean's hearing: fragments of home talk, tendernesses, economies, intimate first names, and dinner hours; and whether it was joy or sadness, it was in common; the world seemed knit in a single skein of home ties. Two or three came by whose purses must have been slender, and whose purchases were humble and chosen after much nice adjustment. And when one plain man dropped a word about both ends meeting, and the woman with him laid a hand on his arm, saying that his children must not feel this year was different, Lin made a step toward them. There were hours and spots where he could readily have descended upon them at that, played the role of clinking affluence, waved thanks aside with competent blasphemy, and tossing off some infamous whisky, cantered away in the full, self-conscious strut of the frontier. But here was not the moment; the abashed cowpuncher could make no such parade in this place.

The people brushed by him back and forth, busy upon their errands, and aware of him scarcely more than if he had been a spirit looking on from the helpless dead. And so, while these weaving needs and kindnesses of man were within arm's touch of him, he was locked outside with his impulses. Barker had, in the natural press of customers, long parted from him, to become immersed in choosing and rejecting; and now, with a fair part of his mission accomplished, he was ready to go on to the next place, and turned to beckon McLean. He found him obliterated in a corner beside a life-sized image of Santa Claus, standing as still as the frosty saint.

"He looks livelier than you do," said the hearty Governor. " 'Fraid it's been slow waiting."

"No," replied the cowpuncher, thoughtfully. "No, I guess not."

This uncertainty was expressed with such gentleness that Barker roared. "You never did lie to me," he said, "long as I've known you. Well, never mind. I've got some real advice to ask you now."

At this Mr. McLean's face grew more alert. "Say, Doc," said he, "what do you want for Christmas that nobody's likely to give you?"

"A big practice—big enough to interfere with my politics."

"What else? Things and truck, I mean."

"Oh—nothing I'll get. People don't give things much to fellows like me."

"Don't they? Don't they?"

"Why, you and Santa Claus weren't putting up any scheme on my stocking?"

"Well—"

"I believe you're in earnest!" cried His Excellency. "That's simply rich!"

Here was a thing to relish! The Frontier comes to town "heeled for a big time," finds that presents are all the rage, and must immediately give somebody something. Oh, childlike, miscellaneous Frontier! So thought the good-hearted Governor; and it seems a venial misconception. "My dear fellow," he added, meaning as well as possible, "I don't want you to spend your money on me."

"I've got plenty, all right," said Lin, shortly.

"Plenty's not the point. I'll take as many drinks as you please with you. You didn't expect anything from me?"

"That ain't—that don't—"

"There! Of course you didn't. Then what are you getting proud about? Here's our shop." They stepped in from the street to new crowds and counters. "Now," pursued the Governor, "this is for a very particular friend of mine. Here they are. Now, which of those do you like best?"

They were sets of Tennyson in cases holding little volumes equal in number, but the binding various, and Mr. McLean reached his decision after one look. "That," said he, and laid a large muscular hand upon the Laureate. The young lady behind the counter spoke out acidly, and Lin pulled the abject hand away. His taste, however, happened to be sound, or, at least, it was at one with the Governor's. But now they learned that there was a distressing variance in the matter of price.

The Governor stared at the delicate article of his choice. "I know that Tennyson is what she—is what's wanted," he muttered, and, feeling himself nudged, looked around and saw Lin's extended fist. This gesture he took for a facetious sympathy, and dolorously grasping the hand, found himself holding a lump of bills. Sheer amazement relaxed him, and the cowpuncher's matted wealth tumbled on the floor in sight of all people. Barker picked it up and gave it back. "No, no, no!" he said, mirthful over his own inclination to be annoyed; "you can't do that. I'm just as much obliged, Lin," he added.

"Just as a loan, Doc—some of it. I'm grass-bellied with spot cash."

A giggle behind the counter disturbed them both, but the sharp young lady was only dusting. The Governor at once paid haughtily for Tennyson's expensive works, and the cowpuncher pushed his discountenanced savings back into his clothes. Making haste to leave the book department of this shop, they regained a mutual ease, and the Governor became waggish over Lin's concern at being too rich. He suggested to him the list of delinquent taxpayers and the latest census from which to select indigent persons. He had patients, too, whose inveterate pennilessness he could swear cheerfully to—"since you want to bolt from your own money," he remarked.

"Yes, I'm a green horse," assented Mr. McLean, gallantly; "ain't used to the looks of a twenty-dollar bill, and I shy at 'em."

From his face—that jocular mask—one might have counted him the most serene and careless of vagrants, and in his words only the ordinary voice of banter spoke to the Governor. A good woman, it may well be, would have guessed before this the sensitive soul in the blundering body; but Barker saw just the familiar, whimsical, happy-go-lucky McLean of old days, and so he went gaily and innocently on, treading upon holy ground. "I've got it!" he exclaimed. "Give your wife something."

The ruddy cowpuncher grinned. He had passed through the world of woman with but few delays, rejoicing in informal and transient entanglements, and he welcomed the turn which the conversation seemed now to be taking. "If you'll give me her name and address," said he, with the future entirely in his mind.

"Why, Laramie!" and the Governor feigned surprise.

"Say, Doc," said Lin, uneasily, "none of 'em ain't married me since I saw you last."

"Then she hasn't written from Laramie," said the hilarious Governor, and Mr. McLean understood and winced in his spirit deep down. "Gee whiz!" went on Barker, "I'll never forget you and Lusk that day!"

But the mask fell now. "You're talking of his wife, not mine," said the cowpuncher very quietly, and smiling no more, "and, Doc, I'm going to say a word to you for I know you've always been my good friend. I'll never forget that day myself—but I don't want to be reminded of it."

"I'm a fool, Lin," said the Governor, generous instantly. "I never supposed—"

"I know you didn't, Doc. It ain't you that's the fool. And in a way—in a way—" Lin's speech ended among his crowding memories, and Barker, seeing how wistful his face had turned, waited. "But I ain't quite the same fool I was before that happened to me," the cowpuncher resumed, "though maybe my actions don't show to be wiser. I know that there was better luck than a man like me had any call to look for."

The sobered Barker said, simply, "Yes, Lin." He was put to thinking by these words from the unsuspected inner man.

Out in the Bow Leg country Lin McLean had met a woman with thick, red cheeks, calling herself by a maiden name, and this was his whole knowledge of her when he put her one morning astride a Mexican saddle and took her 50 miles to a magistrate and made her his lawful wife to the best of his ability and belief. His sagebrush intimates were confident he would never have done it but for a rival. Racing the rival and beating him had swept Mr. McLean past his own intentions, and the marriage was an inadvertence. "He jest bumped into it before he could pull up," they explained, and this casualty, resulting from Mr. McLean's sporting blood, had entertained several hundred square miles of alkali.

For the new-made husband the joke soon died. In the immediate weeks that came upon him he tasted a bitterness worse than in all his life before, and learned also how deep the woman, when once she begins, can sink beneath the man in baseness. That was a knowledge of which he had lived innocent until this time. But he carried his outward self serenely, so that citizens in Cheyenne who saw the cowpuncher with his bride argued shrewdly that men of that sort liked women of that sort. And before the strain had broken his endurance, an unexpected first husband, named Lusk, had appeared one Sunday in the street, prosperous, forgiving, and exceedingly drunk. To the arms of Lusk she went back in the public street, deserting McLean in the presence of Cheyenne. And when Cheyenne saw this, and learned how she had been Mrs. Lusk for eight long, if intermittent, years, Cheyenne laughed loudly.

Lin McLean laughed, too, and went about his business, ready to swagger at the necessary moment, and with the necessary kind of joke always ready to shield his hurt spirit. And soon, of course, the matter grew stale, seldom raked up in the Bow Leg country where Lin had been at work; so lately he had begun to remember other things besides the smoldering humiliation.

"Is she with him?" he asked Barker, and musingly listened while Barker told him. The Governor had thought to make it a racy story, with the moral that the joke was now on Lusk. But that inner man had spoken and revealed the cowpuncher to him in a new and complicated light. Hence he quieted the proposed lively cadence and vocabulary of his anecdote about the house of Lusk. Instead of narrating how Mrs. beat Mr. on Mondays, Wednesdays, and Fridays, and Mr. took his turn the odd days, thus getting one ahead of his lady, while the kid Lusk had outlined his opinion of the family by recently skipping to parts unknown, Barker detailed these incidents more gravely, adding that Laramie believed Mrs. Lusk addicted to opium.

"I don't guess I'll leave my card on 'em," said McLean grimly, "if I strike Laramie."

"You don't mind my saying I think you're well out of that scrape?" Barker ventured.

"Shucks, no! That's all right, Doc. Only—you see now. A man gets tired pretending—oncet in a while."

Time had gone while they were talking, and it was now half after one and Mr. McLean late for that long-plotted first square meal. So the friends shook hands, wishing each other Merry Christmas, and the cowpuncher hastened toward his chosen companions through the stirring cheerfulness of the season. His play hour had made a dull beginning among the toys. He had come upon people engaged in a pleasant game, and waited, shy and well disposed, for some bidding to join, but they had gone on playing with each other and left him out. And now he went along in a sort of hurry to escape from that loneliness where his human promptings had been lodged with him useless.

Here was Cheyenne, full of holiday for sale, and he with his pockets full of money to buy; and when he thought of Shorty, and Chalkeye, and Dollar Bill, those dandies to hit a town with, he stepped out with a brisk, false hope. It was with a mental hurrah and a foretaste of a good time coming that he put on his town clothes, after shaving and admiring himself, and sat down to the square meal. He ate away and drank with a robust imitation of enjoyment that took in even himself at first. But the sorrowful process of his spirit went on, for all he could do.

As he groped for the contentment which he saw around him he began to receive the jokes with counterfeit mirth. Memories took the place of anticipation, and through their moody shiftings he began to feel a distaste for the company of his friends and a shrinking from their lively voices.

He blamed them for this at once. He was surprised to think he had never recognized before how light a weight was Shorty, and here was Chalkeye, who knew better, talking religion after two glasses. Presently this attack of noticing his friends' shortcomings mastered him, and his mind, according to its wont, changed at a stroke. *I'm celebrating no Christmas with this crowd,* said the inner man. And when they had next remembered Lin McLean in their hilarity he was gone.

Governor Barker, finishing his purchases at half-past three, went to meet a friend come from Evanston. Mr. McLean was at the railway station, buying a ticket for Denver.

"Denver!" exclaimed the amazed Governor.

"That's what I said," stated Mr. McLean doggedly.

"Gee whiz!" went his Excellency. "What are you going to do there?"

"Get good and drunk."

"Can't you find enough whisky in Cheyenne?"

"I'm drinking champagne this trip."

The cowpuncher went out on the platform and got aboard, and the train moved off. Barker had walked out too in his surprise, and as he stared after the last car, Mr. McLean waved his wide hat defiantly and went inside the door.

"And he says he's got maturity," Barker muttered. "I've known him since 'seventy-nine, and he's kept about eight years old right along." The Governor was cross, and sorry, and presently crosser. His jokes about Lin's marriage came back to him and put him in a rage with the departed fool. "Yes, about eight. Or six," said His Excellency, justifying himself by the past. For he had first known Lin, the boy of nineteen, supreme in length of limb and recklessness, breaking horses and feeling for an early mustache. Next, when the mustache was nearly accomplished, he had mended the boy's badly broken thigh at Drybone.

His skill (and Lin's utter health) had wrought so swift a healing that the surgeon overflowed with the pride of science, and over the bandages would explain the human body technically to his wild-eyed and flattered patient. Thus young Lin heard all about tibia, and comminuted, and other glorious new words, and when sleepless would rehearse them. Then, with the bone so nearly knit that the patient might leave the ward on crutches to sit each morning in Barker's room as a privilege, the disobedient child of twenty-one had slipped out of the hospital and hobbled hastily to the hog ranch, where whisky and variety waited for a languishing convalescent. Here he grew gay, and was soon carried back with the leg refractured. Yet Barker's surgical rage was disarmed, the patient was so forlorn over his doctor's professional chagrin.

"I suppose it ain't no better this morning, Doc?" he had said humbly, after a new week of bed and weights.

"Your right leg's going to be shorter. That's all."

"Oh, gosh! I've been and spoiled your commiunated fee-mur! Ain't I a son-of-a-gun?"

You could not chide such a boy as this, and in time's due course he had walked jauntily out into the world with legs of equal length after all, and in his stride the slightest halt possible. And Doctor Barker had missed the child's conversation. Today his mustache was a perfected thing, and he in the late end of his twenties.

"He'll wake up about noon tomorrow in a dive, without a cent," said Barker. "Then he'll come back on a freight and begin over again."

At the Denver station Lin McLean passed through the shoutings and omnibuses, and came to the beginning of Seventeenth Street, where is the first saloon. A customer was ordering Hot Scotch; and because he liked the smell and had not thought of the mixture for a number of years, Lin took Hot Scotch. Coming out upon the pavement, he looked across and saw a saloon opposite with brighter globes and windows more prosperous. That should have been his choice; lemon peel would undoubtedly be fresher over there. And over he went at once, to begin the whole thing properly. In such frozen weather no drink could be more timely, and he sat, to enjoy without haste its mellow fitness.

Once again on the pavement, he looked along the street toward uptown beneath the crisp, cold electric lights, and three little boot-blacks gathered where he stood and cried, "Shine? Shine?" at him. Remembering that you took the third turn to the right to get the best dinner in Denver, Lin hit on the skillful plan of stopping at all Hot Scotches between; but the next occurred within a few yards, and it was across the street. This one being attained and appreciated, he found that he must cross back again or skip number four.

At this rate he would not be dining in time to see much of the theater, and he stopped to consider. It was a German place he had just quitted, and a huge light poured out on him from its window, which the proprietor's fatherland sentiment had made into a show. Lights shone among a well-set pine forest, where beery, jovial gnomes sat on roots and reached upward to Santa Claus. He, grinning, fat, and Teutonic, held in his right hand forever a foaming glass, and forever in his left a string of sausages that dangled down among the gnomes.

With his American back to this, the cowpuncher, wearing the same serious, absent face he had not changed since he ran away from himself at Cheyenne, considered carefully the Hot Scotch question, and which side of the road to take and stick to, while the little bootblacks found him once more and cried, "Shine? Shine?" monotonous as snowbirds. He settled to stay over here with the south-side Scotches, and the little one-note song reaching his attention, he suddenly shoved his foot at the nearest boy, who lightly sprang away.

"Dare you to touch him!" piped a snowbird, dangerously. They were in short trousers, and the eldest enemy, it may be, was ten.

"Don't hit me," said Mr. McLean. "I'm innocent."

"Well, you leave him be," said one.

"What's he layin' to kick you for, Billy? 'Tain't yer pop, is it?"

"Naw!" said Billy in scorn. "Father never kicked me. Don't know who he is."

"He's a special!" shrilled the leading bird sensationally. "He's got a badge, and he's goin' to arrest yer."

Two of them hopped instantly to the safe middle of the street, and scattered with practiced strategy; but Billy stood his ground. "Dare you to arrest me!" said he.

"What'll you give me not to?" inquired Lin, and he put his hands in his pockets, arms akimbo.

"Nothing; I've done nothing," announced Billy firmly. But even in the last syllable his voice suddenly failed, a terror filled his eyes, and he, too, sped into the middle of the street.

"What's he claim you lifted?" inquired the leader, with eagerness. "Tell him you haven't been inside a store today. We can prove it!" they screamed to the special officer.

"Say," said the slow-spoken Lin from the pavement, "you're poor judges of a badge, you fellows."

His tone pleased them where they stood, wide apart from each other.

Mr. McLean also remained stationary in the bluish illumination of the window. "Why, if any policeman was caught wearin' this here," said he, following his sprightly invention, "he'd get arrested himself."

This struck them extremely. They began to draw together, Billy lingering the last.

"If it's your idea," pursued Mr. McLean alluringly, as the three took cautious steps nearer the curb, "that blue, clasped hands in a circle of red stars gives the bearer the right to put folks in the jug—why, I'll get somebody else to black my boots for a dollar."

The three made a swift rush, fell on simultaneous knees, and clattering their boxes down, began to spit in an industrious circle.

"Easy!" wheedled Mr. McLean, and they looked up at him, staring and fascinated. "Not having three feet," said the cowpuncher, always grave and slow, "I can only give two this here job."

"He's got a big pistol and a belt!" exulted the leader, who had precociously felt beneath Lin's coat.

"You're a smart boy," said Lin, considering him, "and you find a man out right away. Now you stand off and tell me all about myself while they fix the boots—and a dollar goes to the quickest through."

Young Billy and his towheaded competitor flattened down, each to a boot, with all their might, while the leader ruefully contemplated Mr. McLean.

"That's a Colt .45 you've got," ventured he.

"Right again. Some day maybe you'll be wearing one of your own, if the angels don't pull you before you're ripe."

"I'm through!" sang out Towhead, rising in haste.

Small Billy was struggling still, but leaped at that, the two heads bobbing to a level together; and Mr. McLean, looking down, saw that the arrangement had not been a good one for the boots.

"Will you kindly referee," said he, forgivingly, to the leader, "and decide which of them smears is the awfulest?"

But the leader looked the other way and played upon a mouth-organ.

"Well, that saves me money," said Mr. McLean, jingling his pocket. "I guess you've both won." He handed each of them a dollar. "Now," he continued, "I just dassent show these boots uptown, so this time it's a dollar for the best shine."

The two went palpitating at their brushes again, and the leader played his mouth-organ with brilliant unconcern. Lin, tall and brooding, leaned against the jutting sill of the window, a figure somehow plainly strange in town, while through the bright plateglass Santa Claus, holding out his beer and sausages, perpetually beamed. Billy was laboring gallantly, but it was labor, the cowpuncher perceived, and Billy no seasoned expert. "See here," said Lin, stooping, "I'll show you how it's done. He's playin' that toon cross-eyed enough to steer anybody crooked. There. Keep your blacking soft, and work with a dry brush."

"Lemme," said Billy. "I've got to learn." So he finished the boot his own way with wiry determination, breathing and repolishing; and this event was also adjudged a dead heat, with results gratifying to both parties. So here was their work done, and more money in their pockets than from all the other boots and shoes of this day. Towhead and Billy did not wish for further trade, but to spend this handsome fortune as soon as might be. Yet they delayed in the brightness of the window, drawn by curiosity near this new kind of man whose voice held them and whose remarks dropped them into constant uncertainty. Even the omitted leader had been unable to go away and nurse his pride alone.

"Is that a secret society?" inquired Towhead, lifting a finger at the badge.

Mr. McLean nodded. "Turruble," said he.

"You're a Wells & Fargo detective," asserted the leader.

"Play your harp," said Lin.

"Are you a—a desperaydo?" whispered Towhead.

"Oh, my!" observed Mr. McLean, sadly, "what has our Jack been readin'?"

"He's a cattle-man!" cried Billy. "I seen his heels."

"That's you!" said the discovered puncher, with approval. "You'll do. But I bet you can't tell me what we wearers of this badge have sworn to do this night." At this they craned their necks and glared at him.

"We—are—sworn—don't you jump, now, and give me away—sworn—to—blow off three bootblacks to a dinner."

"Ah, pshaw!" They backed away, bristling with distrust.

"That's the oath, fellows. You may as well make your minds up—for I have it to do!"

"Dare you to! Ah!"

"And after dinner it's the Opera-house, to see 'The Children of Captain Grant.' "

They screamed shrilly at him, keeping off beyond the curb.

"I can't waste my time on such smart boys," said Mr. McLean, rising lazily to his full height from the window sill. "I am goin' somewhere to find boys that ain't so turruble quick stampeded by a roast turkey."

He began to lounge slowly away, serious as he had been throughout, and they, stopping their noise short, swiftly picked up their boxes and followed him. Some change in the current of electricity that fed the window disturbed its sparkling light, so that Santa Claus, with his arms stretched out behind the departing cowpuncher, seemed to be smiling more broadly from the midst of his flickering brilliance.

On their way to turkey, the host and his guests exchanged but few remarks. He was full of good will, and threw off a comment or two that would have led to conversation under almost any circumstances save these. But the minds of the guests were too distracted by this whole state of things for them to be capable of more than keeping after Mr. McLean in silence, at a wary interval, and with their mouths, during most of the journey, open. The badge, the pistol, their patron's talk, and the unusual dollars, wakened wide their bent for the unexpected, their street affinity for the spur of the moment. They believed slimly in the turkey part of it, but what this man might do next, to be there when he did it, and not to be trapped, kept their wits jumping deliciously. So when they saw him stop, they stopped instantly too, ten feet out of reach.

This was Denver's most civilized restaurant—that one which Mr. McLean had remembered, with foreign dishes and private rooms, where he had promised himself, among other things, champagne. Mr. McLean had never been inside it, but heard a tale from a friend; and now he caught a sudden sight of people among geraniums, with plumes and white shirt-fronts, very elegant. It must have been several minutes that he stood contemplating the entrance and the luxurious couples who went in.

"Plumb French!" he observed at length; and then, "Shucks!" in a key less confident, while his guests ten feet away watched him narrowly. "They're eatin' patty de parlty-voo in there," he muttered, and the three bootblacks came beside him. "Say, fellows," said Lin, confidingly, "I wasn't raised good enough for them dude dishes. What do you say! I'm after a place where you can mention oyster stoo without givin' anybody a fit. What do you say, boys?"

That lighted the divine spark of brotherhood!

"Ah, you come along with us—we'll take yer! You don't want to go in there. We'll show yer the boss place in Market Street. We won't lose yer." So, shouting together in their shrill little city trebles, they clustered about him, and one pulled at his coat to start him. He started obediently, and walked in their charge, they leading the way.

"Christmas is comin' now, sure," said Lin, grinning to himself. "It ain't exactly what I figured on." It was the first time he had laughed since Cheyenne, and he brushed a hand over his eyes, that were dim with the new warmth in his heart.

Believing at length in him and his turkey, the alert street faces, so suspicious of the unknown, looked at him with ready intimacy as they went along. And soon, in the friendly desire to make him acquainted with Denver, the three were patronizing him. Only Billy, perhaps, now and then stole at him a doubtful look.

The large Country Mouse listened solemnly to his three Town Mice, who presently introduced him to the place in Market Street. It was not boss, precisely, and Denver knows better neighborhoods; but the turkey and the oyster stew were there, with catsup and vegetables in season, and several choices of pie. Here the Country Mouse became again efficient, and to witness his liberal mastery of ordering and imagine his pocket and its wealth, which they had heard and partly seen, renewed in the guests a transient awe. As they dined, however, and found the host as frankly ravenous as themselves, this reticence evaporated, and they all grew fluent with oaths and opinions. At one or two words, indeed, Mr. McLean stared and had a slight sense of blushing.

"Have a cigarette?" said the leader, over his pie.

"Thank you," said Lin. "I won't smoke, if you'll excuse me." He had devised a wholesome meal, with water to drink.

"Chewin's no good at meals," continued the boy. "Don't you use tobaccer?"

"Oncet in a while."

The leader spat brightly. "He ain't learned yet," said he, slanting his elbows at Billy and sliding a match over his rump. "But beer, now—I never seen anything in it." He and Towhead soon left Billy and his callow profanities behind, and engaged in a town conversation that silenced him, and set him listening with all his admiring young might. Nor did Mr. McLean join in the talk, but sat embarrassed by this knowledge, which seemed about as much as he knew himself.

I'll be goshed, he thought, *if I'd caught on to half that when I was streakin' around in short pants! Maybe they grow up quicker now.* But now the Country Mouse perceived Billy's eager and attentive apprenticeship. "Hello, boys!" he said, "that theater's got a big start on us."

They had all forgotten he had said anything about theater. Other topics left their impatient minds while the Country Mouse paid the bill and asked to be guided to the Opera-house. "This man here will look out for your blackin' boxes and truck, and let you have it in the morning."

They were very late. The spectacle had advanced far into passages of the highest thrill, and Denver's eyes were riveted upon a ship and some icebergs. The party found its seats during several beautiful lime-light effects, and that remarkable fly-buzzing of violins which is pro-

nounced so helpful in times of peril and sentiment. The children of
Captain Grant had been tracking their father all over the equator and
other scenic spots, and now the north pole was about to impale them.
The Captain's youngest child, perceiving a hummock rushing at them
with a sudden motion, loudly shouted, "Sister, the ice is closing in!"
and she replied, chastely, "Then let us pray." It was a superb tableau.
The ice split, and the sun rose and joggled at once to the zenith. The
act-drop fell, and male Denver, wrung to its religious deeps, went out
to the rum shop.

Of course, Mr. McLean and his party did not do this. The party
had applauded exceedingly the defeat of the elements, and the leader,
with Towhead, discussed the probable chances of the ship's getting
farther south in the next act. Until lately Billy's doubt of the cowpuncher had lingered; but during this intermission whatever had been
holding out in him seemed won, and in his eyes, that he turned
stealthily upon his unconscious, quiet neighbor, shone the beginnings
of hero-worship.

"Don't you think this is splendid?" said he.

"Splendid," Lin replied, a trifle remotely.

"Don't you like it when they all get balled up and get out that way?"

"Humming," said Lin.

"Don't you guess it's just girls, though, that do that?"

"What, young fellow?"

"Why, all that prayer-saying an' stuff."

"I guess it must be."

"She said to do it when the ice scared her, an' of course a man had
to do what she wanted him."

"Sure."

"Well, do you believe they'd've done it if she hadn't been on that
boat, an' clung around an' cried an' everything, an' made her friends
feel bad?"

"I hardly expect they would," replied the honest Lin, and then,
suddenly mindful of Billy, "except there wasn't nothin' else they could
think of," he added, wishing to speak favorably of the custom.

"Why, that chunk of ice weren't so awful big anyhow. I'd've shoved
her off with a pole. Wouldn't you?"

"Butted her like a ram," exclaimed Mr. McLean.

"Well, I don't say my prayers any more. I told Mr. Perkins I wasn't
a-going to, an' he—I think he is a flubdub anyway."

"I'll bet he is!" said Lin, sympathetically. He was scarcely a prudent guardian.

"I told him straight, an' he looked at me an' down he flops on his knees. An' he made 'em all flop, but I told him I didn't care for them putting up any camp-meeting over me. An' he says, 'I'll lick you,' an' I says, 'Dare you to!' I told him mother kep' a-licking me for nothing an' I'd not pray for her, not in Sunday school or anywheres else. Do you pray much?"

"No," replied Lin, uneasily.

"There! I told him a man didn't, an' he said then a man went to hell. 'You lie; father ain't going to hell,' I says, and you'd ought to heard the first class laugh right out loud, girls an' boys. An' he was that mad! But I didn't care. I came here with fifty cents."

"You must have felt like a millionaire."

"Ah, I felt all right! I bought papers an' sold 'em, an' got more an' saved, an' got my box an' blacking outfit. I weren't going to be licked by her just because she felt like it, an' she feeling like it most any time. Lemme see your pistol."

"You wait," said Lin. "After this show is through I'll put it on you."

"Will you, honest? Belt an' everything? Did you ever shoot a bear?"

"Lord! Lots."

"Honest? Silver-tips?"

"Silver-tips, cinnamon, black; and I roped a cub oncet."

"O-h! I never shot a bear."

"You'd ought to try it."

"I'm a-going to. I'm a-going to camp out in the mountains. I'd like to see you when you camp. I'd like to camp with you. Mightn't I some time?" Billy had drawn nearer to Lin, and was looking up at him adoringly.

"You bet!" said Lin; and though he did not, perhaps, entirely mean this, it was with a curiously softened face that he began to look at Billy. As with dogs and his horse, so always he played with what children he met—the few in his sagebrush world; but this was ceasing to be quite play for him, and his hand went to the boy's shoulder.

"Father took me camping with him once, the time mother was off. Father gets awful drunk, too. I've quit Laramie for good."

Lin sat up, and his hand gripped the boy. "Laramie!" said he, almost shouting it. "You—you—is your name Lusk?"

But the boy had shrunk from him instantly. "You're not going to take me home?" he piteously wailed.

"Heaven and heavens!" murmured Lin McLean. "So you're her kid!"

He relaxed again, down in his chair, his legs stretched their straight length below the chair in front. He was waked from his bewilderment by a brushing under him, and there was young Billy diving for escape to the aisle, like the cornered city mouse that he was. Lin nipped that poor little attempt and had the limp Billy seated inside again before the two in discussion beyond had seen anything. He had said not a word to the boy, and now watched his unhappy eyes seizing upon the various exits and dispositions of the theater; nor could he imagine anything to tell him that would restore the perished confidence. *Why did you lead him off?* he asked himself unexpectedly, and found that he did not seem to know; but as he watched the restless and estranged runaway he grew more and more sorrowful. "I just hate him to think that of me," he reflected.

The curtain rose, and he saw Billy make up his mind to wait until they should all be going out in the crowd. While the children of Captain Grant grew hotter and hotter upon their father's geographic trail, Lin sat saying to himself a number of contradictions. *He's nothing to me; what's any of them to me?* Driven to bay by his bewilderment, he restated the facts of the past. *Why, she'd deserted him and Lusk before she'd ever laid eyes on me. I needn't to bother myself. He wasn't never even my stepkid.* The past, however, brought no guidance. *Lord, what's the thing to do about this? If I had any home—*

"This is a stinkin' world in some respects," said Mr. McLean aloud, unknowingly. The lady in the chair beneath which the cowpuncher had his legs nudged her husband. They took it for emotion over the sad fortune of Captain Grant, and their backs shook. Presently each turned and saw the singular man with untamed, wide-open eyes glowering at the stage, and both backs shook again.

Once more his hand was laid on Billy. "Say!"

The boy glanced at him, and quickly away.

"Look at me, and listen."

Billy swervingly obeyed.

"I ain't after you, and never was. This here's your business, not mine. Are you listenin' good?"

The boy made a nod, and Lin proceeded, whispering: "You've got no call to believe what I say to you—you've been lied to, I guess, pretty often. So I'll not stop you runnin' and hidin', and I'll never give it away I saw you, but you keep doin' what you please. I'll just go now. I've saw all I want, but you and your friends stay with it till it quits. If you happen to wish to speak to me about that pistol or bears, you come around to Smith's palace—that's the boss hotel here, ain't it?—and if you don't come too late I'll not be gone to bed. But this time of night I'm liable to get sleepy. Tell your friends good-by for me, and be good to yourself. I've appreciated your company."

Mr. McLean entered Smith's Palace, and, engaging a room with two beds in it, did a little delicate lying by means of the truth. "It's a lost boy—a runaway," he told the clerk. "He'll not be extra clean, I expect, if he does come. Maybe he'll give me the slip, and I'll have a job cut out tomorrow. I'll thank you to put my money in your safe."

The clerk placed himself at the disposal of the secret service, and Lin walked up and down, looking at the railroad photographs for some ten minutes, when Master Billy peered in from the street.

"Hello!" said Mr. McLean, casually, and returned to a fine picture of Pike's Peak.

Billy observed him for a space, and, receiving no further attention, came stepping along. "I'm not a-going back to Laramie," he stated, warningly.

"I wouldn't," said Lin. "It ain't half the town Denver is. Well, good night. Sorry you couldn't call sooner—I'm dead sleepy."

"Oh!" Bill stood blank. "I wish I'd shook the darned old show. Say, lemme black your boots in the morning?"

"Not sure my train don't go too early."

"I'm up! I'm up! I get around to all of 'em."

"Where do you sleep?"

"Sleeping with the engine-man now. Why can't you put that gun on me tonight?"

"Goin' upstairs. This gentleman wouldn't let you go upstairs."

But the earnestly petitioned clerk consented, and Billy was the first to hasten into the room. He stood rapturous while Lin buckled the belt round his scanty stomach, and ingeniously buttoned the suspenders outside the accouterment to retard its immediate descent to earth.

"Did it ever kill a man?" asked Billy, touching the six-shooter.

"No. It ain't never had to do that, but I expect maybe it's stopped some killin' me."

"Oh, leave me wear it just a minute! Do you collect arrowheads? I think they're bully. There's the finest one you ever seen." He brought out the relic, tightly wrapped in paper, several pieces. "I foun' it myself, camping with father. It was sticking in a crack right on top of a rock, but nobody'd seen it till I came along. Ain't it fine?"

Mr. McLean pronounced it a gem.

"Father an' me found a lot, an' they made mother mad laying around, an' she threw 'em out. She takes stuff from Kelley's."

"Who's Kelley?"

"He keeps the drugstore at Laramie. Mother gets awful funny. That's how she was when I came home. For I told Mr. Perkins he lied, an' I ran then. An' I knowed well enough she'd lick me when she got through her spell—an' father can't stop her, an' I—ah, I was sick of it! She's lamed me up twice beating me—an' Perkins wanting me to say 'God bless my mother!' a-getting up and a-going to bed—he's a flub-dub! An' so I cleared out. But I'd just as leave said for God to bless father—an' you. I'll do it now if you say it's any sense."

Mr. McLean sat down in a chair. "Don't you do it now," said he.

"You wouldn't like mother," Billy continued. "You can keep that." He came to Lin and placed the arrowhead in his hands, standing beside him. "Do you like birds' eggs? I collect them. I got twenty-five kinds—sage-hen, an' blue grouse, an' willow-grouse, an' lots more kinds harder—but I couldn't bring all them from Laramie. I brought the magpie's, though. D'you care to see a magpie egg? Well, you stay tomorrow an' I'll show you that an' some other things I got the engine-man lets me keep there, for there's boys that would steal an egg. An' I could take you where we could fire that pistol. Bet you don't know what that is!"

He brought out a small tin box shaped like a thimble, in which were things that rattled.

Mr. McLean gave it up.

"That's a kinni-kinnic seed. You can have that, for I got some more with the engine-man."

Lin received this second token also, and thanked the giver for it. His first feeling had been to prevent the boy's parting with his treasures, but something that came not from the polish of manners and experience made him know that he should take them. Billy talked away, laying bare his little soul. The street boy that was not quite come made place for the child that was not quite gone, and unimportant words and confidences dropped from him disjointed as he climbed to the knee of Mr. McLean, and inadvertently took that cowpuncher for some sort of parent he had not hitherto met. It lasted but a short while, however, for he went to sleep in the middle of a sentence, with his head upon Lin's breast. The man held him perfectly still, because he had not the faintest notion that Billy would be impossible to disturb.

At length he spoke to him, suggesting that bed might prove more comfortable, and, finding how it was, rose and undressed the boy and laid him between the sheets. The arms and legs seemed aware of the moves required of them, and stirred conveniently; and directly the head was upon the pillow the whole small frame burrowed down, without the opening of an eye or a change in the breathing. Lin stood some time by the bedside, with his eyes on the long, curling lashes and the curly hair. Then he glanced craftily at the door of the room, and at himself in the looking-glass. He stooped and kissed Billy on the forehead, and, rising from that, gave himself a hangdog stare in the mirror, and soon in his own bed was sleeping the sound sleep of health.

He was faintly roused by the church bells, and lay still, lingering with his sleep, his eyes closed, and his thoughts unshaped. As he became slowly aware of the morning, the ringing and the light reached him, and he waked wholly, and, still lying quiet, considered the strange room filled with the bells and the sun of the winter's day. "Where have I struck now?" he inquired, and as last night returned abruptly upon his mind, he raised himself on his arm.

There sat Responsibility in a chair, washed clean and dressed, watching him.

"You're awful late," said Responsibility. "But I weren't a-going without telling you good-by."

"Go!" exclaimed Lin. "Go where? You surely ain't leavin' me to eat breakfast alone?" The cowpuncher made his voice very plaintive. Set Responsibility free after all his trouble to catch him? This was more than he could do!

"I've got to go. If I'd thought you'd want for me to stay—why, you said you was a-going by the early train!"

"But the durned thing's got away on me," said Lin, smiling sweetly from the bed.

"If I hadn't a-promised them—"

"Who?"

"Sidney Ellis and Pete Goode. Why, you know them; you grubbed with them."

"Shucks!"

"We're a-going to have fun today."

"Oh!"

"For it's Christmas, an' we've bought some good cigars, an' Pete says he'll learn me sure. O' course I've smoked some, you know. But I'd just as leave stayed with you if I'd only knowed sooner. I wish you lived here. Did you smoke whole big cigars when you was beginning?"

"Do you like flapjacks and maple syrup?" inquired the artful McLean. "That's what I'm figuring on inside twenty minutes."

"Twenty minutes! If they'd wait—"

"See here, Bill. They've quit expecting you, don't you think? I'd ought to waked, you see, but I slep' and slep', and kep' you from meetin' your engagements, you see—for you couldn't go, of course. A man couldn't treat a man that way now, could he?"

"Course he couldn't," said Billy, brightening.

"And they wouldn't wait, you see. They wouldn't fool away Christmas, that only comes oncet a year, kickin' their heels and sayin', 'Where's Billy?' They'd say, 'Bill has sure made other arrangements, which he'll explain to us at his leesyure.' And they'd skip with the cigars."

The advocate paused, effectively, and from his bolster regarded Billy with a convincing eye.

"That's so," said Billy.

"And where would you be then, Bill? In the street, out of friends, out of Christmas, and left both ways, no tobaccer and no flapjacks. Now, Bill, what do you say to us putting up a Christmas deal together? Just you and me?"

"I'd like that," said Billy. "Is it all day?"

"I was thinkin' of all day," said Lin. "I'll not make you do anything you'd rather not."

"Ah, they can smoke without me," said Billy with sudden acrimony. "I'll see 'em tomorrow."

"That's you!" cried Mr. McLean. "Now, Bill, you hustle down and tell them to keep a table for us. I'll get my clothes on and follow you."

The boy went, and Mr. McLean procured hot water and dressed himself, tying his scarf with great care. "Wished I'd a clean shirt," said he.

But I don't look very bad. Shavin' yesterday afternoon was a good move. He picked up the arrowhead and the kinni-kinnic, and was particular to store them in his safest pocket. "I ain't sure whether you're crazy or not," said he to the man in the looking-glass. "I ain't never been sure." And he slammed the door and went downstairs.

He found young Bill on guard over a table for four, with all the chairs tilted against it as warning to strangers. No one sat at any other table or came into the room, for it was late, and the place quite emptied of breakfasters, and the several entertained waiters had gathered behind Billy's important-looking back. Lin provided a thorough meal, and Billy pronounced the flannel cakes superior to flapjacks, which were not upon the bill of fare.

"I'd like to see you often," said he. "I'll come and see you if you don't live too far."

"That's the trouble," said the cowpuncher. "I do. Awful far." He stared out of the window.

"Well, I might come some time. I wish you'd write me a letter. Can you write?"

"What's that? Can I write? Oh, yes."

"I can write, an' I can read, too. I've been to school in Sidney, Nebraska, an' Magaw, Kansas, an' Salt Lake—that's the finest town except Denver."

Billy fell into that cheerful strain of comment which, unreplied to, yet goes on contented and self-sustaining, while Mr. McLean gave amiable signs of assent, but chiefly looked out of the window. And when the now interested waiter said respectfully that he desired to close the room, they went out to the office, where the money was got out of the safe and the bill paid.

The streets were full of the bright sun, and seemingly at Denver's gates stood the mountains sparkling; an air crisp and pleasant wafted from their peaks. No smoke hung among the roofs, and the sky spread wide over the city without a stain. It was holiday up among the chimneys and tall buildings, and down among the quiet ground-stories below as well; and presently from their scattered pinnacles through the town the bells broke out against the jocund silence of the morning.

"Don't you like music?" inquired Billy.

"Yes," said Lin.

Ladies with their husbands and children were passing and meeting, orderly yet gayer than if it were only Sunday, and the salutations of

Christmas came now and again to the cowpuncher's ears. But today, possessor of his own share in this, Lin looked at everyone with a sort of friendly challenge, and young Billy talked along beside him.

"Don't you think we could go in here?" Billy asked. A church door was open, and the rich organ sounded through to the pavement. "They've good music here, an' they keep it up without much talking between. I've been in lots of times."

They went in and sat to hear the music. Better than the organ, it seemed to them, were the harmonious voices raised from somewhere outside, like unexpected visitants; and the pair sat in their back seat, too deep in listening to the processional hymn to think of rising in decent imitation of those around them. The crystal melody of the refrain especially reached their understandings, and when for the fourth time "shout the glad tidings, exultingly sing," pealed forth and ceased, both the delighted faces fell.

"Don't you wish there was more?" Billy whispered.

"Wish there was a hundred verses," answered Lin.

But canticles and responses followed, with so little talking between them they were held spellbound, seldom thinking to rise or kneel. Lin's eyes roved over the church, dwelling upon the pillars in their evergreen, the flowers and leafy wreaths, the texts of white and gold. *Peace, good will toward men,* he read. *That's so. Peace and good will. Yes, that's so. I expect they got that somewheres in the Bible. It's awful good, and you'd never think of it yourself.*

There was a touch on his arm, and a woman handed a book to him. "This is the hymn we have now," she whispered, gently; and Lin, blushing scarlet, took it passively without a word. He and Billy stood up and held the book together, dutifully reading the words:

> It came upon the midnight clear,
>   That glorious song of old,
> From angels bending near the earth
>   To touch their harps of gold;
> Peace on the earth—

This tune was more beautiful than all, and Lin lost himself in it, until he found Billy recalling him with a finger upon the words, the concluding ones:

> And the whole world sent back the song
> Which now the angels sing.

The music rose and descended to its lovely and simple end, and, for a second time in Denver, Lin brushed a hand across his eyes. He turned his face from his neighbor, frowning crossly; and since the heart has reasons which Reason does not know, he seemed to himself a fool. But when the service was over and he came out, he repeated again, " 'Peace and good will.' When I run on to the Bishop of Wyoming I'll tell him if he'll preach on them words I'll be there."

"Couldn't we shoot your pistol now?" asked Billy.

"Sure, boy. Ain't you hungry, though?"

"No. I wish we were away off up there. Don't you?"

"The mountains? They look pretty, so white! A heap better'n houses. Why, we'll go there! There's trains to Golden. We'll shoot around among the foothills."

To Golden they immediately went, and after a meal there, wandered in the open country until the cartridges were gone, the sun was low, and Billy was walked off his young heels—a truth he learned complete in one horrid moment, and battled to conceal.

"Lame!" he echoed, angrily. "I ain't."

"Shucks!" said Lin, after the next ten steps. "You are, and both feet."

"Tell you, there's stones here, an' I'm just a-skipping them."

Lin took the boy in his arms and carried him to Golden. "I'm played out myself," he said, sitting in the hotel and looking lugubriously at Billy on a bed. "And I ain't fit to have charge of a hog." He came and put his hand on the boy's head.

"I'm not sick," said the cripple. "I tell you I'm bully. You wait an' see me eat dinner."

But Lin had hot water and cold water and salt, and was an hour upon his knees bathing the hot feet. And then Billy could not eat dinner!

There was a doctor in Golden, but in spite of his light prescription and most reasonable observations, Mr. McLean passed a foolish night of vigil, while Billy slept, quite well at first, and, as the hours passed, better and better. In the morning he was entirely brisk, though stiff.

"I couldn't work quick today," he said. "But I guess one day won't lose me my trade."

"How d'you mean?" asked Lin.

"Why, I've got regulars, you know. Sidney Ellis an' Pete Goode has theirs an' we don't cut each other. I've got Mr. Daniels an' Mr. Fisher an' lots, an' if you lived in Denver, I'd shine your boots every day for nothing. I wished you lived in Denver."

"Shine my boots? You'll never! And you don't black Daniels or Fisher, or any of the outfit."

"Why, I'm doing first-rate," said Billy, surprised at the swearing into which Mr. McLean now burst. "An' I ain't big enough to get to make money at any other job."

"I want to see that engine-man," muttered Lin. "I don't like your smokin' friend."

"Pete Goode? Why, he's awful smart. Don't you think he's smart?"

"Smart's nothin'," observed Mr. McLean.

"Pete has learned me and Sidney a lot," pursued Billy engagingly.

"I'll bet he has!" growled the cowpuncher; and again Billy was taken aback at his language.

It was not so simple, this case. To the perturbed mind of Mr. McLean it grew less simple during that day at Golden, while Billy recovered, and talked, and ate his innocent meals. The cowpuncher was far too wise to think for a single moment of restoring the runaway to his debauched and shiftless parents. Possessed of some imagination, he went through a scene in which he appeared at the Lusk threshold with Billy and forgiveness, and intruded upon a conjugal assault and battery. "Shucks!" said he. "The kid would be off again inside a week. And I don't want him there, anyway."

Denver, upon the following day, saw the little bootblack again at his corner, with his trade not lost; but near him stood a tall, singular man, with hazel eyes and a sulky expression. And citizens during that week noticed, as a new sight in the streets, the tall man and the little boy walking together. Sometimes they would be in shops. The boy seemed as happy as possible, talking constantly, while the man seldom said a word, and his face was serious.

Upon New Year's Eve Governor Barker was overtaken by Mr. McLean riding a horse up Hill Street, Cheyenne.

"Hello!" said Barker, staring humorously through his glasses. "Have a good drunk?"

"Changed my mind," said Lin, grinning. "Proves I've got one. Struck Christmas all right, though."

"Who's your friend?" inquired His Excellency.

"This is Mister Billy Lusk. Him and me have agreed that towns ain't nice to live in. If Judge Henry's foreman and his wife won't board him at Sunk Creek—why, I'll fix it somehow."

The cowpuncher and his Responsibility rode on together toward the open plain.

"Suffering Moses!" remarked His Excellency.

The Bullpuncher

James Stevens

"Bullpuncher" is one of several old-fashioned terms for a logger—that brawling, lusty son of the Big Woods. What was Christmas like for one of that breed a hundred years ago? James Stevens (1892–1971), who for many years was head of public relations for the old West Coast Lumberman's Association, a trade organization once among the most powerful in the world, provides the surprising answer in the fine, memorable story which follows. Stevens was the author of the first and most famous book-length account of the legendary exploits of Paul Bunyan *(1925); of two first-rate novels,* Brawnyman *(1926) and* Big Jim Turner *(1948); of many short stories set in the Pacific Northwest, some of the best of which can be found in his 1928 collection* Homer in the Sagebrush; *and of half a dozen nonfiction books and a long-running newspaper column called "Out of the Woods."*

A thousand miles of timberland. Cedar and spruce, hemlock and Douglas fir. The forest sweeps down from Alaska, fringes the Fraser River, skirts Puget Sound, makes a great green ruff for Mt. Tacoma, blankets the Olympic Peninsula for millions of acres, walls Gray's and Willapa Harbors, hedges the Columbia, and rolls on over the Oregon valleys and hills to meet the sequoias of California. This is the timber country of the Pacific Northwest. It is the last American wilderness. Here Paul Bunyan died.

Here the Herculean hero of the loggers lived the last of his glory among his choppers, sawyers and bullpunchers from Michigan, Wisconsin and the State of Maine. Paul Bunyan and his glory did not fade into the dark of far timber until the machine made the logger a timber mechanic, until the strapping Northwestern sisters of the Lake States river towns took the veil and became "lumber capitals."

In the bullpunching days Paul Bunyan survived in tremendous tales. Then there were also mortal heroes in the land. One Black Larrity was an Achilles of the Gray's Harbor logging towns; in his highest renown he was known as the bulliest performer that ever splintered the plank streets of Aberdeen with calks. The frame of Black Larrity vanished with that of Paul Bunyan at the end of the nineties. What became of old Paul and Black Larrity? Nobody knows. Your great characters must disappear, if they are to be greatly remembered.

The old-timers say that Black Larrity left the Gray's Harbor country when the first whistle of a donkey engine was heard along the Wishkah River. The saloons of Aberdeen were clean, decent and tame by that time. A performer like Black Larrity couldn't go through a blow-in without landing in jail. So he went over the hump. Where he ended, the old-timers do not know. They tell of his first Christmas blow-in in Aberdeen, of his battle with Swede Henry, that tough bull of the woods, and they say:

"He disappeared. Most of the famous old characters disappeared. Just like that."

II

A wind roared up the Wishkah from the foggy harbor and the great boughs of virgin cedars, hemlocks and Douglas firs dripped from a cold December drizzle. The sixteen oxen—the "bullteam"—stood with drooping heads, the log chain hanging slack under the eight yokes. Black Larrity, the bullpuncher, and his second man were heaving the turn of logs together by the power of jackscrews. The skids, small logs sunk in the earth in intervals of four feet, were smeared with oil and the riding side of the log turn was peeled and slick. But it was always tough going around this bend of the skidroad and the shod hoofs of the big bulls slipped in the soaked earth between the skid logs. The turn was struck, and Black Larrity, being in a fair humor, was giving his bulls the best of it by jacking the logs together, slacking the coupling chains, just as a locomotive engineer jams the cars of his train together for an easy start.

It was a ten-minute job for the bullpuncher and his second. Then Black Larrity shoved a brown plug under his sweeping, coaly mustache, ground off a chew that bulged his right cheek—the cheek that had a gashlike scar running over it from high bone down to chin—, stuck the plug in a pocket of his black-and-red-checked mackinaw, and picked up his goad.

The goad was a thick oak stick over six feet long and tipped with iron. By itself the goad was a club but in Larrity's gloved hand it looked like a switch. He held it straight up while he scowled and figured over the bullteam and the turn of logs. His sweep of mustache, the deep scar, the thick, fishhook eyebrows, the heavy muss of black hair over his forehead, made the scowl a tremendous one. Larrity fired a stream of tobacco juice that hit the butt log squarely in the heart, then he swung springly for the bullteam.

"Yee-ay, bulls!" His growly bellow brought a slow shiver from the low-headed bulls. "Yee-ay, Buster—Tramper—Li-*on!* Yee-*ay,* you juggy dead-eyed, hump-backed critters of the old hell! H'ist, Tramper, or I'll chew your hocks off! Snub—Hogan—Sawbuck—Hols—you leaders! Heave on 'er or I'll burn and blast ye from muzzle to tail! H'ist! Yee-ay, bulls!"

At each bellow Black Larrity sprang from yoke to yoke, the sharp iron tip of the goad raking the ribs of the bulls and gouging their shoulders. The wheelers lumbered against their yoke, the swingers tightened the chain, the leaders heaved. The eyes of every aroused animal rolled as the team took the butt-log ahead with a heavy lunge. The second log of the turn slowed them a little, the third one made them labor—and again Black Larrity's profane roars and the bite of his goad made them paw mud.

"There she skids! Gee, Hols!"

The bullteam now had a start that should have taken the turn of logs on around the bend. But a squeal of brake shoes on iron tires made Black Larrity glance through the bush. The road to a new settlement ran close to the skidroad here. Through the bush he saw two shaggy horses braced back in mangy breeching to keep a lumber wagon from running over them on a sharp pitch of the road. An old woman in a floppy felt hat and a man's rusty overcoat was driving the team from a spring seat. Beside her was a girl in a yellow slicker. A pale oval face shone through the gray mist. Wide blue eyes gazed into Larrity's black ones. What in the holy old mackinawed devils—she seemed to be scared! Her lips were parted like she was going to scream. And damn' if she wasn't holding her hands over her ears! It was just a glimpse through the bush—then only the green boughs dripping from the heavy mist—and the bulls were slowing down. Tramper, the near wheeler, grunted, stopped, and sank to the ground.

For a few seconds Black Larrity stared dumbly at the stalled bullteam. She'd heard him giving the bulls old Billy-hell. That's why she'd looked scared and put her hands over her ears. Scared of him, was she? Well, she'd better be scared, if she belonged to this lousy sanctimonious gang of settlers that had begun stump-ranching along the Wishkah. If that outfit tangled up with him a few deacons would get their ribs broke. As for the women folks—what in the name of the slippery old saints did church women want to come into this wild timber country for? Here one had to come along and hear him giving it to the bulls in the only language bulls could understand. She had looked at him like a rabbit looks at a wolf. And he'd let the log turn stall again. Tramper was down. By the holy old, jumping old, whistling old, high-tailed, bald-headed, blue-bellied Jerusalem H. Slim!

"H'ist! H'ist, you, Tramper!"

The scar in Black Larrity's right cheek was scarlet and his whole face was an Indian red. He h'isted Tramper with his goad, then he leaped to the butt log. It was five feet thick, on a level with the wide hips of the wheelers. Black Larrity jumped on those hips. His right calked boot struck Buster's back, his left one struck a white spot on Tramper's ribs. Using the goad for a balance, Black Larrity leaped high and came down with raking kicks on the backs of the plunging beasts. Little streams of blood oozed over Tramper's white spot. Buster bawled like he was being butchered. Larrity leaped on to the next yoke, raked and kicked—on to the next—on to the leaders—and to the ground.

"Yee-ay bulls!"

The bullteam heaved against their yokes like stampeding cattle. The log turn plunged over the skids and around the bend. As Black Larrity took it on down to the river landing he muttered and swore to himself about Christian women.

Swede Henry, the bull of the woods, was at the landing.

"What the hal you ban blood 'em up foor?" he grumbled.

"Who's punchin' these bulls?" said Larrity coldly.

"Ay tank maybe you don' punch 'em after Christmas."

"That's what you 'tank,' hey? Maybe this outfit'll have another boss logger after Christmas. Y'ever 'tank' of that, Swede Henry?"

"Ay gas we settle that plenty soon enough."

Swede Henry bristled his pale bushy eyebrows in a threatening frown and squinted his small gray eyes in a hostile stare. Swede Henry was not afraid of any black Irishman of a bullpuncher alive. Yellow hair jutted out from under his cap like wheat stubble. His nose was flat and his face was pitted with calk scars. He was a Wisconsin man. It had taken a dozen lumberjacks to put those scars on his face. A river town king he had always been in Wisconsin and no Gray's Harbor logger had yet rassled him down. He was not afraid of Black Larrity. After Christmas he would still be the boss logger of this Wishkah camp and there would be a new bullpuncher on the skidroad.

Larrity paid no more attention to the bull of the woods. As he turned the bulls back up the skidroad he was scowling over his own dark thoughts. A girl had looked at him like a rabbit looks at a wolf. That was about it. A religious girl and a lousy timber beast. The bullteam lumbered up the skidroad with a slow jangle of chains. Yeah, that's what he was, what he always had been, boy and man. That was what you had to be to punch the bulls and to hold your own in the timber town saloons. He might go join the settlers, get their religion— Campbellites, wasn't they?—and go stump-ranching. A religious girl would smile at a religious man. But he was a lousy timber beast, heart, soul and hide. The bulls were to punch. Swede Henry was to be licked. He'd never had a blow-in in Aberdeen yet, as he'd come to this country since the Fourth of July. The Christmas blow-in was just ahead; in it he'd have to show what a star performer he was, take Swede Henry to his cleaning—so what the hell, Bill, what the hell!

Swede Henry stood with his hairy red fists resting on his hips until the bullteam had vanished around the bend and into the drizzle and mist. The bull of the woods grunted and turned to meet the curious gaze of the boom boss.

"You better look out for Black Larrity," said the boom boss earnestly. "He's a bad one and he don't like Swedes."

"Ay give a gude damn," growled Swede Henry.

"I allow you can handle him," said the boom boss politely. "But he'd be a bad un to meet in a dark alley. Slab Gilkerson used to know him on the Menominee. He'd punched bulls in Maine, but in Michigan he was a star sleigh teamster and a white water bucko. Tough black Irish all the time. They was a Swede bartender in one of the river towns. He had corkscrew mustaches that was bigger'n Larrity's coaly ones. When Larrity first saw them he bellered, 'Chop 'em off!' 'Go to hal!' says the Swede. Larrity overs the bar and beats him rumdum. 'Have 'em chopped when I get back from the spring drive,' he ordered when he left. Sure enough, end of the drive, here come Larrity into the saloon. The Swede still has his mustaches. Larrity overs the bar for him again. The Swede has a hatchet stashed and he out and ups with it and puts that gash in Larrity's map. Cut him up otherwise too. But Larrity leaves him a dead Swede. Had to take out from the Michigan timber country, though. Headed for Minnesota or sommers, then for Washington and the big sticks of the Olympic Peninsula. And here he is. Look out for his Christmas presents, Swede Henry."

"Ay give a gude damn," repeated the bull of the woods. "Well, we got to be loggin' noo. Yump back to your boom sticks."

III

That night the wind roared into a storm that beat from the open sea over the Gray's Harbor bar and up the Wishkah. It rattled the shakes that roofed the bunk shanty and it puffed and whistled through the cracks between the rough boards of the walls.

"Might as well be bunkin' inside a picket fence," grumbled an old faller, as he tramped in from supper and lit his pipe.

The remark was spoken to Larrity but the bullpuncher paid it no mind. The mist and drizzle had turned into rain before dark. His mackinaw was wet and it was hanging on a line above the pot-bellied heater. The fire snapped and snarled around pitchy knots and the fat sides of the heater bloomed red. The mackinaw hung to dry, Larrity sat on a bench and gnawed a mouthful off his plug. He pulled off his calk boots and threw them over to his bunk. Then he sat with his sock feet perched on the edge of the two by six frame which enclosed the ash-filled heater bed. They were big feet but the sweat-stained toes of the gray wool socks curled out and drooped down. Larrity kept the toes elevated above the ashes, which were brown with tobacco juice.

He spread his knees apart, rested his forearms on them, and let his hairy hands dangle between his legs. He scowled solemnly at the three triangle holes in the door of the heater through which the flames flickered and snapped. Every so often he spit a brown stream at one of these holes. There was always a sharp hiss for a second, as Larrity never missed. After each discharge Larrity would lift a hand, part his mustache, and wipe his mouth. Then he would start scowling and thinking again.

The shakes overhead rattled from the rain and the wind. The loggers crowded the benches around the stove. They were all in their sock feet. All of them were wearing overalls or ducking pants stagged just below the knee. Red strips of drawers legs were revealed between pants ends and sock tops. Heavy suspenders stretched over backs covered with wool shirts, red, green or blue. There were several bald heads, but every man had mustaches. There were no cigarettes. Pipe smoke of a stinging smell curled over the bowed heads of the loggers, who were tired out from their eleven hours in the wet cold. Fresh tobacco juice soon made small puddles in the ashes of the heater bed. From rafters, beams and lines hung wet mackinaws, stagged shirts, paraffin pants, and underclothes which had been boiled to kill the latest crop of lice. The windows were shut tight and the steam from the drying clothes mixed its powerful various smells with that of bitter root tobacco burning in caked pipes. The coal oil lamps with rusty tin reflectors behind them smoked from shelves in each end of the bunkhouse. The light was so dim around the heater that its red sides shone and sparkled. A mumble of talk arose. Somebody was grouching about the cook.

"That belly burglar's so greasy he has to use sandpaper to pick up the dishes."

An old faller complained of his rheumatism.

"It was better for a while here on the Coast. Never bothered me at first like she used to in Michigan. But now it's misery all the time."

A swamper had a lame ankle.

"Widder-maker dropped from a snag. Come nigh gettin' me. But I dodged. Turnt so quick, though, I spraint my lousy ankle. Warn't so close to Christmas, I'd mope."

Christmas. . . . The mumble of talk turned to the good time to come. . . .

"Hope I meet up with that woman in the Eagle I had last Fourth."

"Not me. Three drinks a day this trip is my limit. Got to save up for my old age."

"Yeah, you'll save, lad. You'll get the other ear chawed off this blow-in, that's how you'll save."

"Hear they's a new place opened where they sell the real double-stamp."

"Yeah. Paul Bunyan's runnin' it, ain't he? Redeye, rotgut, bug juice and forty-rod—that's the licker for loggers all the time. Double-stamp stuff for loggers? Don't tell me!"

"I learnt last Fourth how they mix their bar licker. First they take hundred eighty-eight proof alcohol, then English breakfast tea for color, then prune juice for flavor—"

"You mean finecut for both color and flavor, don't you, lad? That was it back in the river towns."

"I'll bust the faro bank this trip, then I'll buy a bullteam of my own."

"You'll buy a trip to hell ridin' out on the ebb tide if you don't steer clear of the tinhorn joints, old settler! The bustin'll be done by some-body with a blackjack and you'll join the floater fleet!"

"Hear they got a new bar in the Heron Cribs. Built like a horseshoe. Some nights they gets one of the sportin' women out, strip her off, grease her with vaseline, put her and some cockeyed bum inside the bar, and then have a chase for your whiskers."

"Yeah? That makes me think of the time I went from Saginaw to Chicago. . . ."

Larrity's scowl grew deeper and darker as the talk went on and the loggers began to boast and brag about their great drunks and perfor-mances with dance hall women. At last he grunted sourly and got up.

"You are the bulliest drunks and performers with the women that ever was—here in camp. But let you get to town and you'll line up in some redeye joint and log your heads off. Whistlin' old Jemima Jeezus, you make my tailbone ache! I'm goin' to roll in."

He turned with one springy movement and strode between the rows of three-decked bunks. Larrity didn't mind the smells from the tumbled gray blankets in each bunk. He had been used to them since he was a boy. Beans, salt pork, and sourdough bread for grub. From ten to sixteen hours a day in the woods. The stink of drying work clothes and heaps of dirty blankets at night. That was the life of a logger, a timber beast, a camp man, for you, and Larrity didn't ques-tion the right of it. He pulled off his socks, overalls and shirt. The muscles of his arms, shoulders and back made bulging ridges in his red undershirt. He was a moose of a man, this star bullpuncher of the Wishkah. He crawled into his blankets and tried to think of Christmas —four days more and he'd show these Aberdeen bullies how he'd performed on the Menominee and the Kennebec. When he was done with Swede Henry the name of Black Larrity would be known all over the Gray's Harbor timber country. . . . A pale oval face drifted before him. . . . Blue eyes. . . . Scared eyes. . . . A religious girl like that, living so close to a bullteam camp. . . . Timber beasts. . . . The loggers around the heater heard a growly mutter from among Larrity's blankets.

"Puncher's in a mean humor to-night."

"Yeah. Prob'ly dreamin' he's takin' the bulls down a thirty-per pitch."

"More likely dreamin' he's chewin' on Swede Henry's ear."

" 'Low they'll tangle, right enough."

"Juh hear Slab Gilkerson tell how a stickup tried to lay Larrity out with a dray stake once? Well, Larrity went down, but when the stickup went to make his frisk Larrity hooked him. Come to that quick and choked him dead with one hand. Come clear of course. That was back in Saginaw."

"Good ol' Saginaw, where they was a sawdust mountain forty miles long and a saloon and dance hall every quarter."

"All run by Paul Bunyan, wasn't they?"

Larrity snored. He had to roll out every morning at four to feed and rub down the bullteam and nothing could keep him awake long after he was once in his blankets.

The others soon drifted to their bunks. At nine o'clock the lights were blown out. The ding-dong would rouse the men for breakfast at five. Long hours in the big timber made men sleep hard. The bunk shanty sounded with a chorus of hearty snores. The glow on the sides of the heater soon died out. The smells thickened and settled in the cold, dead air.

Down at the docks of the tidewater town of Aberdeen the storm rattled through the rigging of schooners moored to load cargoes of lumber. It romped among the houses of the town. The dance hall girls slouched about empty tables. The bartenders loafed over their bars. Aberdeen was a dead town now. But Christmas was only four days off. Just wait!

IV

All of the loggers from the Wishkah camp were on the road the day before Christmas, but Black Larrity tramped into Aberdeen alone. The December wind was still on a rampage, blowing in a drizzle from Gray's Harbor. Heron Street was veiled in the foggy rain. Lights were shining through the windows of stores, restaurants, dance halls and saloons. The calked boots of a thousand loggers scrunched the wet boards of sidewalks as the bearded and mustached men in mackinaws and stagged pants roved from one saloon to the other. They straggled across the planks of the street to meet friends on the other side. Gangs gathered, whoops and laughs filled the air, bottles were passed around. Shingle-weavers, mill hands, fishermen and sailors stood aside for the men of the woods. Hard-looking customers eased among the gangs, searching for those who might be relieved of their rolls without too much trouble.

Amid this scene Larrity lost the black scowl he had worn for the past four days; his eyes got a hot gleam, he threw back his bulky shoulders, tossed his head, and seemed to snort. This was the good old stuff. The town didn't know him yet, but it wouldn't be long now until he'd be a king of performers here, just as he had been in the old timber towns.

In the first blocks from the left bank of Wishkah the saloons packed Heron and Hume Streets—the Humboldt, the Mug, the Whale, the Eagle, the Combination, the Gem, the North Pole, the Blazer, the Circle, and many more. Square-fronted one- and two-story buildings of wood in rusty paint, all resting on piling or on ground made by a fill of sawdust and edgings. The best bars, such as the Humboldt and Blazer, had new floors, but already these were freckled and splotched from the calks of the loggers' boots. Twice a year these popular saloons had to lay new floors. Such tough joints as the Circle had iron-bound bars and sawdust floors. The sidewalks had slivery hollows, except where new planks had been nailed down. Aberdeen was still a rough-hewn frontier town.

Larrity cashed his check over the bar of the Blazer. A star bullpuncher was paid the tremendous wage of one hundred and fifty dollars a month and board. Big Al, the boss of the Blazer, counted out twenty twenty-dollar gold pieces for Larrity.

"Bankin' any, Mr. Puncher?" he asked politely.

"Nope."

"Better, lad. Some stickup'll slip you a blackjack or knockout drops and roll you. You can bank what you want in my safe here and I give you a receipt. You're safe in the Blazer but there are joints where you'll be gypped quick."

"I'm safe anywhere," said Larrity. "I like to jingle my gold."

He bought a round for the house, then pocketed the double-handful of gold. Then he went to a barber shop, had his hair trimmed, his face and neck shaved, and got himself magnificently oiled and powdered. Out into the fog, then, and back to the Blazer, where he bought two quarts of bar whisky. He uncorked each one and pushed pinches of finecut into the necks. The liquor took on a richer and darker hue and the tobacco threads curled beautifully as he shook the bottles. Larrity recorked them and stuck one in each mackinaw pocket. A logger always liked to pass around a bottle whenever he bumped into some bunch or other between saloons. And in a gang battle a quart bottle clutched in each fist made powerful weapons. Now he was all set to perform. Now he would show them how to celebrate Christmas!

Two thousand men from the bullteam camps, the lumber and shingle mills, the ships and the fisheries, were also ready. In the Blazer four aproned bartenders rushed and sweated between spigots, bar and till. Big Al, the thick-necked, fierce-eyed owner, who prided himself on running the squarest place in town and on having the muscles to keep it square and peaceable, was cashing check after check and banking for most of the loggers. His safe held twenty thousand dollars before midnight. The loggers were six-deep before the bar. The bottles and glasses were skidded through splashes of beer and furrows of foam. The bartenders picked up wet dollars and half-dollars and the loggers picked up wet quarters and dimes of change. The rush was so heavy that the bartenders had no time to swab off the bar. The fog was thickening outside and the saloon lamps threw a richer glow over the scene. The splattered and foamy top of the bar shone. The mirrors back of it reflected light into the drinkers' faces, making them appear handsome and bright. The rumble of talk and the clink of glasses quickened; shouted jokes and bawls of laughter sounded; all of a sudden there was a blast of hot argument, a hard tramp of feet, a thud, a grunt—and Big Al swung around the bar. He pried the two battlers apart, made them feel the power of his grip, then brought them to the bar.

"Drink together on the house," ordered Big Al. "Then keep the peace, or I'll work you both down with a bungstarter. This ain't no knock-down-and-drag-out joint, my lads."

Somebody smacked a twenty-dollar gold piece on the bar.

"Set up the whisky! Everybody drink on a Michigan man!"

Big All grinned and helped with the setting-up himself. The loggers were starting now, starting to blow 'er hard and fast.

V

The doors never stopped swinging. Loggers tramped in and loggers tramped out. Few were staggering any yet; the night was hardly born. But the street was darkening fast and few gangs were lingering outside now. It was ramble from one saloon to the other; at suppertime head for pork chops and eggs; then to the dance halls and the dance hall girls when the pianos began to thump and the fiddles to squeak foot-teasing tunes.

Dance and drink until midnight. Then in the Eagle, Black Larrity began to get up steam. There was a rich glow inside his head and his thoughts were running high and wild.

Hey, lad, it's a bum dancer you are, in logger boots, heavy and calked! No chance to slick and slide around in a fancy style. No chance to give the girls a treat with a nifty dancing show. But what the hell, Bill, what the hell! You're only a lousy timber beast anyway, here to blow in with the dance hall women! You're a camp man, old settler, a man who has to live away from women most of his days and get the timber out. Religious women look at you like a rabbit looks at a wolf. You've been "timber beast" to the good folks since a way back. So that's how you are what you are. That's why you perform. You got to get your high and mighty times any way you can. Well, lad, here's the fixings for you, here in your roaring old timber town! Redeye to uplift your Jeezus-jimmed soul, booze-mooching whores to ease your heart! Yea, lad, you know they'd spit in your eye if it wasn't for your silver and gold! Love—love hell! But for just the feel of a soft breast against your pitch-streaked mackinaw, for that shaking look of hidden fire which only a woman—and any damned woman—can give—for these your dance hall woman will do—yea, when you're half-shot with the old redeye which'll make you see the woman you've always dreamed about in this painted girl with the circus dress! . . .

Yea, she'll do! She's a plump young one, soft and warm, so hold her close in the dance, grin and dream like an oary-eyed fool—then buy a drink and see her pocket the check. She pockets the check, that girl in the circus dress. There's a red sash around it. Hell, and she's got a schoolgirl ribbon in her hair! A circus doll, a school kid; but look at the paint on her, swabbed on her cheeks, under the brown eyes sizing you up with a sharp stare that pinches the skin into fine little wrinkles around them. Yay, lad, you know what she is! But what the hell, Bill, what the hell! There's that soft look that smites you all over with the fire that smolders behind it—take 'er on, lad, for she's a soft, warm woman. Hold the flesh and smash the dream. . . .

So the hot thoughts swam in Black Larrity's head as he began to dance the early hours of the night away. It was good for awhile; he was having a high and mighty old time of it. Tramping and swinging around in calk boots to the sound of piano-thumping and fiddle-squeaking, bumping into loggers dancing so with other girls; it was just that, and between dances slap down four bits for the drinks and see her pocket half; but that is her trade, so come on, girl, for another dance!

They talked . . . her name was Babe, that was all . . . she bet he could lick any ten men in the dance hall . . . oh, so he was a bullpuncher; he must have a big stake, lucky man . . . she got awful sick of this dance hall life sometimes, so many of the men were brutes when they were oary-eyed . . . it was wonderful when she could meet somebody like him. . . .

But her eyes kept wandering to a slim, hard-mouthed young man in a handsome checked suit, a young man with shiny hair slicked and curled elegantly over a pasty forehead. Larrity saw her glances . . . but he wouldn't see. Hell, he knew how it was, right enough. But Babe was in his arms now. She was his woman . . . for awhile. . . .

At two o'clock Babe went with Larrity to the Blazer, as the dancing was stopped. The wind was higher than ever. Larrity breathed deep of the fresh wet air. Two o'clock in the morning and time for a bully logger to perform. He swung his legs in a long stride and Babe's slip-pered feet pattered on the soggy boards. The Blazer was jammed with a roaring mob. Six bartenders were handling the rush. The glasses of beer and whisky were passed back from hand to hand. The shrill voices of dance hall girls sounded among the chesty rumble of logger talk. Above the drab shades of the hanging coal oil lamps a drift of blue smoke hid the ceiling. On kegs and in chairs men who had drunk themselves off their feet lolled and snored. Big Al stood at the end of the bar, grinning from the corner of his mouth whenever a joke was shouted at him from the crowd, keeping his eyes peeled for pimps and stickup men. His was a logger's saloon and he protected his trade. A young logger staggered up to him, seized one of Al's suspenders to steady himself, and asked for fifty dollars from the safe.

"You'll get nothin' till in the mornin', you polluted Siwash!" growled Big Al, and pushed him away.

The young logger weaved through the crowd, looking for sympathy.

"Won' give me my own money, the suhvabish! Call' me p'luted Siwash! Juh hear him, Bill? Call' me p'luted Siwash! An' I jus' wanna woman. Tha's all. An' I gotta have money to get a woman. An' he call' me—"

Larrity had elbowed through the crowd, and now he swung Babe up and set her on the bar. With one foot on the rail and one elbow on the bar, he faced the loggers. The red and black checks of his mackinaw sleeve flashed up, then down, and the bar shook as his fist smacked a twenty-dollar gold piece on it.

"Whisky for the house!" he bellowed.

"Who's that bully?" the loggers were asking one another as they poured the treat down.

Larrity heard and looked for a chance to show them. It soon appeared, in the person of Swede Henry, the broad-beamed bull of the woods. He was roaring drunk and the loggers respectfully made way for him. He crowded toward Larrity, and he leaned both thick elbows on the bar beside Babe.

"Ay got money to burn!" his chesty voice boomed. "Ay skal set 'em oop for house, too. Bartender, you got Swedish whisky? Ever'body don' drink Swedish whisky ay ban go'n' roll in sawdust wit'!"

Then he stared at the splatters of beer and rolls of foam on the bar.

"Clean off de bar for Swedish whisky!" he ordered.

"Swab it yerself," said a weary bartender.

Swede Henry's gray eyes glittered; then he saw Babe perched at his elbow and he grinned.

"All right. Ay tank ay do."

Swede Henry grabbed Babe by a foot and an arm, leaped like he was on a boom of logs, and slid the dance hall girl over the bar's flooded surface, crashing glasses to the floor, rolling a tide of beer and foam before her. She screamed. Swede Henry started a laugh. It ended when his right jawbone seemed to be driven through the other. The bar mirror exploded before him in a blaze of stars. The blaze turned into a cloud of milk-white smoke—then Big Al was shoving him out to the street. Swede Henry began to bawl cusswords in his native tongue and tried to push back past Big Al.

"Out with ye, Swede Henry, till you can be decent. You try a performance like that in my place again and I'll smoke you up with my four by five! Take yerself to bed, or go fall off the dock."

With Babe perched beside him again, Larrity was leaning beside her as a hero. Some bullpuncher from the state of Maine had set 'em up in his honor. He heard the old Aberdeen loggers saying that this was the first time Swede Henry had ever been knocked loose from himself. "Never saw him go down from one sock before." "A fightin' devil, that black Irishman, you ask me." "Yeah, where's he from?" "You know 'im, Sully?" "Yeah, he's been punchin' bulls in Swede Henry's camp. They ain't done with each other yet. One of 'em's gettin' a new job after this shutdown. Slab Gilkerson used to perform with Larrity in Michigan. Says he bumped off a bartender with his bare hands back there." "The hell! Some bully, hey?"

Larrity heard, and gloried. So it was in the timber country. You got glory with your muscles and your fists. A star sleigh teamster and white water bucko in the Lake States, a star bullpuncher here on the West Coast, a star performer in both the river and tidewater towns. That was him, all the time. All the time. . . . His head was afire with liquor and the heat the short battle had aroused. His knuckles ached. Enough for to-night. Yep, performing enough for this time. To-morrow was Christmas—hell, it was Christmas already! Christmas, logger, Christmas! Blow in! Blow in! Booze up and battle and get a woman for yourself! That was Christmas for a logger—have a high and mighty time until his silver and gold are gone. That was it for a logger, bully one or not. Just a time in town, then out to the timber, eleven-hour labor, salt pork, tough beans and sourdough bread to eat, a stinking bunk shanty to sleep in, and lousy blankets for a lonesome sleep. Back to the life of a timber beast! But what the hell, Bill, what the hell! A pocketful of gold, and it's time to perform! Come on, Babe. . . . Got a soft, warm woman for Christmas. . . .

VI

The wind never rested on Christmas day, and there was always rain in the hard wind. The restaurants had their turn at the loggers' stakes between noon and night. "Roast turkey with dressing and cranberry sauce. Home-made mince pies." In the hotel dining room there were white cloths on the tables. And the diners were served with wines. Calk boots, stagged pants and mackinaws were not wanted there. But the loggers didn't care a damn. To hell with the highfalutin stuff! At the hotel bar you could have Tom and Jerries and eggnog, drinks rich and hot. But to hell with that too. Redeye was good enough. Redeye in a joint where a man can whoop and sing and perform—come on, bullies, to the Blazer! We've got our money in Big Al's safe!

All of Christmas day loggers streamed through Heron Street, flowed in and out of the saloons. The Christmas blow-in reached its high tide at night. Big Al had kept the peace in the Blazer, but in the joints it had been a different story. In one a logger had taken a swing at a crooked faro-dealer and got a bullet in the groin in return. He was in the hospital now, the bullet still in him. A doctor had probed for it for an hour, and then given it up. Probably he'd die. Two brothers were looking for their younger one. Last anybody'd seen of him was in the Eagle. Probably he'd been slipped some knockout drops, rolled, and then eased through a trapdoor into the river. Yep, prob'ly. That was the way she went. A pore damn logger certainly had to look out for himself in this tough town.

But most of the talk along the bar of the Blazer was roared boasts of performances of the night before and promises of the performances that were to come to-night. It was Christmas, the great day of the blow-in. To-morrow the loggers would calm down and talk logging as they lined the bars. But to-day they had to perform. Black Larrity had a gang around him and he was buying most of the drinks, as a bullpuncher lousy with gold was supposed to do. But he didn't brag. He only scowled and wiped his mustaches as he listened to the others. He was waiting to show them what real performing was like.

"Hey, big fellow, Swede Henry's out again! He's oary-eyed and all primed for you this trip! He's lookin' for you, big fellow, and out for blood!"

"Where's he now?"

"Over't the Circle. Better steer clear of him, big fellow!"

But Black Larrity was already on his way. There was no Big Al at the Circle. Anything went in the Circle, from frisking to bloody murder. The bar was in a black, foul room. In the back of it were tables of gambling games. Swede Henry was bending over a roulette wheel when Black Larrity swung over the sawdust floor and jammed against him.

"What are you peddlin' about me, hey?" Larrity's voice was hoarse from the rage into which he had worked himself coming from the Blazer. "You ready to settle, squarehead?"

Swede Henry stepped back from the roulette table, glared at Larrity for a short second, hunching his head down between his shoulders, and then he charged.

It was no stand-up-and-knock-down battle. The two giants clinched, dug their calks through the sawdust and strained to pull each other down. Larrity's arms were on the inside and he worked his paws to get a clutch on Swede Henry's bull throat. But there was tremendous strength in the arms and shoulders under that neck and Larrity had to grip the mackinaw collar just to hang on. He swung his knee for the Swede's groin. As he did, Swede Henry yanked savagely; both fighters were thrown off balance; they hugged each other and heaved, twisted, staggered, reeled, swayed, lunged, from the bar to the kegs along the wall, from the kegs to the bar again, up and down, their calks gouging splinters out of the rough plank under the sawdust, while they grunted and growled like two fighting bears. Larrity's struggles grew savager every minute. The red snapped in his black eyes and his bared teeth shone under his coaly mustache. He unloosed the grip of his right hand from the mackinaw collar and clawed for the Swede's ear. Swede Henry forced his right arm on around Larrity's neck, clamped it in a stranglehold, and as Larrity heaved back against it the two went down, with Swede Henry on top.

Bartenders, gamblers, dance hall girls, loggers, everybody in the saloon, crowded around the prone fighters. Men streamed in from the street. The news spread to the other saloons. Two bullies were putting on a regular old-time riot of a fight in the Circle.

On the floor Larrity was throwing every move into breaking the choking hold that Swede Henry had clamped on his neck. He did loosen it enough to gasp in some air, but the powerful Swede still had him foul as they threshed over the floor, sending up clouds of sawdust with their kicking feet. Had him foul and was going for his ear. That was the mark of a man who had been licked in a logging town fight— an ear mangled or missing. Larrity's head was slowly being forced against Swede Henry's teeth. He felt hot breath on his cheek. A desperate lunge lifted his head farther out of Swede Henry's hold just in time, but he felt a grinding pain in his neck. A violent lust for murder blasted through his head, spread a blaze of red before his eyes and shot his muscles with fresh fire. He rammed a hand above the Swede's shoulder, his clawing stubby fingers felt an ear, the thumb pushed into an eyesocket, jabbed against a soft ball, and into the grip and push of that hand Larrity forced all his strength.

An animal-like bawl of anguish roared in his ears. The big bulk on top of him went limp, rolled away. Larrity got to his feet. He heard his own breath coming in hoarse wheezes. Faces rocked, madly before him. One, lower than the rest, had its left cheek covered with a bloody smear.

There was the door—yep, there she was—and now here he was, out in the dark, the rain wetting his face, the wind fanning his burning eyes. Coming back to himself now. Was nearly choked under. First time any man had ever taken him off his feet. Nearly marked him as a licked man. He put his hand up to his throbbing neck. Swede Henry'd bloodied him some, after all. Teeth marks to carry—but they were in his neck—there was the Blazer. Now that mob'd have something to talk about! He could hear 'em. . . . "Swede Henry was goin' for his ear and Black Larrity popped his eye out on his cheek just like you'd squeeze a pit out of a prune! There's a performer for your whiskers!"

Yep, popped it out just like you'd squeeze the pit out of a prune. That was performing for anybody's whiskers. For anybody's—holy Jeezus, but his neck did ache! It'd be stiff as a board in the morning. Well, let 'er be stiff. He'd go on performing. Other bullies would try to fight him down, go for him with teeth, calks and claws. He'd clean 'em all. He, Black Larrity, was the fightingest fool on the Menominee—but this wasn't Michigan. He was logging on the Wishkah, blowing his stake in the tidewater town of Aberdeen. No further West for him or any other logger. The last timber country, the last land for a lousy timber beast. Here he'd have to stick. This was the town for the rest of his blow-ins. This was the end of the cruise. . . .

VII

Where the light shone out from the windows of the Blazer the rain slanted in fine gleaming lines. Larrity stopped to feel his wounded neck again. His hand brought away a fresh smear of blood. The rain trickled it between his fingers. He wiped his hand with a bandanna, then wrapped his neck and turned up his mackinaw collar. The wind slapped rain around him with a sudden lusty puff. It carried a smell of the sea and of the timber. The old timber . . . the skidroad . . . the bulls heaving around the level bend, loping down a steep grade . . . the old stable was warm at four in the morning and then coffee and beans were good . . . and at night gabbing around the heater. . . .

Hell, he was going soft. It was a lousy old life. Nothing else. You had to have blow-ins to look ahead for, or you couldn't stand it. Any way you stood it you was a timber beast. Nothing else. A man whose folks had forgot him and whose woman was never any better than a dance hall girl. A religious girl would look at a timber beast like a rabbit looks at a wolf. He'd seen one do it. But he knew he could be good to a woman like that. He might bloody up the bulls and go to the floor with a Swede Henry but he'd never hurt a woman, not even one like Babe. He could never forget how that religious girl had looked at him. Funny he had to think of her now.

Hell, he was going soft. And getting sober. You can't go soft when you're a timber beast, lad! And to get sober on Christmas! Come on, bully! Remember what you are! Perform! Perform!

There's a gang tramping up the boards from the Circle Saloon. Swagger into the Blazer now, plank down a twenty, set 'em up, as a bullpuncher should, set 'em up for five straight rounds, and listen to 'em tell how you took Swede Henry to his needin's. Hear 'em tell how there's going to be a new bull of the woods in the Wishkah camp! Yea, lad, you got to perform! You're a timber beast from now to the end. So what the hell, Bill, what the hell!

Standing Alone in the Darkness

Arthur Winfield Knight

Arthur Winfield Knight is an acclaimed poet, playwright, and fiction writer whose work deals with many different subjects and eras, including prominent Western historical figures. He has authored numerous Western poems, some of which appear in his 1988 collection Wanted!, *and two plays about the Old West:* Blue Earth, *about Jim and Cole Younger; and* Burning Daylight, *about Jesse James's relationship with his sister. A particular enthusiasm of Knight's, Jesse James is also the subject of "Standing Alone in the Darkness"—an insightful look at the famous outlaw's life told in his own words, in a series of Christmas letters written between 1864 and 1881.*

Scyene, Texas
Christmas Day 1864

Dear Frank,

Probably you were smart not to come here, but I had to get away from the war, at least for a while. Even though I miss Missouri, it's been good to see Myra Belle Shirley again. (These days she gets mad if you don't refer to her as Belle.)

Her mother has retreated into herself. She can look right at you and you have the feeling she doesn't know you're there. I suppose it's one way to cope with losing a son and being run off from a place you love. Her voice always gets softer when she talks about Missouri.

Belle's father is tired. Beaten. When the weather's nice, he just sits on the porch with his feet up on the railing. You can hear him chewing and spitting, chewing and spitting, or sometimes when he doesn't have any tobacco, he just sighs.

Last night Cole and I helped them decorate the tree. When it was done, they lit the candles on it and everyone sang "Silent Night, Holy Night," and everything almost seemed "calm" and "bright" as we stood there.

I don't think anyone else noticed, but Cole had his huge arms around Belle, his hands on her breasts. I think she took big breaths on purpose as she sang, "Sleep in heavenly peace."

Cole was smiling and his voice joined hers, booming out "heavenly peace," then he whispered something that made Belle blush. You could see the candles burning in Cole's eyes.

Sometimes I think Cole laughs and drinks too much, swearing when he doesn't have to. He's too casual about the way other people feel, using them, and I worry about him and Belle. But when I see them together like that, I don't know; maybe we should get any happiness we can, where we can.

Sometimes I don't know why I love the man so much. In some ways, he's everything I'm not—everything I don't want to be—but there's something basic about him. Honest. Elemental. I know he'd never betray a friend. You can trust him. You don't have to look behind your back.

Later on last night I got him alone on the porch (he went out there to smoke a cigar) and said, "Cole, don't do anything to hurt Belle."

He puffed on his cigar for a long time, then he held it between his thumb and index finger, standing there like a politician ready to have his picture taken. He said, "Jesse, learn to lighten up. Have some fun. I know your father was a minister, but you can't spend all your time thinking about going to hell."

"Sometimes I just . . . feel so lost," I said, gesturing at nothing, my arm curving like a bird flying in the dark. "I don't really feel grown-up, but none of us are kids now. I don't know who I am."

"Hell, you sound like Frank now. Trying to philosophize. Come in, let's drink and have some fun."

"Yeah, fun."

When we went back inside, Belle was still fighting the war. She said, "It doesn't matter who wins it. I'll never kiss some Yank's ass." It surprised me to hear her swear.

Cole paced back and forth, his footsteps heavy-sounding on the floor. The boards shook, and as he spoke, his voice got louder and louder. "The goddamn Yanks run everything now, and the war isn't even over yet. Next thing you know, they'll be telling us how to live. Holding a gun between our eyes. Next thing you know we'll have to ask their permission to piss, like kids in elementary school."

Belle said, "I'll piss on their foot and say it's raining if I want to."

"I have a gun of my own," Cole said, "and the Yanks aren't the only ones who know how to point. I tell you, I'd like to get some goddamn Yankee banker in my sights and pull the trigger.

"That son-of-a-bitch at the Liberty Bank would have a hole where his belly button used to be if it were up to me. I went in there to get change for a hundred-dollar bill and Bird looked at me like I was something dirty. He said, 'Where did you get that? I see men like you all the time. Drifters. Riffraff. You've never worked a day in your life.' Greenup Bird should talk about work. The only place he has a callus is on his ass."

Belle put her arms around Cole. The tips of her fingers barely touched by the time they circled his chest. She said, "In a few minutes it'll be Christmas, and we ought to be rejoicing. There's plenty of time to fight the Yanks."

I know Pa left for California when I was only three, but I still remember that last Christmas he was with us. At least I think I remember, and that's just as good. Maybe better, 'cause I can have it my way. He and Ma and you and I stood around the tree and little Susan was lying in her crib.

I think Ma and Pa were singing "Silent Night, Holy Night," and maybe you were, but I was too little to know the words, so I just stood there with my mouth open, pretending to sing.

I thought about that after I'd said goodnight to Cole and Belle. Then I blew out the candles, one by one, until there was only one left. If it had been the evening star, I'd have made a wish, but it wasn't a star, so I blew it out, too. Anyway, it was too late for wishes.

JESSE

Kansas City, Missouri
December 26, 1865

Dear Belle,

I proposed to Zee yesterday, and she said she'd marry me.

We were sitting at the foot of the huge spruce tree we'd decorated for Christmas, and the smell of the tree and the candy being made in the kitchen filled the house, and I don't know that I've ever been happier.

I'd read Dickens' *Christmas Carol* to her while she lay on the floor, her head on my lap, and I told Zee I feel like an unredeemed Scrooge except for those moments I'm with her.

I am unredeemed. I was even rebaptized at the New Hope Baptist Church, the one my father was pastor at, in an attempt to leave the war behind, but I can't forget it, maybe because I don't want to. At least I was alive then.

Now, each day is pretty much the same.

At dawn I'm out in the field, plowing.

I have blisters on my hands, my back aches and my butt feels like I rode a mule a hundred miles. Bareback.

Is this what we fought the war for?

Sometimes I think I'd like to spread the word of God, becoming a minister like the father I never knew. He left for California when I was three. He never came back, although we were told he died in the gold fields there. The last letter Ma received said he found consolation that, through the art of writing, he could converse as if "face to face."

I understand that, although I sometimes think I'm writing most of my letters to myself. I keep hoping I'll find out who I am: the Jesse James who was born in Kearney 18 years ago or the legendary Jesse who rode with Anderson and Quantrill.

Ma says I'll never make a good preacher, and she's probably right. If my parishioners didn't get "the word," I'd probably stick a gun in their face and say, "Look at God." Sometimes I don't think I know how to live without violence.

Sometimes, Frank and I ride into Liberty, spurring our horses at full gallop, racing back and forth up the streets, hurrahing people (I hate myself later) because we don't know what else to do. Sometimes I'll even fire my pistol because I don't want to forget what a gunshot sounds like.

I know it's wrong, but sometimes I think I want to die. That, maybe, I'd have been better off if I'd died from the wounds I got when I rode into Lexington to receive amnesty and the blue bellies ambushed me. I can still see the sun glinting from the barrels of their rifles. But I got a few of them, too. I can still see the spurts of blood on the blue of those Yanks' uniforms each time I hit one. It was like roses blossomed from their chests.

Everyone's dead, it seems: Todd, Anderson. I heard Quantrill was half crazy at the end. He was going to take some men to Washington so he could assassinate President Lincoln, turning the Union victory into defeat. Some of the men who were with Quantrill at the end say he foamed at the mouth like a mad dog.

Maybe I would be better off dead. I have absolutely no idea what I'm going to do. I don't think I can become a farmer, settling down after everything I've been through.

When Lee surrendered, I told myself he'd betrayed the Confederacy, that the war wasn't over yet, but then Taylor gave up too; when General Kirby-Smith surrendered in Texas, I knew it was really over. We were through.

The Union papers like to say how the guerrilla soldiers raped and pillaged, but I never saw a woman raped and the only real pillaging that took place was at Lawrence—and Quantrill was just getting back at the people who'd used it as a base to raid and kill Missourians.

Cole and Frank and I got together a couple of months ago.

"Where'll we go?" Cole asked.

I stared into the fire we'd built, wishing I could see into the future. Probably I should be glad I can't. I said, "Maybe we could go back to Texas or drift down into Mexico."

"I don't know," Cole said. "I can't imagine spending the rest of my life hanging around a cantina with a bunch of guys wearin' serapes."

"Why shift about in search of unseen lands heated by other suns?" Frank said. "Who, exile-bound, escapes himself as well?"

"What the hell does that mean?" Cole asked.

"You can't run away from your troubles, I guess."

"Then why didn't you say that?"

You know Frank. Always reading a book. If there's a fancy way to say something simple, he'll find it.

"I liked the sound of it," Frank said. "It's like a poem. We'll need to hang onto everything we can to get through."

"We'll need more than poetry to turn our lives around."

"Well," I said, "we still haven't answered the big question. What are we going to do?"

"I don't know," Frank said. "I guess we go home and get on with our lives."

I keep telling myself this is a new beginning for us, but each night I sit near the fire, exhausted, and listen to the earth humming. Last week Ma asked if I was all right and I said, "Yeah, I'm fine," but I was lying.

When I tell Zee about the war, she says, "You have to put it behind you. Forget about it."

"At least I was alive then."

"You're alive now."

"Most of the time, I'm just pretending. I go through the motions."

"Are you pretending now?"

We'd gone into the kitchen and I was cranking the handle to make ice cream.

I could feel the tiredness setting in, but it wasn't the good tiredness we had after a battle with the blue bellies. It was something else. Numbing. Insidious. It creeps in on you like the night.

Zee asked, "Are you happy now?"

It was almost dusk and my arm and my chest ached and I knew I'd have to take some morphine to make it through dinner, but I kept turning the crank: bored, bored, bored. What kind of a husband will I make? Cranking. Going through the motions.

"I've never been happier," I said.

Cole sends his love,
JESSE

Dallas, Texas
December 15, 1872

Dear Zee,

Cole sings in the church choir here and he's even worked for the sheriff as a deputy. It's humorous, but Cole isn't laughing much.

Yesterday he had too much to drink, and Frank and I had to hold

him up when he staggered out onto his porch. When he got there he
yelled, "I HAVE TO PISS."

"Not here," Frank said. "The neighbors will see you."

"PISS ON THE NEIGHBORS."

Cole staggered over to the railing, holding on to it with one hand
while he unbuttoned his pants with the other. He was singing "Bringing in the Sheaves" at the top of his lungs and peeing.

Frank said, "Watch out, you're hitting your pants," but Cole didn't
care.

He stopped singing and said, "Boys, we're pissing our lives away. We
could have been anything. Anything." He gestured grandly with both
hands. A hot wind blew across the prairie; it's hard to believe it's
almost Christmas.

"I saw Belle yesterday," Cole said, and suddenly, he almost seemed
sober. He stood up straight, wiping at his eyes. I thought he was going
to cry, but he just stood there with a faraway look and his voice got
softer. "She calls herself the Outlaw Queen now, and she's married to
someone named Starr who's a horse thief."

"Well, we can't live other people's lives for them," Frank said. "You
can't interfere with the way someone wants to live."

"The Outlaw Queen," Cole said again. "You should have seen her.
She was riding sidesaddle. She was on Venus and she was wearing a
velvet gown and shiny boots and she was holding a pistol. Someone
was even taking her picture. It was the damndest thing. You should
have seen her astride that horse. The sky behind her was as blue as
the rest of our lives."

I remember telling Cole not to hurt Belle. Now I don't know what
to say.

"She's a good woman, Cole. But you kept leaving her. And finally,
you came around too late."

"It's too late for all of us. Belle. Me. Pearl."

Then I knew what was wrong with Cole.

"Jesse, she's three now. And she looks like me. A little."

"I know."

We sat on the steps, and suddenly, he seemed tired, broken, although he's only three years older than me. He hadn't shaved for a
couple of days and his hands shook, and he was getting fat around the
middle. For the first time I noticed he had a double chin, and his hair
was thinning.

Cole said, "We used to talk about going away together."

"I know. Belle mentioned it to me once . . . a long time ago. She said something about the Pacific Northwest and wondered where it was."

"We should have gone, Jess."

"Yeah. Maybe. I don't know. We do what we do, and it's useless to look back."

"You can say that. You and Zee are engaged and happy, and hell, I don't know. You have it all."

The blue bellies or the Pinkertons or the law have been dogging me since the war, so how can I have it all? I know a lot of people have made me into a legend (and I'm not even dead), but they don't know what it's like to have to look behind you everywhere you go.

I told Cole, "No one has it all."

"When I talked to Pearl, she didn't even know who I was. I was just some man who was a friend of her Ma's. It almost killed me when she called Sam Starr daddy. I wanted to say, 'That heathen bastard ain't your daddy,' but what good would that have done?"

"Maybe you would have felt better," Frank said.

"I don't think I'll ever feel good again."

"Sure you will," I said. "Sure."

"The only thing that will help me is some more to drink. That's what I need," and Cole stood up painfully and went into the kitchen to get what was left of the bottle.

I'll be home for Christmas.

JESSE

Kearney, Missouri
Christmas Day 1875

Dear Susan,

I love being married. But after sleeping alone so many years it's strange to go to sleep, and to awaken, with someone by my side. The bed is the same size as the one I've always slept in—here, it is the same bed—but now, with an extra person, the bed seems too big. I want to stay close to Zee. Want to hold her. I don't want any space between us.

I didn't want you to marry Allen, as you know, didn't want the two of you to go off to Texas. It almost killed me when you left, especially with someone I didn't approve of, but he obviously cares about you and I'm glad you're happy.

I love being married.

I love watching Zee comb and braid her hair, and I keep telling myself she's really my wife because it's so hard to believe.

So much has changed in the last couple of years. You and Allen getting married. Then Zee and me. ("It's about time," she said. "You kept me waiting for nine years." Now I don't know why.) Then Frank and Annie.

Frank's wife didn't have the nerve to tell her parents she was marrying him—a man with a price on his head—so Annie just wrote her mother. All she said was "I am married and going West." But they're back here with us now for the holidays.

Yesterday morning Frank and I went out into the woods and cut down a Christmas tree. It was six above zero and there was close to a foot of snow. Our breath hung in the air and the snow glittered like the sand on the beach at Galveston at high noon (I'd never seen anything so dazzling) and our laughter and the sound of the axe must have carried for miles. Everything would have been perfect if little Archie was there.

I realize the Pinkertons have a job to do, that they want to get me, but they should have checked to see if I was there that night they threw the bomb into Ma's house. It was more terrible than anything I saw in the war. At least there a man had a gun—a chance. Here, there was just Ma and Dr. Samuel and their child.

How can anyone cut off the life of an eight-year-old?

Ma held him in her arms as his life leaked away and she almost went crazy at the funeral. Frank led her away, sobbing.

Zee and I stayed behind. Neither of us said anything for several moments, then, finally, I said, "Damn it. Damn it," over and over again. I felt so helpless I didn't know what else to do. In a way I felt it was my fault because I was the one they wanted.

Zee and I broke a branch from the juniper tree, since it was the only green thing there, and laid it on little Archie's grave.

Susan, it broke my heart.

Zee said, "Don't cry, Jesse."

"I'm not crying," I said. "It's the wind," but I don't know if it was. "The wind," I insisted.

Neither of us had ever placed a flower, a branch, anything, on someone's grave because we feel you should honor people while they're living, but we didn't know Archie's life was going to be so short.

Zee said, "It seems so unfair."

We weren't sure why we put the branch of juniper there. We knew it wouldn't bring Archie back, knew it wouldn't change his being dead but. . . .

It was a gesture that somehow seemed important.

Frank and I stopped laughing when we mentioned Archie, and the tree seemed heavier than it should have as we dragged it back to the house through the snow.

When we got back, Annie had a huge fire going and Ma was making the beds while Zee cooked breakfast. She seemed to be making toast and coffee and scrambling eggs and frying bacon, all at the same time, and the morning light shone on her dark hair.

When Ma asked me to say grace, I said, "When thou makest a feast, call the poor, the maimed, the lame, the blind: And thou shalt be blessed," then we all began to eat at the same time. I was never hungrier.

Later that morning, I showed Zee how to skeet shoot because it gave me an excuse to put my arms around her, to put my cheek against hers while I showed her how to lead clay pigeons through the air. When they shattered, Zee said, "It's like breaking a China plate."

Today her shoulder was black and blue.

"What have I done to you?" I asked, rubbing the bruised area as if I could erase it.

"It's nothing, Jesse. I'm fine."

"Then tell me your name. See if you know that."

"Don't be silly."

"Tell me."

"It's Zee. You know that."

"Zee what?"

"Zee James, silly. Mrs. Jesse James."

"I love hearing you say it. I don't care if it's silly. Everything about you makes me happy," I said and I grabbed her around the waist, dancing across the kitchen. I felt like I was 18, not 28. Felt like anything was possible now.

"Stop it," she said. "The bacon will burn."

"Let it," I said. "I don't care," and we swirled around and around the kitchen until we were both dizzy and out of breath.

Merry Christmas,

JESSE

Nashville, Tennessee
New Year's Day 1878

Dear Ma,

Zee spends most of her time crying, and I don't know what to say to her. Don't know what to do. The twins meant so much to her, even though we only had them a few days; Zee can't reconcile herself to their loss. Truthfully, neither can I. I keep looking for some passage in the *Bible* that will help me to understand, help me to assuage my grief. But my grief's huge.

Yesterday, I tore a page out of the *Bible,* crumpling it up and throwing it into the yard. Like Job, I wondered how a just God could let things like this happen. Wondered if there even is a God.

I've begun eating my dinner on the back porch so that I don't have to listen to Zee crying. I feel helpless when I'm not able to console her, and I feel guilty when I leave her. But I tell myself she's getting better. Tell myself she'll be all right. But almost nothing has been right since Northfield, since Cole and his brother were locked up. I've asked myself a thousand times what good it would have done for Frank and me to stay with the others when they couldn't go on, but I wonder how Cole would answer that.

Sometimes Frank and I will walk around town, our hands in our pockets. It's dusk and we'll watch people lighting their lanterns, watch the lights come on in Nashville. I think we've walked five or six miles without saying a word.

Sometimes I wonder why anyone has children, but then I think of Jesse Junior's birth. Nothing went wrong there, although it was the strangest New Year's Eve I've ever spent. Wandering around the house, waiting for him to be born. I tried to play solitaire, tried to read. Waiting. I was so befuddled I even tried to play cribbage with myself, and stumbling once, I almost knocked the Christmas tree down.

Around eleven I heard a cry from the other room, then the doctor came into the front room and said, "You have a healthy son, Mr.

Howard. Congratulations." For a moment I wondered who he was talking to. I've used so many names.

"Happy New Year," I said.

That was three years ago.

Now I'm afraid to go to bed at night. I don't know why, but I feel like I can't breathe when the door's closed. I think I've felt like that since I was a kid, since the time I was sick for weeks and you'd shut the door, so people moving around the house wouldn't disturb me.

I thought I was going to die, and I guess I still feel shut-in when I'm in a room with a closed door.

Sometimes Zee awakens in the night, and she'll shut the door to keep out intruders, even though she knows no one will get into the house. Those are the times I'll wake up sweating.

Last night I woke up, perspiration dripping from my face, and I asked Zee, "Why'd you shut the door?"

She sat beside me, leaning back against her pillow in the darkness. "I heard noises downstairs."

"It's your imagination."

"I thought I heard the babies crying."

"Zee, the twins are dead."

She didn't say anything for a long time, and I almost thought she'd fallen asleep sitting up. I almost wished I had a cigarette to smoke—or a cigar—although you know I've never used tobacco. It would have given me something to do. Lighting up.

"Do you think the dead know what time it is?" Zee asked.

I didn't know what to say to that. I put my left arm around her. Finally, I said, "Why don't I make you a glass of warm milk? Maybe it'll help you sleep."

"Yes, maybe it would. I'd like that."

While the milk was warming, I went out onto the back porch. It was cold, but the sky was as clear as I'd ever seen it and I tried to find the constellations.

I remember Dr. Samuel showing them to me when I was a child. I remember there was a lion and a pitcher and a hunter, but I don't remember their names anymore and I couldn't find them, even though I looked up into the sky until my neck was sore.

By the time I went back into the house, the milk was boiling and I poured Zee a glassful and watched her drink it. Then we lay back down and I held her, neither of us saying anything. (I learned to go a long time without talking when I was sick.) Finally, I felt her body relax and I knew she was asleep.

I lay there telling myself the Lord is my shepherd, I shall not want, I will lie down beside green pastures, the Lord is my shepherd, I shall not lie down beside the Lord, jumbling the words until I got up and came back downstairs, sinking into the big chair beside the Christmas tree.

Love,
JESSE

St. Joseph, Missouri
Christmas Day 1881

Dear Susan,

Billy the Kid was killed five months ago.

Two months ago there was a gunfight in Tombstone, Arizona. It only lasted thirty seconds, but when it was over, three men were dead and another two were badly wounded.

Wyatt Earp and two of his brothers, along with a dentist named Holliday, shot it out with the Clanton-McLaury faction at the O.K. Corral. Some people claim the Earps opened fire without giving the others a chance, but you know what people say about me. It's hard to determine the truth, even about yourself.

Sometimes I think an era's coming to an end.

Sometimes I'll walk down the hill toward the site of the old Pony Express station. It's been gone more than twenty years. They claim they could have galloped around the world twenty-four times in the year and a half they existed. And now the stables are boarded up and weeds are growing through the cracks in the cobblestones out front. I stand there, trying to bring it all back: the smell of the horses and the hay and the men sweating, but it's all gone. Like the twins. Like Cole. Like so many things.

Gone.

The street down the road from our house is covered with snow. I look down the long hill from our house in the twilight; the sky looks like a bloody rose, getting redder and redder. I think it's going to burst into flame, the clouds shriveling up like burning petals, but the light just gradually fades, the way our lives do.

The snow looks like it's on fire. Outside, Jesse Jr. and Mary are making a snowman. He has eyes made out of lumps of coal and a carrot for a nose.

For a while, I helped with the snowman, but I'm more sensitive to cold than I used to be, and there's a pain behind my eyes that never goes away unless I take enough morphine.

I even tried to get Bob Ford to go out with us, but he looked at the snow and said, "It's just a bunch of white crap you have to shovel. I don't see why people get so excited about it. A cousin of mine fell down and broke his leg on the way to the outhouse, and to make things worse, while he was lying there he crapped in his pants."

I couldn't help smiling. "It can be a cruel world, Bob."

Last night, I dressed up in a Santa Claus suit. The kids and Zee had just finished decorating the tree when I came into the front room. "Ho, ho, ho, what have we here?" I asked.

"Daddy, Daddy, you look funny," little Jesse cried.

"I told you it was a dumb idea," Bob said.

I just ignored him, though.

We turned down the lanterns until the wicks were almost smoking, then we lit the candles on the tree and exchanged presents. Mary tried to eat the paper her jacks were wrapped in, but little Jesse took it away from her and said, "No, you don't eat *that.*" I could tell it made him feel grown-up, counseling a two-year-old.

I've been trying to remember what it was like when we were kids. I know we weren't moving from place to place—there was a sense of stability in our lives—and we weren't friendless. Perhaps this life hasn't damaged Jesse or Mary yet, but we can't keep moving the way we have been.

There's a farm for sale near Lincoln, Nebraska. If I can raise the money, I'd like to buy it. ("Just one more job," I tell Zee. "That's why I need Bob.") Maybe we can finally stop running. You and Allen have done it. And it looks like Frank has. Why can't I?

Next year my son will be in the first grade, and I want him to have a normal life. It's something I pray for.

After the presents were opened, we stood around the tree. Even Bob did, although I had to nudge him. If they ever make a play out of *A Christmas Carol,* they can get Bob to play Scrooge.

Zee and I held hands and we began singing. "It came upon a midnight clear,/ That glorious song of old." Our voices rose and fell. Rose and fell. "From angels bending near the earth,/ To touch their harps of gold."

Bob stood there, moving his lips a little, but I could tell he wasn't singing.

At the end of the song there was something about peace and good will, but no matter how hard I tried, I couldn't remember the words.

Maybe it was the morphine.

When Zee and the kids had gone to bed, Bob said, "I think I'll go out for a walk. Do you want to join me?"

"You go ahead, Bob."

I don't know why we've had him live with us. I guess it gives me someone to talk to now that I'm away from everyone I love—you, Frank, Ma—except Zee and the kids. Bob's like a dog. You could kick him and he'd wag his tail.

I get so lonely . . . Sometimes I'll just sit, oiling my pistol and wiping it down. Counting the number of shells I have left. Sometimes I think that's about all I have left: bullets.

I sat next to the window, watching Bob disappear into the snow. It reminded me of the time I was visiting Belle in Texas. She and Cole and the rest of the folks had gone to bed and I was left to snuff out the candles on the Christmas tree. Seventeen years later, things end the same way.

I'm still standing alone in the darkness.

JESSE

Winter Harvest

John Prescott

John Prescott knows well the history and people of his adopted state of Arizona, and writes of frontier life there with both realism and compassion. One example is this tale of a hard-luck homesteading family and their very special "Winter Harvest." Two other notable examples are his novels Renegade *(1954) and* Ordeal *(1958). He is also the author of* Journey by the River, *a superior tale of heroism and adventure along the Oregon Trail, which earned him a Western Writers of America Spur Award for Best Historical Novel of 1954.*

In the first year, the strange land where Amos Lake and the others had settled down was a fair place: one favored in deep stands of grama grass that fell away from the cliffs of the Mogollon Rim in long, rolling swells mottled with piñon and juniper trees. Passing through it from the Rim, a creek made its easy way in broad curves, quiet in deep pools where trout appeared as puffs of smoke, full of chatter where dark, glossy rocks upset the even flow, and at other times, in silent haste, ridged above strong sinews of deep current. All along its course were groves of fat trees—sycamore, cottonwood, oak; deer and bear, turkey and antelope were plentiful, and wandering bands of Indians came there to winter.

The second year was that way, too.

But now in the fall of their third year the creek had shrunk, and the water lay in pools, mostly shallow and in some places separate. For days on end, the dry winds of early October came over the cliffs to harry the trees and to bluster the scalded grasslands into clouds of chaff and dust. Standing on the ridge behind his house to watch the Tuppers leave, Amos saw the crowns and shoulders of the evergreens stained in the rusted reds of the country's color.

The wagon soon came yattering along the stony ridge, and drew to a halt. John Tupper sat on the seat beside his woman, glaring down at Amos while a gaggle of children peered out of the hooped tarpaulin behind them. A little, bristling man, his face and words were shaped by defeat.

"Amos, you're a prideful fool!" he shouted against the wind. "You'll soon be blighted as bad as the damned land!"

Sounding like a jaybird, his woman cried out, "You'll see! Be your death, and the death of your coming child, too!"

Amos heard them out, standing solid while their ranting churned the wind's passage. He'd long since got used to such talk.

Way last March, when the Wilson family had thrown their hands up, he'd come to the ridge to shout, "Wait! Don't give up yet! There's sure to be rain by April!"

In rainless April, when the Stones had hitched their wagon to pull out for Iowa, he'd cried, "Summer rains are always the best! Don't quit now; you got to have faith!"

And in August, when the Hendersons had ground along the ridge, he'd come running up to shout, "Winter ain't too far! You'll see how the melt brings the roots back to life!"

On coming here, dreary memories of the plow in Illinois and Iowa and Indiana had conspired with the sight of waving grass to lure them into stock raising. Their eyes had near popped to see the wealth of grass and space that lay for the taking.

Why, they had asked each other, should they spend their lives in study of a mule's rear end when, with time enough, a bull and some cows could make them a living?

Amos found himself the only one among them not excited by such notions. And while the others thought him queer to hold to farming the meadows and benches along the creek, he only laughed and said that there was time enough to go into cattle. Someday, he'd say, he might; but until he came to know the country, he might better work in known ways for a time.

And anyhow, his fingers had always itched for the soil.

And now the Tuppers were on their way. Saving the Lakes, the Tuppers were the last to pull out, and Amos knew he had good cause for anger with them, for they'd promised him they'd stay on until Maria's time. Yet it always pained him to think badly of others, so instead, he pitied them. And as if they sensed this, they now rained their bitterness upon him.

"You're a fool!" Tupper yelled again into the wind. "You'd damn well better clear out of here, too!"

"This is our home," Amos said simply.

"What about your missus?" Tupper's wife shrilled, as if guilt now took hold of her, too. "Who'll you get for midwife?"

"Myself," answered Amos. "Other men have tended their wives."

"Another month and that creek could be dry," Tupper warned. "What'll you do for water, then?"

"There's still plenty to drink in the pools. And the melt from the Rim will fill the creek with water for the fields in time for spring growth." Amos glanced at the peaks of the mountain range, still showing dark and forested above the cliffs of the Rim. "San Xavier should have a good snowfall, too, given time."

Lifting her raddled face to the sky, Tupper's woman sang out, "Saintly names in the devil's country!"

Her husband now stood and whipped his blacksnake backward over the canopy. "Shut up!" he yelled at her; and then to Amos, "So you say about your snow!" His arm slammed down and the snake shot forward, cracking. "Ha! You won't last till Christmas!"

Amos raised his hand and stood aside as the ladder-sided animals lurched ahead and the turning wheels began to scuff the red dust from the trace. The wagon jolted along beyond him, and then a lanky boy went by, on horseback, herding a dozen stringy cows along. After three years, they were the last of twenty good head.

Amos watched the wagon yaw and heave along until a swell of land hid it; then he went down the ridge to the house on the bench below. Hanging his hat on a peg, he poured out coffee at the stove and sat down with his cup at the room's only table.

In the bedroom doorway, Maria idled her broom for a moment.

"Where did he go this time, Amos?"

"Go?" Amos felt his mind go blank for an instant. Then he laughed. He'd told her that one of their oxen had strayed. "Ah, Blue."

"You needn't hide it, Amos. It's no surprise, and no matter that they said they'd stick it out, either. The Tuppers were bound to leave like everyone else."

Amos felt himself smiling; she always found him out so easy. Still, Blue did often stray; a born drifter, he was.

"Now, Maria, they had it pretty much against them—stock raising didn't come natural," he said. "They ranched dry range; we farm bottomland."

"You've said that of all of them," Maria told him while she swept under his chair. "I suppose it's so, and yet they could have shored themselves against it. Raise your big feet, Amos."

"Now, Maria, nobody gave a thought to drought until it struck," he said; but it was true he made excuses for them. It embarrassed him to have good fortune while others dealt with bad luck.

"We had your instinct to help us. Not that we've made it yet."

"I know. But we will. Given snow when winter comes on."

Sweeping the dust to the door, Maria stood with her hand on the latch, awaiting a pause in the wind to pull it open. "Suppose we don't get snow?"

"We've food enough until spring; then, if need be, we can travel. The child should be old enough by then."

"It can travel now, if you wish," Maria said. "I've carried it past six months. Amos, do you think we ought to stay on here alone?"

Grinning, Amos stood up, took a step, and put his big arm around her shoulders. Women got flighty with a young'un coming; especially their first. Or, so he'd heard.

"Now, girl, they'll be back. And if not them, then somebody else. This is good country here; it only needs knowing." Bending down, he kissed her cheek. "And after all, it's home to us now."

"Yes, I know . . ." She brightened quickly, as she almost always did. "It was just a notion, Amos. Women have them, you know, at these times."

By November, the wind had lessened, the nights were colder and longer, and in the mornings and evenings a fire felt good. The days stayed sunny, yet they had a feel of winter, too—a briskness. And while it still might be too early for them, Amos kept an eye peeled for snow clouds piling over the cliffs of the Rim.

He liked to busy himself, make things with his hands—one of the strange urges that had turned his face toward this country in the first place—and fall was the time to take up tasks held over from more busy summer months: splitting cedar shakes to fill gaps in the roof left by the wind; tightening up his implements against the shrink of dry mountain air; grinding his plow blades, and honing his axes and knives and other edged tools. And fence had to be mended.

He enjoyed these doings, for there was more involved than the simple occupation of his hands. Holding a plow blade to the grindstone cast up a vision of rich spring earth peeling from the sharpened steel. In putting a razor edge to his axe, he felt the blade chunking into the oak he'd soon be splitting for the deep winter cold. Idle or not, the purpose of the tools still had meaning for him.

Then there were the ditches to be cleaned, and the flume that carried water from the creek had to be repaired; and while they'd had small use this year, he went at the jobs anyway, ignoring the fact of the drought. It was hard for him to explain why he felt driven to do these things that might never be needed, but he had the feeling that not doing them would be like confessing to a loss of faith in this country to which he still stubbornly clung. And then there would no longer be a point in staying in it.

It was a busy time for Maria, too. Throughout all of the waiting weeks, she sewed and knit clothing for the child to come. Often, when she came outdoors to sit in the sunlight, Amos took his secret pleasure in watching her, while he worked at some chore close by. Sometimes she sang quietly to herself; other times she sat as still as a statue and gazed away as if in dreamy contemplation of some far vista known only to her.

She was apt to have moods now, and he could only wonder at her thoughts. Radiant one day, she would be downcast on another. On occasions, she seemed to live within herself altogether; and although these were mysterious—even resented—moments for Amos, he nevertheless learned to smile and to shrug them off when they came.

Though a farmer all of his years, the bearing of new life in the world never ceased to hold marvel for him.

Now, with their last neighbor gone, Amos traveled less to the grasslands than in past times and so wasn't aware of the full extent of the drought until early December, when hunting time came. Each fall he'd pick a day when all the chores around home were finished, and set out to garner his supply of winter meat.

But this year, all that was changed. Though he tramped the hills all day, he found them bare of any living creature. And nigh on bare of browse, too. Like the stands of grama that once had fattened now-vanished cattle, the browse had withered and died; and the game—deer, antelope—had gone elsewhere to find forage.

A day or two later, he went to the top of the Rim; but it was no different there from down below. The scattered alpine grass had burned out, the draws where oak thrived held no acorns, and the forest carpet of dry pine needles crunched and rattled under his boots. He camped for two nights on the Rim, and while the cold at that height froze his drinking water, the hopeful signs of snow were as scant as those of game.

He returned to the valley feeling uneasy; but he was careful not to let it show before Maria.

"Maybe I'd have better luck fishing," he told her, as a joke.

"No harm to try," she answered. "Anyhow, I'd rather face winter without meat than have you go hunting again on the Rim. It's too lonely down here all alone."

Amos hugged her against him, then stroked her hair.

"Well, now," he said awkwardly, "I guess in a pinch we could always butcher Blue or Patch for meat."

"Don't you dare say such things, Amos Lake! Don't even *think* them. We wouldn't be able to leave this place without them."

"It was only a joke," he said. But he knew now that she could think of leaving here, and it sank a chill of foreboding through him.

During the last of that week, the cold of the Rim swept into the valley; rising chimney smoke seemed bluer and sharper, and the inside of Amos' nose became stiff and dry from the icy air. Thick puffs of vapor left his mouth when he cut his winter oak and cleared out pail-sized holes in the fringe of creek ice so that water might be drawn from the few remaining deep pools.

That week, too, the Indians came down to the valley, as they came every winter: a Coyotero Apache clan that camped along the creek until the worst of the mountain cold had passed on. They were wandering, mostly peaceful people who hunted, gathered seeds and nuts, and sometimes planted maize or wild wheat in canyons and draws—crops that might or might not be harvested in summer, depending on the weather.

They traded, too, among themselves and with the whites, exchanging baskets, sometimes pelts and meat and such for old implements or odds and ends of clothing. They would come, barter as they smoked and visited, and then leave, pleased with what was offered them, and finding satisfaction in the simple pleasure of trading.

But as with all else this dry year, that, too, was different. With their lodges and wickiups raised a half mile or so below the house, they one day came marching up the creekside, all in a file, their ragged blankets flapping about them. Amos counted nine squaws and bucks, all told.

They were hungry. They had no goods for trading this year, but they needed food, and a sharp uneasiness threaded Amos as they came up to his door and stood hunched against the wind, while they pointed dolefully at their stomachs.

An old man, one who knew a little English, spoke for them. Gesticulating, he explained that bad times had come to the mountains this year. The game had vanished, and the piñon trees had offered few piñon nuts. No matter how diligently their young men had hunted, they had brought in little meat.

He motioned with his bony arms toward the Rim and the rising peak of San Xavier above, where the young men still hunted; he bent his withered knees in a crouch to demonstrate exactly how the women had searched the brush for berries and nuts. Abruptly opening his blanket, he displayed the prominence of his ribs.

The old man grinned toothlessly, scrawny ropes of gray hair straggling down over one sightless eye. With a finger like an awl, he indicated Amos's house, Amos's fields, Amos's oxen.

Their good white brother, he pointed out, was richly blessed with goods, while they, as he could plainly see, were in tatters. Their white brother had food for his belly, while they, as he could also plainly see, were on the verge of starvation. How would the elders live the winter through?

Amos shuffled his feet and looked down at them. It was difficult for him to tell if this ingratiating and guileful old man was being wholly truthful or not. And yet the obvious misery of these people shamed him.

At his back, Maria's step sounded. "Amos, send them away. Send them away. We need the food."

"But, Maria, a little grain . . ."

"Feeding them once will have them begging here all winter long."

Amos returned his gaze to the Indians; as if sensing his doubt, they stood cringing against the cold, blankets pulled up about their scrawny necks.

He hesitated, looking at them. Clearly, he was better fed than these miserable creatures. Their clothes were rags, giving little warmth; his were of good, stoutly woven wool. In his youth and vigor, he was a conspicuous contrast to their shriveled oldness; people smaller and weaker than he had always made him aware of his size.

Finally, it was enough. Fetching a sack of grain from his stores, he sent them away chattering like a flock of hungry birds. Maria watched him for a long, silent time when he reentered the house, and it was hard to meet her cold glance.

"But, Maria," he said when it was plain that she was not going to speak, "what could I do? Those people were starving."

"So I heard them say." Her hands were knit together at her waist, the knuckles white. "That sly old man knew the manner of fool he dealt with."

"You saw how they stood. As if the cold was in their very bones."

"I've seen old Indians stand so on a summer day. It's a trick of theirs. They *like* to look that way."

But it had not appeared so to Amos, and distress at her mood seemed to strengthen rather than diminish his sympathy for the Indians. He threw out his hands.

"But, Maria, we couldn't let them starve, could we?"

"You're quick enough to fret about them starving! But what about us? There's not a sign of game anywhere, yet you gave away our grain!"

"We've got plenty left; and there'll be game sooner or later, when the earth shows promise."

"How do you know?" Flushed, her voice lifting, Maria stepped away from the cozy warmth of the stove. "How can you tell anything in this dreadful place?" she asked.

"The lack of game's no different for them than it is for us," he replied. "We're all together in this."

The forced calm in Amos's voice seemed only to make Maria angrier. Never before had they quarreled like this, and Amos was frightened to think what might come of it.

"Ah, Maria, how can you be so hard?" he said at last.

"Your softness leaves me no choice!" Then, all at once, she was in his arms, sobbing. "Oh, Amos, please forgive me; I don't feel well today."

That evening she fell ill with fever, and for several days lay hot and parched in bed while Amos brought buckets of ice to chill the cloths with which he bathed her forehead. He sat beside her for hours, making clumsy efforts at cheer, and beginning, now, to have misgivings of his own at having kept her in this bleak wilderness with only a band of starving Indians for neighbors.

He felt guilt, now, that he had stood up so strongly for the Coyoteros, and when they came again to wheedle and beg at the door, he put a cold expression on his face and sent them away empty-handed.

Maria's fever lasted four days before it broke, and in the middle of that night their child was born: a boy, healthy and strong, and yet in Amos's great hands seeming no more than a kitten when he bathed it, wrapped it in a warm blanket and then, with relief, placed it in Maria's arms.

At once, she smiled, weakened and pale though she was. And now she smiled at Amos, too, and never had he been so grateful.

"Another man about the house," she said shyly, her fever-cracked lips drawn against her teeth. "Amos, he looks like you."

"Let's hope he's got a better head," Amos said.

"I was ill, Amos. I was wrong to be so angry—about the Indians."

"No, there's always two sides to a coin."

She touched his arm, smiling faintly. "What will *he* think if we quarrel before him?"

For the rest of the night, Amos kept vigil beside the bed, watching as they peacefully slept. Though dozing at times, he stayed wakeful mostly, for his mind was alive with all that he and his stalwart new son would do together when the time should come: hunting, fishing, tramping through the woods.

And all he'd teach him, too: the way pitch pine would bring an icy room to quick warmth on a winter morning; how an ox could best be made to plow a straight furrow; why trout in the creek were likely to be found below a rapids. And more . . .

All night his mind built air castles. And in the morning he whistled as he drew water at the creek, and then, in pure zest, split up into stove lengths a great oak log he'd set aside a few days earlier.

With afternoon, the child began to cry. Coming into the house, Amos laughed to hear the strange, piping sound.

"Some lungs," he told Maria. "With a set like that, he'll run like a Hopi someday. Let me rock him to sleep, Maria; he needs to know his father, too."

"Oh, Amos, it's not sleep he's crying for; it's food."

"Food?" Amos said blankly. Then he noticed how stricken she looked, and felt his heart pound as though half sick.

"He's taken nigh all I have for now," she said simply. "I'm sorry. It must have been the fever."

A bad time now began. For hours, at Maria's direction, Amos rattled about the stove. A crudely made pacifier was convincing only until the child discovered the deception. Mixed sugar and water administered with a spoon was rejected with screams; molasses thinned with water fared no better. Gruel, flavored with a little jerked venison, was swiftly rejected.

Now and again, Maria made efforts to nurse, but the results were sporadic, and in no way satisfying.

At last, the child cried without letup. The shrill wailing seemed to follow Amos wherever he went, and nothing they could think of was of any apparent use.

"Oh, why did we ever leave home?" Maria cried out.

Back and forth across the room Amos paced, the shrieking, livid child cradled in his arms. "Now, Maria, we are home; *this* is home."

"Home is this barren wilderness?"

"It won't always be barren," Amos said.

"Home is where the grass has burned to a crisp and there's almost no water?"

"Now, Maria, it's only the year that's bad."

"You call it home to step out of your own door and have to stumble over thieving Indians?"

"I tell you it will all work out, Maria. A drought can't last forever."

Maria laughed hysterically, then began to weep, her head lolling on her pillow. "How can you talk like that with our son starving? Why did you have to make us stay in this place alone?" She flung her hand up from the blanket. "Can't you see it as it *really* is—the way the others saw it? John Tupper saw it clear enough. I doubt we *will* last till Christmas!"

"Now, Maria . . ." Amos began, then checked himself as the infant screamed again, turned the color of blood, and held its breath.

Maria raised her hands and covered her face. "Please, Amos—don't! Don't say 'Now, Maria' again."

The child shrieked on and Amos walked the floor, back and forth. The floor was made of flagstones and Amos paced them like a caged animal, stepping on each separate stone until he came to know them all as separate landmarks in a journey of no end or destination.

But Maria finally slept, and when at last exhaustion battled hunger into silence, the child, too, fell into a sighing sleep. Then, feeling as if he had just been released from prison, Amos laid it in the cradle that he'd built for it and went outdoors to breathe the still, icy air when first light is about to break upon the world.

For a long time he stood relishing the blessed cold silence, marveling at the total absence of sound. Then, as the first of day began to sneak in under the edge of night, he could see the shape of red earth that he'd loved and had labored in—and that now he hated. Overhead, the sky seemed swollen with the clouds that for weeks he'd hoped and looked for; but now he hated them, too. In the growing light, he loathed the sight of his ditches and flume, his fields and fences and woodpile.

In the meadow, he saw Patch—and he hated Patch—but he could make out no sign of Blue. True to form, Blue seemed to have drifted off again. For a moment, he relished a hatred of the absent Blue; then he found hatred turning to affection.

No question but that Blue must be found, and the time needed for the search would set him free of the house and all in it.

Then awareness of the relief he felt made him hate himself, for Maria had spoken the truth, he reflected now as he took up Blue's aimless trail. Everything she'd told him was true, and in this hour of self-illumination, he made himself face the fact.

They should have left this godforsaken wilderness months ago. Left with the Stones—safe in Iowa by now—or the Wilsons, or when the Hendersons pulled out. Even had they held on until the Tuppers quit, they'd be in Kansas now, most likely, and maybe in Kansas City, where they could winter over.

Handy to doctors there, he thought; and warmth and store food and helpful folks. Now that it was nigh on Christmas—which had left his mind until Maria's outburst—there'd be all the song and laughter, and creature comforts of the season, too. There'd be windows winking with festive lights, children prancing about, and their elders maybe raising a toast or two after church.

But if it was so for all those people who romped and sported in his mind, it wasn't so for him, or for Maria, or for their child. No, not for them. In his pride and folly, he'd waved the others on their way, and had remained. He, Amos Lake, in mortal and surely sinful arrogance, had so decided. Amos Lake—dreamer and prince of fools!

He climbed a stony ridge and plunged into scattered clumps of piñon and juniper beyond; here one track showed the way, there another. Sometimes, in shadow, he felt along the ground for impressions with his bare hands. Then, back in open light, he walked upright, scanning the baked earth as he moved along.

After a lengthy while he reached a place where Blue's trail was joined by other tracks—those of Indians. The moccasin prints were soft, but still visible in the growing light. These didn't come from the creek, but were from the west and northwest, where the Rim reared starkly. Seven or eight, by rough count, they merged with Blue's trail so plainly that no doubt could exist as to what was happening.

What with all his wool gathering and self-blaming, he must have been gone for an hour, and now Amos ran as hard as he could along the widening band of these many new tracks. As if in flight from danger, he maintained a headlong pace through piñon groves, red with dust, and across bare, grassless flats, his breath heaving and his heart pounding. And then he broke through a motte of incense cedar, and coming into the flat beyond, stopped as if bludgeoned.

Blue, stout puller of plows, power to heavy wagons, mover of rock and stump, crafty drifter and comrade and friend, lay before him on the earth in the ruin of his yellow bones and wet crimson hide. Little remained beyond that. All that could be eaten had been taken. The very blood, a good deal at any rate, had been drained off at the throat.

Amos stood frozen, his heart pounding, a sudden limpness in his whole body, staring down in stunned disbelief.

He turned at last—toward the direction of the wickiups. Then he remembered about the hunters, and stopped. He could go among the elders with his bare hands, but he'd need his rifle with the hunters back in camp. So he headed north.

He walked rapidly, and after a while, his heart steadied and his breathing neared normal. He reached the piñon grove, passed through it, and now the ridge appeared, looming grayly.

He scaled it, and reaching the top, looked up and saw a sky suddenly choked with snow. At any other time he would have tossed his hat in the air and shouted in jubilation; now, against the terrible dark anger swelling in him, the miracle of the snow no longer seemed important.

He strode along the crest of the ridge to the north.

The air by now seemed one vast wall of snow. The feathery flakes mantled his head and shoulders and enveloped the red rust on the crowns of the trees. Already, the earth was a carpet of white, and as the cover swiftly thickened, his steps muffled and the forest world took on a ghostly stillness. Though he knew it was nearby, the Rim had vanished. He tramped on in a milky smother through which he could see only dimly.

He came to the end of the ridge, and passing down the flank, saw beyond him a vague yellow glow. Soon, it was bounded by a window frame, and then his house was in view, and in another moment some dim linear shape, like a hedge. Only Amos had no hedge before his doorstep, and as he advanced with quickened steps, the hedge became a row of standing Indians.

The terrible dark anger came back on him now, intensifying as he strode with deadly purpose toward the figures huddled at his doorstep. These were the murderers of Blue; thieves and worse, on whom he'd squandered his compassion. And they had come between him and his wife, and so were at the root of his quarrel with Maria.

The colossal gall of them—daring to stand at his door now, begging for more grain!

He passed the meadow and saw Patch, alone now, his great head furred with snow and bent to the wind. Amos passed the ditches he'd dug, the hand-split rails of fences he'd built. Reminders of past hopes, dead dreams. When he came to the woodpile, he withdrew the axe he'd left imbedded in a log and strode on, hefting it for balance. He crossed the flume that took water to the fields.

He could see them fairly clearly by now; could identify the hunters by their lances. Others had bows, and buckskin quivers filled with arrows on their backs. All held blankets close.

Let them do what they can, he thought. *At least, I'll take a few of them before they can take me.* He felt exalted, and wholly strange to himself.

He saw the elders, too, a few hugging deeper into their blankets, and for them, he thought, death would be a blessing.

Until he halted among them, none had known he was near. Then they saw him and drew back in startled recognition. One of the hunters slowly lowered his lance. An elder, blanket raised as if to ward off evil spirits, stared at him in terror.

But now Amos had seen the children. Hidden from him before, one by one they emerged timidly from concealment and stood staring at him with great round eyes, more with curiosity and surprise than any fear. They were new to him, for there had been no children with the elders before. Plainly, these young ones had come down from the mountains with the hunters.

The axe seemed to gather weight in his hands as a soft, nebulous feeling of doubt came over him.

As if awaiting a sign, the children kept their quiet, unfearful gaze upon him. He could see stains of blood on their blankets—the blood, no doubt, from his slaughtered ox. Yet the feeling of softness grew in him—and now he recognized it as the same feeling he'd had when he'd given grain to the elders when they'd come begging to his door.

These people had slaughtered his ox. And, yet, would he not steal one, too, if Maria and the baby were starving and there was no other way to feed them?

A creaking sound turned him around, and as the door swung open, he saw Maria standing there, looking shaken and pale.

Amos advanced a step, then stared past Maria through the door opening. Inside the cabin, firelight gleamed on a swatch of raven-black hair framing a dark female face. The visitor who sat before his hearth had a blanket tumbled from her naked shoulders and a baby nursing at her breast.

The baby was his.

Amos gaped. Then, slowly, the axe slid from his fingers and dropped unnoticed into the snow. Maria's face, as she stood in the doorway, was radiant.

"They came just after daylight," she told him. "They heard him crying and knew what was wrong."

Amos felt the snowfall on his face, saw the thick clumps of it that had built on the soles of his boots. Behind him, he heard the elders titter, caught sounds of stirring among them.

With a sense of daze, he stared through the doorway again. His son —their son—still clung to the squaw's breast. The woman's own child lay strapped to its cradleboard nearby, observing the proceedings with a bright gopher eye.

"Well," he said. It was all he could think of at the moment; a man could only handle so much at a time.

"I know," Maria said, and her face was still softly radiant as she raised her face to the chilled kiss of the snow. "I'm glad you've got your ditches cleaned out, Amos; the spring melt should be good."

Then she stood back, and her smiling glance embraced him, along with the shivering Coyoteros. "And now, Amos, let me bring these people in by the fire, while you pick up your axe and go find us a Christmas tree."

Mainwaring's Gift

Ed Gorman

Ed Gorman wears three different hats, all of them well: advertising executive, editor and publisher of Mystery Scene *magazine, and writer of quality Western, mystery, and horror fiction. His Western novels include three in an evocative series about sometime bounty hunter Leo Guild,* Guild *(1987),* Death Ground *(1988), and* Blood Game *(1989); and two nonseries books set in old Cedar Rapids, his hometown—*Graves' Retreat *(1989) and* Night of Shadows *(1990). "Mainwaring's Gift," a moving and highly unusual Christmas tale, demonstrates his considerable ability with the Western short story.*

He had been nine hours riding to get here, Mainwaring had, and now that he was here, he wondered if he should have come at all.

Stover was little more than two blocks of false fronts, a railroad depot, telegraph lines, and a big livery stable to handle all the drovers who came through here in the hot months.

Not even on Christmas Eve was the plain ugliness of the little town softened any. The covered candles that should have given the main street a soft glow only succeeded in showing up the worn look of the buildings and the hard, hostile faces of the people. Stover was a boastfully religious town where no liquor was served except at one hotel and a man should know better than to trouble the ladies. There were long-standing tales of men who had done such and had found themselves hanging wrist-tied and black-tongued from a tree next to the winding river to the west.

A church half a block away was furious with yellow light and even more furious with a choir singing Christmas songs. Out here on the prairie the little white box split the night with its light and sound.

Mainwaring's horse sounded lonely coming down the street, its metal shoes striking the cold-hardened ground and smashing through occasional patches of silver ice. The horse smelled of manure and sweat. Mainwaring probably didn't smell much better.

Mainwaring was a cowhand when he could be and a farmhand when he needed to be. The hell of it, here in the Territory of 1892, was that with all the bank failures, tending sheep and pigs and crops paid a lot more than tending beeves. Too many big beef men had gone bust for bankers to climb right back on.

Most of this year, his thirty-sixth, Mainwaring had spent on sixty-three acres raising shell corn and soybeans and ocra. He had been to town here twice, once in March when one of the other farmhands was afraid he'd come down with cholera (but hadn't), and the other to celebrate his birthday. For only the second time in his life, Mainwaring, who'd been raised to believe in the Bible himself, had found his way to a bottle of rye. Most of that night was fuzzy but he did remember making the acquaintance of a certain woman and that was what brought him here tonight. Though he'd written her several times since going back to the farm, he'd received no reply. He figured that maybe he'd use the night of Christmas Eve to sort of accidentally see her. Maybe in his drunkenness he had offended her in some way. He hoped not.

At the end of the first block he found the hotel where he'd met the town woman.

The lobby was nearly as bright as the church. Piney-smelling Christmas decorations hung from walls and doors, and a holiday tree that seemed to be near as high as the church spire stood in one corner, casting off the warm yellow-blue-red-green hues of Christmas candles.

The people in the lobby were about what you'd expect, relatively prosperous-looking folks in three-piece banker suits and silk and organdy dresses. Only prosperous people could afford such clothes.

Within thirty seconds of him entering the lobby, a glass of hot apple cider was thrust into Mainwaring's hand by the desk clerk, a stout man with a walrus mustache, a bald and shiny head, and a genuinely friendly manner.

As he handed Mainwaring the cider, he squinted one eye and said, "You look familiar."

Mainwaring, who was usually too embarrassed to talk when he was in gatherings like this—he was well aware that he was a yokel and that these townspeople were his betters—muttered something about spending his birthday here last spring.

"Why, that's wonderful!" said the desk clerk. "I hope you enjoyed the festivities!" he said, poking Mainwaring playfully in the ribs.

Then, abruptly, the clerk stopped himself, looked around at the other guests, who were just now starting to sing more Christmas favorites, and said, "My God, you're the one."

"The one?"

"This is an unbelievable coincidence."

"What is?"

"That you're here."

"It is?"

"Tonight of all nights."

"What is?"

Even though he knew the cider to be nonalcoholic, Mainwaring wondered if somebody might not have put something in this fellow's drink because he just wasn't making any sense.

The desk clerk looked even more furtive now, as if he were afraid somebody might overhear their conversation. He took Mainwaring by the sleeve and drew him closer to the counter. "You came to see her, didn't you?"

"Who?"

"Who? Why Jenny, of course."

Mainwaring felt like a ten-year-old. His face got hot with blood at the implication linking them together. "Well," he said.

The clerk whispered even more softly. "Believe me, friend, you don't know how glad she's going to be to see you."

"She tell you so?" Mainwaring felt his head and heart thrum with excitement, though he tried to give the impression of being indifferent.

The clerk stared at him. "You don't know, do you?"

"Know what?"

"What happened to her."

"I guess maybe I don't."

The clerk leaned into him and nodded toward the group of people now starting to sing "Silent Night." "The people here have been awful to her."

"They have?"

"They point and they whisper and they condemn."

"Condemn?"

"Most all of them."

"But why?"

The clerk shook his head. "My God, man, can't you figure it out?"

He felt dense and more of a yokel than ever, Mainwaring did. But no matter how he berated himself for being stupid, he couldn't figure out what this man was talking about.

"Do you remember what you did that night?" the clerk asked.

Mainwaring tried a grin. "Got a little drunk."

"But that's all you remember?"

Mainwaring shrugged.

"She wasn't what she pretended to be," the clerk said.

"Huh?"

"Jenny. Don't you remember when she came into the saloon in the back there."

Mainwaring thought back and then flushed once more. "Oh. Yes. I sort of do now."

"She pretended to be a scarlet lady."

"Yes."

"But she wasn't."

"No, I didn't think so."

"She's the daughter of a man who was hanged here about a year ago for rustling some cattle. She went a little crazy after that and took to drink and wandered the streets here and gave everybody the impression that she'd become a lady of easy virtue. Sometimes she'd go out to where the mob hung him that night, and she'd stand under the tree and call out for her daddy as if he were gonna appear to her and answer." The clerk shook his head. "He never did, of course. Appear, I mean. But Jenny went right on cozying up to men and enjoying herself, so that she'd become a scandal in a town that was supposed to be without scandal. They threw her out several times but she kept coming back, kept cozying up to men in the saloon back there. But she never actually did anything with any of them."

"No?"

"No. Not until that night with you, that is."

"With me?"

"With you. She told me later on, after I'd given her some coffee and a cigarette, that she'd done it with you because there was an innocence about you that she liked and trusted. Something in your eyes, she kept saying." The clerk frowned. "Well, now that I've met you, I'd have to say you *are* a mite innocent—or something."

Somehow, Mainwaring didn't feel he was being complimented. "So what happened to her?"

"What happened? What do you think happened, fellow? She is got with child. And that made her even more of a scandal. She'd walk everywhere, this unmarried woman with child, and say hello and nice day and how're you doing just as nice as pie, just as if nothing was wrong at all."

"They didn't like that, the townspeople?"

"Didn't like it? They tried threatening her out of town, and bribing her out of town, and even dragging her out of town. You know, they didn't feel it was fitting for a woman like her to show herself to our children."

"They didn't, huh?"

"Nope. But it didn't do any good. She was just as obstinate as ever. She might be gone for a day or two, but she always showed up again. Always. Then the accident happened and there wasn't much they could do, and still call themselves Christians and all."

"Accident?"

"Out near the tree where her daddy was hung."

"What happened?"

"Stagecoach. Running a couple hours late as usual and top speed. She'd been under the tree and wailing and carrying on the way she usually did, and she didn't hear the stage in the road and it ran her down."

"My Lord."

The clerk paused, his jowly face fallen into a look of despair. "She almost lost the baby. Would have if I hadn't took her in, put her in a guest room on the third floor. That's where she's been ever since."

Mainwaring raised his slate-blue eyes to the sweeping staircase before him.

"She's gonna have the baby any time now."

"She got a doctor?" Mainwaring asked.

The clerk glowered. "Nope. Only doc in town's afraid to help her because the good Christian people hereabouts won't like it. Oh, that isn't what he says, of course—he's got some other cock and bull explanation—but that's what it comes down to."

Mainwaring said, gently, "So what're you gonna do?"

The desk clerk popped his Ingram from the watch pocket of his vest and said, "Any time now, a granny woman from a farm ten miles north of here is comin' by. She's going to help her."

Mainwaring said, "You're trying to tell me this baby is mine, aren't you?"

The desk clerk laughed without humor. "Well, it took you a while to figure out what was going on here, but maybe it was worth the wait." He nodded to the stairs. "Come on."

The room was in the rear, next to a fire exit.

The desk clerk stopped him outside the door. "I'm going in and talk to her a minute. Then I'll come and get you, all right?"

Mainwaring nodded.

While the clerk was gone, Mainwaring went over and looked out the back window. The night was black and starry. A quarter moon cast drab silver light on the small huddled town. Only the singing from the lobby below and the church nearby reminded Mainwaring of what night this was. He was still trying to make sense of this. He had come into town to see Jenny—all innocent enough—and now he was being told he was a father.

"She's ready for you," the clerk said when he came back. He closed the door behind him. "She's real sick, though. I wish that granny woman would get here."

Mainwaring went inside. He saw immediately what the desk clerk was talking about. The frail, blanched woman who lay belly-swollen and sweating in the middle of a jumble of covers was not the pretty, fleshy girl of the spring. She had the look of all dying animals about her. Mainwaring felt scared and sick, the way he'd gotten just recently when he'd seen a foal dying in the barn hay a month ago. Animals, especially young and vulnerable animals, were Mainwaring's way of beating the loneliness of hardscrabble prairie life.

She lay on her back with her hands folded on her belly. Sweat had made her blond hair dark and her gray skin sleek.

He walked up to her and put his hand out and touched her folded hands.

"Hello," he said.

She opened her eyes then and he saw immediately how far gone she was.

She smiled. "I told him you'd come. Somehow."

"I came all right."

"Oscar said he told you about me and the baby."

"Oscar?"

"The desk clerk, Oscar Stern. You believe him?"

"That I'm the father?"

She nodded.

"Yes, ma'am, I do." His hat in his hand, gripping it now, he said, "I hope I didn't—force you into anything that night."

"You didn't." She sounded as if even speaking were difficult. "I got your letters."

"You did?"

"Yes."

"How come you didn't write? I sat there in my cabin at night and thought you didn't want nothing more to do with me."

She closed her eyes. "I guess I was afraid you wouldn't believe me. I figured you'd think that maybe some other man . . ."

She convulsed then, her fragile body threatening to snap in two. She moaned and he saw her eyes begin to dilate.

He turned and opened the door. "That granny lady here yet?" he asked Oscar Stern.

Just as Oscar was about to speak, a short woman in some kind of cape came up the stairs. She had a pipe in one corner of her mouth, a furious glare in her brown eyes, and a curse coming from her lips.

Suddenly, Mainwaring saw what she was angry about.

Right behind her came a tall, severe man in a cleric's collar and three hefty women in their holiday finery.

The granny woman pushed past Mainwaring and the desk clerk and went inside.

The minister spoke first. "Oscar, even though you're of another faith, this town has striven to abide our differences. But we've warned you all along what would happen if you permitted this woman to have her child within these city limits."

Oscar Stern said, "Even though I'm not a Christian, pastor, I'm trying hard to act like one. Somebody's got to care for that girl."

"Not in this town they don't," said one of the ladies.

"We have a wagon downstairs," the minister said. "We plan to take her out to the Kruse farm where a midwife there will take care of her. We just don't want a . . ."

"We don't want an unmarried woman having her child in our town," said another of the women. "What kind of example do you think that sets?"

The minister was getting himself ready for another round of rhetoric, patting his silver hair and swelling his chest, when Mainwaring stepped forward.

"Anybody tries to move that woman," he said, "I'll get my rifle and kill him on the spot."

"My Lord," said the third woman. "Who is this man?"

"I happen," Mainwaring said, "to be the father."

Grave looks of displeasure crossed the faces of the four visitors. The minister looked as if he wanted to spit something awful-tasting from his mouth. He looked Mainwaring up and down and said, "I must say, you're just about the sort of man I would have expected to be the father."

"You get out of here now," Mainwaring told them. "Oscar Stern owns the hotel and it's his rules we abide by here."

One of the women started to say something.

Glaring, Mainwaring pointed his finger at her as if it were a weapon. The woman looked outraged and then she looked frightened.

"After tonight, Oscar," the minister said, "you may as well put this place up for sale. You won't be living in Stover much longer. I can promise you that."

The religious entourage left.

The granny woman, who had obviously been listening, stuck her head out the door and said, "One of you lazybones get in here. I need some help."

Birthing was scissors and thread and cloverine salve; birthing was sulfur and wine of cordia; birthing was cutting the cord and tying it off and dressing the baby; birthing was taking all the afterbirth, including the umbilical cord and placenta, and burying it out in the alley. After all this, the granny woman greased the infant's navel cord with castor oil and then added some powder to the oil.

During all this, Mainwaring sat in the room, terrified and joyous simultaneously, jumping up whenever the granny woman summoned him, carrying hot water and clean rags, ointment and liniment and salve.

When it was all over, when the infant was revealed to be a girl and Jenny herself was collapsed into an exhausted sleep, the granny woman left the child with Oscar and took Mainwaring out into the hall.

"You can see what's going on in there."

"Ma'am?"

"Jenny. She's dying."

Mainwaring felt colder than any winter night had ever made him feel. There was the unaccustomed sting of hot tears in his eyes. He said, "I love her."

"Right now, it's that little girl you've got to worry about."

"But—"

The granny woman said, "I know you love Jenny, son. But now, that don't matter. It's that child that matters."

Mainwaring went back inside the room. The granny woman gave him the infant and then left the room.

For half an hour Mainwaring sat next to the bed with dying Jenny. Occasionally she'd mutter something deep in the down-fathoms of her sleep, something that had the word daddy or father in it.

When the baby squalled, Mainwaring shushed and rocked it, thinking of all the tiny animals he had befriended over the years. This was the tiniest and most special animal of them all. His own daughter.

Finally, Jenny opened her eyes. Her mouth was parched and she could barely speak, but she spoke anyway. She smiled and looked up and touched their little girl there in Mainwaring's arms and said, "My daddy said she's beautiful."

Mainwaring said nothing.

"I saw my daddy just now. He's waiting for me."

Mainwaring felt the tears again and held the baby tighter.

"I'm sorry for how all this happened," Jenny said. "I should've written you back."

Mainwaring just shook his head.

"I want her to love you as much as I love my daddy," she said.

"I'm gonna give her every reason to love me," Mainwaring said. "I'm gonna be the best daddy she could ask for."

Jenny put her long, slender hand to Mainwaring's cheek. "You're not the smartest or the prettiest man I ever saw, Mainwaring, but I honestly do believe you're the best. And that's why I'm so glad I'm leaving her in your care."

He wasn't sure when she died—whether it was when she sighed and her entire body trembled; or when her face turned away from her little girl, toward the wall; or when her hand stretched out briefly in the air as if she were taking an unseen hand in her own—but when he leaned down to kiss her forehead and felt the stone coldness there, he knew.

He sat with his child in his arms, not even noticing how she cried now, just gently rocking her and looking at the dead woman, feeling occasionally the tears in his eyes and the hard unbidden lump in his throat.

After a time, Oscar Stern and the granny woman came back in. The granny woman saw to Jenny and the infant, and Oscar saw to Mainwaring.

"Where you going tonight, son?"

Mainwaring shook his head. "I'm not going to stay here. Probably start back for the farm."

"You think you can handle that infant?"

"The owner's got a wife and a young daughter. They'll help."

Oscar frowned. "Don't blame you for wanting to get out of this town. I'll be leaving it myself soon enough."

Mainwaring put out his hand. "I want to thank you."

"I should be thanking you, Mainwaring. You brought Jenny and me together, and she was one of the few decent people I've known in this place."

Mainwaring went back inside the room. Alone there, the door closed, he knelt beside the dead woman and held her hand for a long and silent time. There were no tears now, nor any unbidden lump in his throat, just his wonderment at her goodness and her grace, and his wish that he'd had time to know her well and love her as all his life he had longed to love a woman.

He stood up, went out and said good-bye to Oscar and the granny woman, and then he set off with the child.

Just as he was leaving town, he heard the church bell celebrate another birth on this night nearly two thousand years ago, and he wondered if people so soured by righteousness and so empty of compassion would love even Jesus if he were to come back.

He rode on, Mainwaring did, hard into the dark night and on Christmas morning crested a hill from which he could see the farm below. He could see smoke from its chimney and hear children singing carols. Farmers from all over the valley had gathered in this house.

Just before he took the horse down the rocky hill, he looked at his swaddled baby and smiled. During the night he had realized that he did, after all, have a woman to love.

His daughter.

"Seven-up's" Christmas

Charles Alden Seltzer

*Charles Alden Seltzer (1875–1942) was among the most successful prac-
titioners of the cowboy story during the first four decades of this century.
Beginning in 1900 with the publication of his first novel,* The Council of
Three, *Seltzer wrote highly romanticized—and highly popular—yarns
about the rangelands of Arizona and other parts of the Southwest. Not all
of his novels feature cowboys and cattlemen, but the best ones do:* The
Trail to Yesterday *(1913),* "Drag" Harlan *(1921),* A Son of Arizona
(1931), Silverspurs *(1935), and* Treasure Ranch *(1940). His most accomplished short stories are likewise cowboy adventures: those in his two
collections,* The Range Riders *(1911) and* The Triangle Cupid *(1912),
and the unusual Christmas tale which follows.*

There was a light in Seven-up's dug-out, and the light meant, of
course, that Seven-up was at home.

Breathing his pony on the crest of Gopher Hill, after the long climb,
Laskar glanced eagerly down the trail.

Yes; the light was there. No doubt about that. Its presence meant
that Seven-up was still active; it meant shelter, warmth and companionship—three things which are highly desirable on a long trail in the
middle of a chill November night.

Laskar smiled as he approached the dug-out. He knew as much

about Seven-up as any man in the country knew, which, when a man
got to reviewing his knowledge, was little enough.

Seven-up was riding line for the Double R outfit. Everybody knew
that. Seven-up was sixty-five years old. He had said so himself, and as
there was nothing to be gained by lying about one's age everybody
believed him. Seven-up had been riding for the Double R for about
two years. Everybody knew that, too. It was not much to know about a
man, but in this country it was enough.

When a man is willing to sit up until near daylight with you, playing
cards, even if—as a rule—he succeeds in winning about nine out of
every ten games, you may safely assume that he likes you. An inveterate card player would rather beat a friend in a card game than an
enemy in a fist fight. Therefore, being an inveterate card player,
Seven-up took a keen delight in proving to Laskar that the latter had
still very much to learn before he could hope to master even the
rudiments of "High-Low-Jack and Game."   .

Infrequent as were Laskar's trips to "town" he always managed so
that on his return he would be able to pass the greater part of one
night in Seven-up's dug-out, playing seven up. Passing a night at
Seven-up's saved a camp in the open with its attendant inconve-
niences. Seven-up usually regaled Laskar with hot frijoles and soda
biscuit, which was much better than cold bacon, crackers and canned
tomatoes. And a deep adobe fireplace, in which Seven-up cooked with
Dutch ovens and frying-pans, and before which one might toast one's
feet, was much to be preferred to a wind-whipped fire on the open
prairie, before which a man might nearly freeze.

Therefore, considering the advantages afforded by the geographi-
cally admirable location of Seven-up's dug-out, Laskar might well
smile as he approached the light.

At the noise he made in dismounting Seven-up appeared in the
doorway of the dug-out.

"Well, you got here, did yu? I've been settin' up, waitin' for yu. Saw
yu hittin' the breeze day before yesterday, an' figgered yu'd be slidin'
back this way about now." He emerged from the dug-out and pulled
the saddle from Laskar's pony while the latter removed the bridle and
staked the animal out in the lee of the dug-out wall.

"Got some frijoles in the pot for yu! They've been blubberin' right
smart sense sundown." Seven-up cackled mirthfully as he cleared a
space on the rough board table and set some steaming food upon it.

He sat and smoked while Laskar ate. He asked a few questions about "town". Then, after the remains of the guest's feast had been cleared from the table, came the inevitable invitation to play cards.

"Seven-up?" questioned the inhabitant of the dug-out. "You ain't got no show ag'in me to-night!" he boasted as he caught Laskar's acquiescent nod. "Fit, I tell yu! They ain't no man c'n beat me playin' seven up when I'm fit. I c'n play cards all around the man that made them!"

"You ain't forgettin' to blow your own horn none, anyhow," grinned Laskar, pulling a bench up to the table.

Seven-up cackled. "I'll ketch your Jack for that, first pop!" he threatened—which he did on the very first deal, much to Laskar's disgust.

"Reckon you've got them cards marked," accused Laskar with some heat. It was not so much that he had lost the Jack but that Seven-up had made good on his threat that caused Laskar a flash of anger.

Seven-up laid his cards face down on the table and leaning forward looked straight at Laskar, his bleared eyes full of reproach.

"Yu know a heap better than that, Las," he said, "a heap better. I ain't never cheated no man playin' seven up, nor in any other game. I'm too old to start now. Besides, I wouldn't do it in a friendly game, nohow. But there's men that do mark their cards, Las—I've knowed 'em. I knowed one man which always made a point of markin' all the high cards in every deck he ever played with. It didn't make no difference whether he was playin' for money or not, he always marked the cards. Nobody ever ketched on to him either, except me, an' I ketched on to it too late." He laughed oddly and took up the Jack of Hearts, laying it face down on the table and pressing the end of his thumb nail against the back, creating a deep impression in the card. He held it up so that Laskar might see. His eyes were very bright as he looked at Laskar.

"See that thumb-mark?" he questioned. "Well, you'll see that the thumb-mark is made up in a corner, but it's sorta round like."

"Yes," said Laskar, "a sorta semi-circle."

"That's it," said Seven-up; "a sorta semi-circle. Well, the man I'm tellin' you about didn't make no semi-circle when he marked the cards. He had a thumb which had been smashed some time or other—smashed bad. The nail had come off an' when it growed back on it didn't grow back like an honest, respectable nail, but growed crooked—like the man which owned it.

"It growed square, an' it was the only square thing about the man.

He played cards a heap an' he used to keep the end of that square thumb nail trimmed straight acrost, an' when he'd git a high card which he wanted to know when it was in some other man's hand he'd press that square nail down on to it, close up to one of the corners of the card. Then he'd know it. He had different ways of pressin' the nail down so's he'd know all the cards. Sometimes he'd make a triangle; sometimes he'd stick the two corners of the square together an' make a cross. He'd a dozen different ways of makin' signs, an' he knowed all of them—he had a fine system. Well, I—" Seven-up seemed about to take Laskar into his confidence, but apparently he decided not to, and laughed harshly.

"Your deal, Las," he said, and they resumed playing.

They played for two hours in a silence broken only by monosyllabic grunts that expressed such terms and phrases as "Beg", "Stand", "Give", "Rub"—the latter term being indicative of the progress of the game.

Apparently Seven-up was "fit", for he was a consistent winner. Along about three o'clock in the morning, disgusted with what he was pleased to call his "luck", Laskar signified his intention of quitting the game and "turning in".

"Just one more," pleaded Seven-up. "Yu don't git here often an' I sure do like to beat yu."

At the conclusion of this game Laskar was convinced that Seven-up was unbeatable and he sought his blankets and pulled the ends of them up over his ears to deaden the sound of Seven-up's gloating cackles.

Some time later Laskar sat suddenly up in his bunk, wide awake, listening intently. A wind was whoo-oo-ing and shrieking around the eaves of the dug-out, coming in heavy gusts against the north wall. The fire in the adobe fireplace was low; Laskar was chilled through in spite of the heavy blanket in which he was wrapped. He reached out one hand and brushed it over the blanket and then started up with an exclamation of surprise.

"Snow!" he said.

In an instant he was out of the bunk, throwing the blankets off, striding to the door and opening it.

He was forced back by a bitter, driving, snow-laden wind that filled the world outside. He closed the door and stood against it, scowling. Then he went to Seven-up and shook him savagely.

"Roll out!" he ordered. "The bottom's dropped out of the sky!"

Seven-up clambered out of his bunk rubbing his eyes, and when his vision cleared he fixed his gaze on the window in the side of the dug-out. The glass (Seven-up himself had brought it from town) was blurred, and fine, frozen snow meal swished against it, sifting through the crevices in the sash and drifting thinly into the bunk in which Laskar had been sleeping.

"A norther," said Seven-up, passionlessly. "She's comin' through the window—from the north. That settles two things. I don't ride no line to-day—nor mebbe for several days. An' you don't go home. Forty miles! You'd never make it. You couldn't ride five!"

"Don't I know it?" flared Laskar, scowling. "I don't need you to tell me!" His wife would worry about him. And yet perhaps not. She might think he had delayed starting from town.

Laskar buttoned up his coat and went outside, closing the door after him. A wild, white smother entered the dug-out while the door was open. It swirled and settled, leaving a new chill. Outside, Laskar was nearly swept off his feet by the wind—a whirling, stinging, blinding blast that bit clear through his clothing. The sky was gone, obscured by an impenetrable smother of fleece. Objects—old landmarks that Laskar knew well—were not to be seen.

He tried to peer northward—homeward. The fine flinty snow blinded him, the wind took his breath; he could not see a foot that way. He turned his back with a curse and sought his pony, finding it huddled against the wall of the dug-out. The animal nickered appealingly when it saw him, and he untied it and led it into a windbreak beside Seven-up's horse. He fed both animals from Seven-up's store and then made his way back to the dug-out.

Seven-up was placidly stirring the frijoles in the pot that he had placed over the fire.

"Goin' home?" he questioned at Laskar's entrance, without looking up.

"Home hell!" returned Laskar irritably.

"Tell you what," offered Seven-up, as they breakfasted; "this here norther reminds me of the one we got last year. About this time, too—on the last day of November. Or is this the last?"

"To-day's the first of December."

"Well, I ain't no hand to keep track of time. But that there storm we got last year about this time was sure a hummer. Early for this country, but it stayed a whole month. I didn't get to town for no Christmas last year."

"I'm goin' to go home for Christmas," declared Laskar.

"Why, sure, I reckon this won't last." Seven-up dished up another plate of frijoles for himself, Laskar declining another.

The two passed the remainder of the day playing cards—seven up. They retired early, and the next morning when Laskar arose and eagerly stuck his head out through the doorway the blizzard raged with unabated fury. Closing the door he walked silently back to the fire, throwing a fresh log upon it. Then he sat down on a bench and stared gloomily at the licking flames.

A little later Seven-up rolled out of his blankets. He said nothing to Laskar, but went to the door and looked out. The two breakfasted in silence. They played cards until dinner time, and then, neither man being hungry, they played through until supper time. They had beans again, and soda biscuit. After the table was cleared they resumed their card playing. It was seven up. That was the only game Seven-up knew; the only one he cared to know. He would play no other.

The proportion of Seven-up's victories remained the same—about nine in ten. Laskar had been beaten so much that he no longer saw any humour in Seven-up's uncanny luck. Both ceased to joke about the game, but played in grim earnest, with a concealed animus that presaged trouble. It was midnight when they agreed to quit. Laskar had won three games, Seven-up twenty-seven.

Instead of having abated during the night the next morning they found the blizzard raging with increased fury.

"We're holed up right," mourned Laskar, as he stood peering out through a two-inch opening in the door; "likely we'll stay here till spring. There's some steers driftin'—plenty of them. Fences won't hold them in this storm."

"Nothin'll hold them," seconded Seven-up. "If this storm keeps up the greasers'll have plenty stock next season—if the cattle don't freeze to death."

Laskar closed the door and came toward the table yawning. "Might as well play seven up," he said.

"Want some frijoles?" queried Seven-up.

Laskar turned on him fiercely. "To hell with your beans," he said; "I'm sick of them!"

"Shucks," said Seven-up, placatively; "they're good enough when you ain't got anything better."

"Eat 'em then," sneered Laskar. "Some folks don't want nothin' better. It all depends on how a man's been raised."

Seven-up did not answer, but gave his attention to the portion of beans that he had helped himself to.

Table etiquette was a thing with which Seven-up had never bothered. Nor had Laskar. Seven-up ate as he always ate, with his knife, masticating loudly, with open mouth. It was not a pretty spectacle, nor were the noises nice things to hear, and Laskar himself practised the same method. Yet he watched Seven-up furtively, a sneer on his lips, his gaze malevolent.

"Maybe you'd just as soon stop eatin' like a pig at a swill trough," he said presently, his voice writhing with suppressed rage.

Seven-up looked at him with a smile of mild defiance. "There ain't nothin' wrong with my eatin'," he said; "I've always et this way, an' I ain't stoppin' it now." He prepared another knife-full of the beans and lifted them, preparatory to placing them in his mouth.

"Put 'em down, damn you!" flared Laskar. He jerked out his forty-five and shoved its muzzle close to Seven-up, his eyes burning with anger. "I don't care how you've et," he declared; "you ain't goin' to do no swillin' whilst I'm lookin' at you!"

Seven-up slowly lowered the knife. "Las," he said gently, "you ain't naturally mean. Bein' holed up here has got on your nerves. So soon, too. I was hopin' we'd be able to git along. Why last year, when I was holed up here—alone—I stood it twenty days before I got to quarrelin' with myself, an' seein' things."

Laskar reluctantly sheathed his gun, grinning with embarrassment. "I reckon that's right," he agreed. "It ain't your eatin', it's me. It's curious how a little thing like bein' holed up will bother a man."

"Right curious," affirmed Seven-up. He took up his knife again, but though Laskar was apparently mollified, Seven-up took care not to rouse him again, mincing his food delicately.

During the day they took turns at the window and door, watching cattle drift by. There was an endless procession of them—now a mere dribble—now a surging wave of gaunt bodies and tossing horns—a tide that no human agency could stop.

Late in the afternoon Seven-up gave up watching them and turned his attention to the pot of frijoles. Laskar paid no attention to him,

standing beside the window, watching steadily, frowning at this thing
which was keeping him from going home.

Seven-up did not invite him to partake of the frijoles, when he lifted
them, steaming from the pot, fearing a recurrence of his anger. He ate
his own meal stealthily, keeping a watchful eye on his companion and
quietly removing the dishes when finished.

But he need not have been concerned over Laskar's probable con-
duct. The latter was master of himself now. His clash with Seven-up
had merely provided an outlet for the bitter rage and disappointment
he felt over being caught forty miles from home by the norther. He
was not likely to lose his temper again. So he told himself as he
thought over the incident.

Seven-up had boasted of his self-possession on a former occasion,
but on the morning of the tenth day of their imprisonment he crawled
out of his bunk and looked at Laskar with a strange light in his eyes.

"Them cattle has been goin' past here all night," he said; "black
cattle—all black. They must have been a million of them—with a
woman drivin'. It was my daughter—she done waved to me an' said
she'd be comin' back this way 'fore long. Told me to wait for her. But I
don't reckon she'll come back—I've waited twenty years!" He went to
the door, opened it and was about to go outside when Laskar seized
him by the arm and drew him away, closing the door.

Seven-up struggled, though his strength was not what it should
have been and he was a child in Laskar's grasp.

"Lemme be," he argued; "I'm goin' to look for her. Why, man, I
can't let her go like that!" he fought with Laskar, but he was carried
bodily to his bunk and placed in it muttering: "She'll sure freeze to
death out there."

"I reckon she would—if she was out there," agreed Laskar. "But she
ain't there and your own gizzard would be a hunk of ice before you'd
travel a quarter of a mile."

Seven-up cackled. And on the morrow, when he regained control of
himself and remembered, he was not exactly pleased. He tried to be
pleasant to Laskar, but the two had been cooped up together so long
that being pleasant was a difficult matter.

The dusk in the dug-out was perpetual; the air stale. But there was
no relief. Indeed, as the days passed the norther seemed to encompass
them more surely; the snow piled in huge drifts against the walls of
the dug-out; they watched the drift by the window grow gradually

higher and creep toward the top, slowly shutting out what little light they had.

"Ought to get that snow away from there," observed Seven-up on the morning of the fifteenth day. "Pretty soon we won't have no light at all."

"Get it away then, you," answered Laskar shortly, and returned to his bunk to sleep.

Seven-up did not reply. He was slowly beginning to believe that Laskar was imposing on him. He reasoned that Laskar had accepted his hospitality, was eating his food and sharing his fire, and therefore he ought to do something toward running the establishment. Why couldn't he have gone out and shovelled the snow away from the window? He was stubborn—that was why. Well, let him be stubborn, and let the snow stay there. He would never go out and shovel it away.

During his two years' acquaintance with Laskar he had never seen him in the light in which he saw him now. He had thought Laskar to be a whole-souled fellow, energetic and eager to do anything to help a friend along. But here he was proving himself a small, mean, narrow-minded, contemptible lazy-bones. Why, he didn't want to do anything! He had loafed in the dug-out while Seven-up had gone to the spring for water—not once but several times. And it was a good hundred yards to the spring, and it was frozen over, and there was ice to be chopped before the water could be secured. He wouldn't cook or wash the dishes, and he complained of the food. Laskar had been feeding the horses though—which was something. But the more Seven-up meditated over this fact the more convinced he became that Laskar had some ulterior purpose in exhibiting industry in this particular chore. He began to suspect that Laskar was favouring his own beast in the matter of feed. He decided to investigate and waited until he thought Laskar was asleep. He was opening the door when he heard Laskar's voice:

"Where you goin'?"

Seven-up's eyes blazed with anger. Laskar suspected the object of his errand and did not want him to investigate. Wasn't that proof?

"You're starvin' my horse," he snarled; "I'm goin' out to feed him."

Laskar threw himself back in the bunk, laughing huskily. "Sure," he said, his lips quivering with the anger that he was trying to suppress, "I'm starvin' your horse. If you knowed that why ain't you been doin' your own feedin', instead of dependin' on me to do it for you. You're too damned lazy, that's why."

Seven-up halted with his hand on the door. "I wouldn't say that ag'in, Las, if I was you," he said.

"Why wouldn't you?" Laskar raised himself on one arm and leered at Seven-up.

"Because I'm tellin' you not to." Seven-up's voice sank to a furious, throaty whisper. "Because I'm tellin' you—that's why," he repeated. "If you chirp one little wee chirp ag'in about me bein' lazy I'm lettin' daylight through you a-plenty. I ain't tellin' you ag'in."

Such clashes did not encourage harmony. They erected a barrier of distrust and suspicion which almost reached a climax when one night, about the twentieth of their enforced companionship, the two men lay in their bunks, opposite each other, glaring an unspeakable hatred.

Hatred was bound to develop sooner or later. These two men had been accustomed to riding forth on their daily rounds in the open. They had been free to come and go as they pleased, living frugally, enjoying the clear, pure, wholesome air of the plains, sleeping out of doors, revelling in their limitless world; being a part of the general bigness of things.

Here they were cooped up. It would not have made so much difference if they could have gone on an occasional ride—if they could have avoided seeing each other for even one night. They would have succeeded in securing a new grip on themselves then; would have taken a new delight in each other's company. But they had seen too much of each other. Even a bridal couple on their honeymoon soon tire of the monotony of being left to their own devices, and if someone does not save them from themselves discord soon spoils the dream.

But no one came to save Laskar and Seven-up. And they had no dream to wake from. It was all stern, bitter, unlovely reality. Their minds dwelt on trivialities; dormant fires of passion, primitive and uncontrollable, flared forth constantly, threatening an eruption. Laskar would lie for hours in his bunk, his gaze fixed on Seven-up, watching the way the latter puffed at his pipe, sneering when the smoker's lips curled around the stem of the pipe, sneering when they were in repose. Nothing that Seven-up did suited Laskar; Seven-up found nothing in Laskar's actions and general demeanour at which he could not cavil. They had reached the breaking point.

For hours they lay in their bunks watching each other furtively.

Laskar would feign sleep and then suddenly open his eyes to catch Seven-up looking at him. The action would be reversed. Suspicion grew quickly in this fertile field. But along toward morning Laskar's eyelids grew heavy—he could stay awake no longer. He sneered at Seven-up.

"Oh, hell," he said. "Stick a knife in me if you want to." And he deliberately rolled over, turning his back to Seven-up.

The latter lay quiet for a long time, certain that Laskar was pretending sleep in order to invite an attack so that he might kill him. But Seven-up was not to be caught thus. He waited, fighting sleep, until there was no further doubt that Laskar was really unconscious. Then he crept noiselessly out of his bunk and deftly removed Laskar's knife and gun. Then with a subdued cackle he slipped back into his bunk and dropped off to sleep—satisfied.

But his dreams were troubled. He kept seeing cattle—black cattle. His daughter was driving them—in the storm—her slight figure cringing from the wind. He talked in his sleep of many strange things—of a troubled past, of a dead wife and motherless girl—a girl whom he worshipped and who had been led away by a card player. Aroused from sleep by Seven-up's mutterings Laskar turned his face and listened.

"Twenty years," said Seven-up mournfully and despairingly, "it's been twenty years an' I ain't seen no sight of her. Likely she's dead—or worse—or she'd have been back before this. Bill Henley—he's got her. Henley couldn't play square; the only thing that was square about Henley was his damned thumb nail . . . an' he cheated with that."

Then he wandered off into incoherence and Laskar resumed his interrupted sleep.

Late the next morning Laskar awoke to hear Seven-up grumbling about the food supply. It was about exhausted. By scraping the pot they obtained enough frijoles for breakfast—and Laskar gagged over these. Once a month the supply wagon visited Seven-up; he would have had plenty to last him until the Double R wagon came again had he not been compelled to share with Laskar. They were both facing starvation now, and it was Laskar's fault. Seven-up yielded to bitterness.

"You've et more than your share," he complained over the table, after the last morsel of food had disappeared. "You've been a damned hog all along, that's what."

"You're a liar!" said Laskar, huskily. His eyes wore a horribly malignant expression as he leered at Seven-up across the table.

"I tell you you're a damned hog!" repeated Seven-up shrilly. If he could goad Laskar into attacking him he would have an excuse to kill him and thus rid himself of a being that he had come to loathe.

He cackled insanely as Laskar clutched at his empty holster and searched in vain for his knife. "I knowed it," he declared with conviction, "you've been wantin' to kill me all along. That's why I took your knife and gun. I've got 'em hid out, but I'm keepin' my own."

"That ain't no way to treat a man," protested Laskar. "Gimme my knife an' gun."

"They're done hid out, I told you," cackled Seven-up. "You don't git 'em. You was goin' to kill me last night; you was waitin' till I got to sleep. But I reckon I done fooled you there, eh? I done fooled you considerable. I got 'em right after my daughter went by, drivin' them black steers."

Into Laskar's eyes came a designing gleam. "Sure, you got 'em then. But I wasn't goin' to kill you, Seven-up—I wouldn't do nothin' like that. Gimme my knife back and my gun an' I'll go out an' ketch your daughter and bring her back. She can't be gone far."

Seven-up laughed discordantly. "You ain't foolin' me none, Las. You don't want to look for my daughter; that's just a game to git back your knife and gun. You don't git 'em. Anyway, my daughter's comin' back. She drives them black steers past here every little while. When she comes past again I'm gittin' her myself."

Laskar went to the window and slowly scraped the frost from the glass. He stood there for a long time, looking out at the swirling snow. There was no indication of a break. "I reckon we're done for," he said, more to himself than to Seven-up; "there ain't no signs of a let-up." He could feel his self-control going; he knew that he would soon be in the same condition as Seven-up, for he could see many things out in the snow that he knew were not there, and strange thoughts flitted through his mind. Once he found himself laughing, though in a flash of sober sense he knew there was nothing at which to laugh.

Once, while looking out of the window, he thought he saw a pony and rider approaching the dug-out and he came very near to calling Seven-up to see, too, so real did they appear. But he knew it was his brain trying to make a fool of him and so he decided to keep silent and not give Seven-up a chance to laugh at him. It was curious, though, how he kept seeing the horse and rider. It was a black horse and he thought perhaps it was the same horse that Seven-up had seen, though there were no black cattle about and the rider of the horse was not a woman but a man. Also, the man appeared to be frozen to the saddle, for, though Laskar could not see his face, the man sat in a queer position, his head bowed and his body strangely slack.

Laskar had been much interested in Seven-up's rambling references to his daughter. Something in Seven-up's recital had struck him as strangely familiar. It sounded like a story that he had heard in the long ago—or had it happened to himself? He was not certain—he could not be certain of anything with his brain forming curious phantasies of thought, drawing odd pictures of unreal things, perplexing him, hurting him. But he felt an overpowering curiosity in the matter of Seven-up's daughter. Then, too, he had heard Seven-up speak of a town named "Milford". He had heard of Milford but could not recollect having been there. Seven-up had said he was from there. But had Laskar been there or had he merely talked to some other person about the town—some person besides Seven-up? If he had been there all well and good, but if he had heard of the town from someone besides Seven-up that would indicate that he might have heard the story of the lost daughter from some other source as well.

He turned to Seven-up, who was sitting in a chair twirling his thumbs and grinning idiotically at them.

Oh, he couldn't talk to that beast! But curiosity forced the question through his lips:

"What's your right name?"

Seven-up stopped twirling his thumbs and looked up at him through blurred, vacuous eyes.

"Which?" he inquired.

"What's your right name?"

Seven-up's eyes flashed with a cunning, maniacal light. "You want to know my name so's you can tell Bill Henley to look out for me. But I ain't tellin'; I ain't tellin' nobody but Bill Henley. I'll find him some day an' then I'll tell him." He resumed twirling his thumbs though he kept a wary eye on Laskar. The latter asked no more questions but crawled into his bunk and went to sleep. For an hour Seven-up sat, watching and twirling his thumbs, then he, too, sought his bunk.

Late that afternoon the sky cleared, the snow ceased, the wind died down. A cold sun, hanging its rim on a mountain peak, bathed the world in a shimmering, glittering, blinding light. Neither Laskar nor Seven-up was conscious of the change. They had sunk into a lethargic state which was so near to complete unconsciousness that they no longer took any interest in anything—not even their hatred for each other.

For two days they lay in their bunks, not stirring out of them, even to feed the horses. During the last day of the storm the snow had drifted above the window in the dug-out, shutting out the light, and when on the morning of the twenty-fourth day Laskar staggered out of his bunk the interior of the dug-out was in semi-darkness. For an instant after getting out of the bunk Laskar stood beside it, glumly surveying the drift at the window.

"Hell," he said; "what's the use of worryin'. It's still snowin' an' we're done for."

Steadying himself he walked across the floor and seized Seven-up roughly by the shoulder.

"Pile out, you old fool—you're sleepin' your head off! We're going to play our harps pretty soon an' we might as well tune up right now. Let's play seven up."

It took Seven-up some minutes to sit erect and when he did it was easy to see that he was not standing the strain of hunger and lonesomeness as well as Laskar. There was an unnatural color in his face and an insane light in his eyes. Only the latter part of Laskar's speech · interested him.

"Seven up?" he said. "Sure, I reckon I'll play seven up. Why, Seven-up's my name, ain't it?"

He slipped down and tottered across the floor to the table. Laskar took a seat opposite him.

The latter's curiosity regarding Seven-up's identity had not abated. He was determined to uncover this mystery before the end came. He hesitated while shuffling the cards and looked at Seven-up. Reaching into a pocket he drew out a handful of currency and laid it on the table.

"We're playin' for somethin'," he said. "I'm putting this roll up. If you win you get it. If you lose you tell me your right name. That go?"

Seven-up braced himself by holding to the table while he looked at Laskar. "My name," he said thickly, his face clouding with incomprehension. Then his eyes flashed craftily. "You can't win, Las. I can beat the man that made the cards."

"It goes then?" suggested Laskar.

"Deal," returned Seven-up. "If you win I tell you my name. But you can't win!" He went off into a gale of wild laughter.

Laskar did not win. Seven-up swept Laskar's money over the table and jeered at him. But Laskar produced more money and they played again. Again Seven-up won; he was a consistent winner. Along toward the middle of the afternoon Laskar announced that he was "broke," and Seven-up started to count his winnings. He was cackling over them, counting and recounting and each time getting a different total, when he saw Laskar fumbling in a pocket and stopped counting to watch him.

Laskar finally pulled out a gold chain and locket and placed them on the table in front of him.

"I'm puttin' this up," he said.

Seven-up dropped the money to the table, seized the locket and drew it over to him. The sight of it wrought a wonderful change in him. The insane light died out of his eyes and was succeeded by a cold, metallic gleam. The hectic colour disappeared from his face and was replaced by a queer, unnatural pallor—the white of cold ashes.

"Las," he said in a low, intense voice; "where did you git this locket?"

"It's my wife's. What's it your business?"

"What's your wife's name?" continued Seven-up, ignoring Laskar's question.

"Amy."

"What was her last name—before she married you?"

"Legget," announced Laskar, his interest finally aroused.

Seven-up's eyes slowly closed. The hand holding the locket was clenched about it so tightly that Laskar was beginning to fear for the delicate thing when he saw that Seven-up was staring at his left hand, staring intensely, his eyes aflame.

"What in hell you lookin' at?" demanded Laskar, a surge of the old anger and hatred sweeping over him.

"I never noticed it before," said Seven-up, paying no attention to Laskar's anger. "It's curious that I never noticed before that you'd lost a part of your thumb. How long ago?"

"When I was thirteen years old," retorted Laskar coldly. "What's it your business?"

"You lost it when you was thirteen years old?" said Seven-up huskily, leaning far over the table, his lips suddenly twitching, his hands working strangely.

"Thirteen, I said," returned Laskar.

"You're a damned liar!" suddenly shrieked Seven-up. The bench upon which he had been sitting was overturned and he swayed against the table, trembling with excitement. "You're a liar!" he screamed again. "You lost it within the last twenty years! You're Bill Henley, damn you—Bill Henley!"

He reached for his holster, to find it empty. Making queer, throaty noises he left the table and tottered to the door, opening it and staggering out into the snow, toward the windbreak where the horses were tethered. Laskar followed, a growing fear in his eyes.

When Seven-up reached the windbreak he fumbled for a moment under a pile of snow-covered straw, bringing forth the knife and gun he had taken from Laskar. He straightened up, evidently thinking that Laskar was still in the dug-out, and, surprised to see Laskar behind him, he hesitated an instant and then flung the six-shooter to a poise. At that instant Laskar hurled himself forward, striking savagely at the hand holding the weapon. He succeeded in knocking the pistol from Seven-up's grasp and it hurtled several feet away and was buried in a snowdrift. Seven-up snarled and tried to use the knife, but Laskar seized his arm. Locked tightly fighting silently and desperately, they reeled around in the snow. Seven-up's advanced age was against him but he was fighting with a ferocity that had twenty years of meditated vengeance behind it and for a time it seemed he would be able to get his knife hand free. A dozen times he came very near to twisting the arm loose, but Laskar's agility saved him and his younger muscles did not fail. They crashed against a corner of the dug-out and rebounded to the edge of a huge snowdrift. There Laskar exerted his strength, forcing Seven-up back into the drift. Seven-up stumbled against something, lost his balance, tried desperately to regain it, dropping the knife. Seven-up's feet slipped and he went down, Laskar on top of him. Laskar, tired with his exertions, lay with his full weight on Seven-up.

"Don't," complained Seven-up feebly; "you're hurtin' me, Las. Git off." He whined with pain. "Git off, Las; I'm layin' acrost a rock."

Laskar wriggled to one side, and fearing that this might be a ruse of Seven-up's to escape and attack him again, he swept a hand around underneath the latter to investigate. The hand came into contact with something that made Laskar withdraw his hand with a suddenness that caused him to roll off Seven-up and into the snow on the other side of him. But he was on his feet in an instant, calling to Seven-up, and together they clawed at the snowdrift, presently disclosing the body of a man—a dead man, rigid and ghastly.

Laskar rose and passed his hand uncertainly over his eyes and forehead. The dead man's eyes, open and staring, seemed to be fixed on him. The face was the face of the man he had seen riding the black horse many nights ago. Or was it yesterday? It did not matter—this was the man. What had become of his horse? Mechanically he looked around at the windbreak. A black horse stood there, snuggled between the other two—his and Seven-up's.

"I reckon I wasn't dreamin'," he said aloud. "He done froze to death right close to the dug-out; he was freezin' while I was lookin' at him and thinkin' I was dreamin'. Hey!" he suddenly shouted, in tones of horror, for Seven-up was astride of the dead man, clutching at his left hand, screaming with rage and calling out that he had found Bill Henley. In proof of this he held up to Laskar's gaze a left hand on which was a curiously deformed thumb nail. Laskar did not stop to examine the nail but pulled Seven-up from the body. He was fighting viciously to keep Seven-up away when he heard shouts and saw a half-dozen cowboys approaching—his own men.

They got Seven-up back into the dugout and regaled him with whisky and food. They told Laskar how his wife had worried about him and how finally she had sent them to look for him. They gave him whisky, too. That night they played cards; they made the dugout ring with hoarse laughter and ribald song. They played poker; they cursed and yelled and danced. It was all sweet music to Seven-up and Laskar —what they heard of it. For early in the evening—before the hilarity had reached its fullness—Laskar and Seven-up were in the bunks, peacefully snoring. Nothing could happen to them now.

Christmas Day dawned clear and cold. The air in the dug-out reeked with the scent of cooking food. Woefully weak, but nearly rational, Seven-up sat up in his bunk and looked around him.

"Say," he said to the figures that flitted about him; "are you real gents or am I still seein' things?"

"See if this is real, you ol'-son-of-a-gun!" said one, passing the whisky bottle to him. Seven-up took a drink of it and smacked his lips. "Didn't think I'd ever get acquainted with that there stuff again," he grinned. He saw Laskar seated at the table, partaking of the steaming food that was on a plate before him.

"Say," he called; "was I dreamin' things or did I hear you say that your wife's name was Amy Legget? Don't lie to me, Las," he pleaded.

"I reckon you wasn't dreamin', father-in-law," grinned Laskar, his mouth full of food.

Seven-up passed a hand over his forehead. "An' was I dreamin' an' seein' things when I thought I'd found Bill Henley—out there in the snow?" he asked, hesitatingly.

"You wasn't dreamin' none then either," returned Laskar. "The boys searched him before they planted him an' there was stuff on him—letters an' such—to prove he was Bill Henley all right."

Seven-up sighed deeply and lay back in the bunk. For a long time he lay there, listening to the sounds made by the punchers as they feasted and drank. Then he sat up again.

"Las," he inquired; "there's something that ain't been explained yet. I always thought Bill Henley had somethin' to do with Amy leavin' home. Did he?"

"Hush, you ol' fool," said Laskar softly; "that's a story that Amy'll tell you when we git back to-night."

Christmas Eve
in San Augustine

Edward D. Hoch

Edward D. Hoch is the award-winning author of more than eight hundred short stories, the bulk of which are in the mystery/detective field. On the infrequent occasions when he turns his hand to the frontier yarn, the result is usually a clever melding of the two genres. His series of stories about enigmatic drifter Ben Snow, who may or may not be Billy the Kid and who solves crimes in various Old West locales, is one example of his prowess with this type of fictional hybrid. Another is "Christmas Eve in San Augustine," which concerns a woman named Angela Ortez who comes to a small east Texas town on a most unseasonal mission—to commit an act of murder.

The stage that brought Angela Ortez to San Augustine in east Texas arrived late on the afternoon of December 23rd. Her first look at the town surprised her a bit until she remembered that this portion of the state was more closely aligned with the cotton kingdom to the east than the cattle country to the west. Even this late in the year the temperature was nearly sixty and the landscape an unaccustomed green. A row of pine trees grew along the muddy town square.

Angela walked across the wide main street to the only visible hotel and took a room for two nights. The room clerk swept his eyes over her hips and breasts, but she was used to that. "Visiting your family for Christmas?" he asked, handing her the key to room 27.

"Just a friend," she replied.

The room showed signs of dust and the curtains were soiled, but the bed seemed comfortable and there was a nice view of the square, which seemed to have been long neglected by the residents. Angela placed her carpetbag on the bed and opened it. First she hung up the two other dresses she'd brought and then put away her underwear and toilet articles. Next she unwrapped a small leather pouch and extracted a tiny short-barreled pistol called a derringer. The man who'd sold it to her in New Orleans said the new weapon was especially popular with riverboat gamblers along the Mississippi.

As soon as she'd seen it and held it in her hand, she knew it was the perfect weapon for the murder she intended to commit.

Texas had been a state for almost eight years by this Christmas of 1853, having been admitted to the Union on December 29, 1845. In places like San Augustine, sometimes the holiday celebrations blended with the statehood observances and became a bit rowdy.

The room clerk told her all this when she asked him for a good place to eat. "I'd suggest right here in the hotel, ma'am. We've got the best food in town anyway, and you won't be bothered by any drunks getting a jump on their Christmas Eve celebrating."

"Thank you," she said, and went off to the dining room. It was a pleasant enough place, decorated for the season.

"What can I get for you?" a tired-looking waitress asked.

Angela made her choice from the handwritten menu and then asked, "Do you know a man named Julius Costigan? I think he has land around here."

"Does he ever! He's the biggest slave owner in these parts, and they say he raises more cotton than anyone else in the state."

Angela nodded. That would be the man she sought. "Does he come to town often?"

"He eats here about twice a week. I'm expecting him tonight." She picked up the menu. "You know him?"

"He's a friend of my sister's."

The food was not very good, but Angela made it last for more than an hour, until she was rewarded by the appearance of two men who came through the door together and walked directly to an empty table against the wall. She had never seen the man she planned to kill, but the tall one looked exactly like the daguerreotype her sister Rose had shown her once. Both men wore dress shirts and string ties, with leather jackets over them. Under the jackets she could see their gun belts.

"That's Mr. Costigan, isn't it?" she asked the waitress.

"That's him."

"Who's the man with him?"

"Perry, his foreman and overseer. Some say bodyguard too. He never goes out among the slaves without Perry at his side."

Angela had gambled on getting close enough to Costigan to take him by surprise. She remembered the words of the gun dealer in New Orleans. "The derringer is not accurate at a distance. You have to be close to your target." With a bodyguard along, that would be difficult, if not impossible.

She was still pondering this turn of events when a male voice said, "Pardon me, but the tables all seem to be taken. Would you mind if I shared this one with you?" His accent was definitely northern, and she looked up to see an attractive man in his early thirties smiling down at her. He was roughly dressed, with a few days' growth of beard, but she could tell he was a well-educated gentleman.

"Of course not," she told him. "I'll be leaving soon anyway."

"My name is Olmsted. Frederick Law Olmsted."

"Angela Ortez. Pleased to meet you."

He pulled out the chair and sat down opposite her. "How's the food here?"

"Not bad. I guess in this town there's not much choice."

"It is small," he agreed. "Not exactly the place to spend Christmas."

"Are you at the hotel, Mr. Olmsted?"

"No, my brother and I are at a rooming house. We've been riding through this part of the state visiting the plantations."

She wondered why anyone would want to visit plantations. "Are you in the cotton business?"

He smiled and shook his head. "I'm a correspondent for *The New York Times*. I'm doing some articles on plantation life which I hope to make into a book later."

Angela finished the last of her coffee. "How come your brother's not with you tonight?"

"He's trying to find a blacksmith to get his horse reshod."

Just then Julius Costigan glanced across at their table and Olmsted exchanged a nod with him. "Do you know him?" Angela asked.

"I visited his plantation a couple of days ago. He claims he does well, selling his cotton for eight dollars a bale in Galveston. In fact, it's the only plantation in east Texas that was worth the visit. Most of them are deserted wrecks. An effort has been made to turn some of them into cattle ranches, but even the cows seem tired and worn out. The Mexicans who used to live in the area have mostly moved away, and there's no one but slaves to work those places."

"Is the entire state like this?" she asked.

"Oh, no! The pine trees here remind one of Louisiana, but they gradually disappear as you ride west. The soil turns to a heavy red clay that sticks to everything. You have to go beyond that to reach the real cattle country."

"You know a great deal about the country," she murmured. She was studying his high forehead and wide-set eyes. He had a studious, almost artistic look about him, a look that she'd often seen among the upper classes in New Orleans. It was something one rarely saw west of Louisiana. He was also slight of build, no larger than herself.

He brushed the wavy dark hair from his eyes and said, "I've traveled a great deal. My brother and I originally planned to ride all the way to California, but I understand there have been Indian outbreaks west of here. We'll probably return to New Orleans soon."

"I know the city well," Angela told him. "You must let me show you around when you return there."

It was an invitation of a somewhat bold nature, but she was beginning to like this slender young man whom she'd only just met. At once he countered with a suggestion of his own. "That's very good, if you'll allow me to show you around San Augustine tomorrow."

"Is there anything to see?" she asked with a laugh.

"The town does hold one or two surprises," he promised, "if you have the time. What brings you here for Christmas?"

"I plan to visit an old friend of my sister's," she answered truthfully.

"Then may I call for you in the morning, Miss Ortez? Possibly at eleven o'clock?"

Angela needed to work out a plan, and she might attract suspicion wandering through the town alone. This man could prove to be the answer to her problem. "That would be delightful, Mr. Olmsted."

Christmas Eve dawned bright and sunny, with a hint of a breeze blowing in from the south. Olmsted was in the lobby promptly at eleven, and Angela descended the stairs to greet him.

He asked, "Did you have a pleasant night's rest?"

"The bed is comfortable, but I have much on my mind. I slept fitfully."

He led her out onto the sunny street. They passed the Lone Star Café and then a general store and several other businesses. The town's residential area came next. Olmsted said there were about sixty houses in all, clapboard dwellings that seemed of better than average quality.

"They're better built than most of the plantation homes," he assured her. "Even Julius Costigan lives here in town rather than on his farm."

"Oh? Which house is his?"

"That one at the end with the picket fence. A nice-looking place. Someone told my brother that he had a lovely wife, but she left him earlier this year and moved away." He led her down one of the few side streets and pointed out a large white house that looked freshly painted. "This is where my brother and I are staying. Come in and meet our landlady."

Mrs. Perkins proved to be a formidable woman with wide shoulders and a loud voice. The Christmas Eve holiday did not keep her from doing the weekly washing, and she glanced up from her task only briefly to acknowledge Angela's presence. "No women in the rooms, Mr. Olmsted," she reminded him. "I run a respectable house."

Angela felt herself blushing, and the young man answered, "Of course, Mrs. Perkins. Is my brother in?"

"I think so. Can't keep track of all your comings and goings!"

John Olmsted, young and slim like his brother, came downstairs just then and Frederick introduced him to Angela. John had a ready smile and bowed to kiss her hand. "The fairest flower in this godforsaken place!"

"Please! I'm blushing already!"

"We're just out for a stroll," Frederick told his brother. "I'm showing Angela the sights of San Augustine."

"That shouldn't take long."

John went off to collect his horse from the blacksmith. "I think he's found a Mexican girl in the next town," Frederick confided. They walked back to look at his horse and then they strolled in the opposite direction through town.

"The stage brought me in this way when I arrived yesterday," she told him.

"I'm surprised he'd even stop. This isn't on their regular route."

"I had to pay five dollars extra."

He paused at the central square acre of neglected mud upon which the handful of business establishments faced. "This could be a lovely community garden," he told Angela, going on to describe his landscaping vision.

"That's very good," she agreed. "You should suggest it to the mayor or whoever runs things here."

"No, I won't waste my ideas on an acre in San Augustine. Up in New York City where I live, they're going to have a competition to design a new Central Park, a huge place for everyone. I plan to enter it with some ideas I've been working on."

"I wish you luck. If you win, I'll come up to see it."

Their eyes met for just an instant. "I hope so," he said.

Out beyond the last of the houses she could see another structure, a three-story edifice that seemed grander than anything else around. "What is that?" she asked, pointing toward it.

Frederick Olmsted told her the story as they walked. "Both the Methodists and the Presbyterians chartered a university here, but of course there weren't enough students for either place. The rivalry between them became so great that the president of the Presbyterian University was shot down in the street. It was like a gunfight between outlaws! Both universities dwindled to nothing and finally sold their buildings to the fraternity of Masons. They are now the Masonic Institute, with this one for boys and the other building, farther out, for girls. Even so, there are only enough male students for one floor of the building."

"How have you learned all these fascinating things about the town?"

"Mainly from our landlady, Mrs. Perkins. She promises one of the most interesting events for this evening. It's a Christmas Eve custom here called the Christmas Serenade. Very late, toward midnight, a group of the town's males, usually more than a little drunk, sets out from the town square, blowing tin horns and banging on pans. They visit every house in San Augustine, kicking in doors if necessary, until all the males have joined them with an instrument of some sort. Then they all march back to the square for a final noisy serenade on their horns and pans."

"It sounds terrible! Will you have to join them?"

"Mrs. Perkins says that John and I will be safe because we're only visitors, but if it looks like fun, we might follow along."

"It's too bad they don't allow females to take part," Angela remarked, gazing off into the distance.

She was surprised to see that it was late afternoon by the time they strolled back to the center of town. Just twenty-four hours earlier the stage had deviated from its regular run to deposit her here. Now she was no closer to killing Julius Costigan than she'd been on her arrival.

But at least she had an idea.

Angela agreed to join Frederick for an early dinner at the hotel. But first she went up to her room for a few minutes, to retrieve the derringer from its leather pouch.

While they ate, a sad-faced Mexican with a guitar strummed an old Christmas carol. Some of the men in the place seemed to have been drinking heavily, but Angela saw no sign of Costigan among them.

"Tell me about yourself," Frederick suggested over coffee. "Did you grow up in New Orleans?"

"Near there. I always loved the city, even as a child. Father would bring my sister and me along sometimes when he went in on business."

"Does your sister still live there?"

"No. She died."

"I'm sorry to hear that."

"What about you? Was it always New York? What made you seek out the frontier life like this?"

"I was born in Hartford, Connecticut, thirty-one years ago, and I believe traveling came naturally to me. When I was fourteen, a bad case of sumac poisoning affected my eyes. My parents wanted me to enter Yale College at that early age, but the eye trouble postponed it. I became a sort of vagabond, shipping out to China on a sailing vessel. Just three years ago I visited England and Europe, and last year I published my first book about that journey, titled *Walks and Talks of an American Farmer in England.* Come back to my room and I'll show you a copy of it."

"No, I couldn't," she answered kindly. "It's already getting dark."

"My brother should be back by now."

"Thank you, but I'll be going up to my room. Thank you for a very pleasant day, Frederick."

"I hope to see you again before you leave."

"Perhaps," she murmured, and shook his hand.

It was much later, toward midnight, when Angela left the hotel alone and hurried along the main street toward Frederick Olmsted's boarding house. She knew he'd be unable to resist the Christmas Serenade, and she wasn't surprised, shortly after she reached the house, to see his lamp go out. A moment later he and his brother left Mrs. Perkin's place and headed toward the center of town. Already she could hear the decidedly unmusical tooting and banging that indicated the Serenade was underway.

Angela waited a few moments until they were out of sight, then crossed the street and entered the front door of the boarding house. She knew there would be no locked doors here. Only Mrs. Perkins might keep her from reaching Frederick's room, and luckily the landlady was in the parlor, playing a Christmas carol on the piano.

Angela went immediately to the door at the top of the stairs from which she'd seen Frederick's brother emerge during their afternoon visit. Though the room was dark and she couldn't risk lighting a lamp, she found their two saddlebags without trouble. She removed her dress and searched through Frederick's bag, easily identified by his notebook on top. The shirt she tried first was a perfect fit, as she'd thought it would be. They were the same size, really, although pulling a pair of his pants over her hips was a bit of a struggle. She found a fringed leather vest that went well over the shirt and helped to hide the swell of her breasts. Her hair was not too long, and with one of Frederick's broad-brimmed hats covering most of it, she decided she could pass as a man in the darkness.

The clamor of the Christmas Serenade was growing closer. She could hear a cheer go up as the crowd paused at each house to be joined by the males from within, each tooting or clanging his own instrument. Angela needed only one more thing—a pair of Frederick's boots. They were too big for her, but they'd have to do. Quietly she slipped out the door and made her way down the stairs. The pouch with the derringer was in her pants pocket. She'd rolled up her dress and hid it with her shoes under the bed.

The piano playing had stopped and Mrs. Perkins was nowhere in sight, perhaps gone to visit neighbors on Christmas Eve. Angela closed the front door carefully so it made no noise, then ran quickly down the steps. She paused only to rub a little dirt onto her face, along the jaw line. In the dark it might appear to be a growth of beard. Then she hurried to the main street to join the serenaders.

Hardly anyone noticed her in the noisy, drunken crowd. One man asked, "Where's your instrument?" When she mumbled a reply, he thrust a tin horn into her hand. She realized it was Costigan's bodyguard.

The growing crowd stopped at one house after another, tooting and drumming and banging on the doors until the male occupants poured out good-naturedly with their makeshift instruments. Angela tooted along with the others, staying toward the rear and well away from Frederick Olmsted and his brother.

Finally the noisy crowd reached the last house on the street. Julius Costigan had been expecting the revelers and he came out almost at once, banging on a pan with a wooden spoon. The crowd gave a cheer and prepared to march back to the center of town. That was when Angela edged forward between the men. In the darkness no one noticed as she slipped the leather pouch out of her pants pocket.

She felt inside the pouch until she found the trigger of the tiny derringer. Then, moving directly in front of Costigan, she pressed the barrel of the weapon against his chest. Above the din of the horns and pans she told him, "This is for Rose Ortez."

His eyes suddenly widened as he understood her words and the meaning of the pressure against his chest. Then she squeezed the trigger and fired through the leather pouch.

One or two in the crowd turned, perhaps believing they'd heard a firecracker, but most went on with their noisemaking, trying to approximate the melody of an old English carol. It was not until Julius Costigan crumpled to the ground that they realized something was wrong, and even then it was too dark for a moment to see the blood. By that time Angela had edged away into the shadows of the pines that lined the street.

By the time she reached Olmsted's rooming house, the crime had been discovered. "Costigan's dead," she heard a man yell. "Somebody shot him!"

Quickly she let herself into the unlocked house and went upstairs to Frederick's room. She pulled her dress and shoes from under the bed and started to change back into them.

That was when the door opened and Frederick Olmsted walked into the room.

"I thought you'd come back here," he told her.

"I—" Her hand was reaching for the derringer, but he was too fast for her. He yanked the weapon from its powder-burned pouch.

"You should have thrown this away or at least reloaded it. It's good for nothing the way it is. A derringer is a single-shot weapon."

"How did you get back here so fast?"

"I recognized my fringed vest in the crowd just before the shooting. Then you disappeared before I could be certain it was you. I figured, if you had borrowed my clothes, you'd come back here to change." His expression hardened. "Costigan's dead, you know."

"It was something I had to do," she told him. "For my sister."

"You'd better explain."

"Rose was Costigan's wife, the one who left him earlier this year. She came to me in New Orleans. Her insides were a mess from his beatings. She left here because she couldn't take it anymore, being treated like one of his slaves. I got her into a hospital, but she died two weeks later from internal injuries. That was when I knew I had to come here and kill him."

Frederick was staring at her. "Did you think that would bring your sister back?"

"No. It was just something I had to do."

"It's still murder. And on Christmas Eve, too."

"Go ahead, call the sheriff! I'll take my punishment."

He continued to stare at her for another moment. "That's up to you to do," he said finally. "I won't tell him, and I won't tell Costigan's bodyguard either. Here, finish changing your clothes and I'll wait in the hall."

When she came out, he asked, "How had you planned to get out of San Augustine?"

"I paid the stagecoach driver to stop here Christmas morning on his way back. I knew if I couldn't do it in two days, I'd never do it."

He took her back to the hotel in silence. When he left her at the door, he said simply, "I hope you do the right thing."

A few diehards had made their way to the town square, undaunted by the killing. They were playing an off-key rendition of "Silent Night" on their tin instruments.

It sounded like a dirge to her.

The stage arrived shortly after eleven on Christmas morning. Angela Ortez climbed aboard alone. On the way out of town she watched for Frederick, but there was no sign of him. He hadn't told the sheriff, but he hadn't come to bid her good-bye, either. She knew she would never see him again.

As the stage was passing the Costigan home at the end of the street, she grew aware of the sound of church bells. And she remembered some of Frederick's words of the night before. *It's still murder. And on Christmas Eve too . . . I hope you do the right thing.*

Suddenly she poked her head out and called to the driver, "Stop the coach and let me out, please! I've changed my mind."

It was a lonely walk back to the center of town. She paused only once, to ask a small boy directions to the sheriff's office.

No Room
at the Inn

Bill Pronzini

Best known for his "Nameless Detective" mystery series, Bill Pronzini is also a successful writer of Western fiction, much of which—as in the case of Edward D. Hoch—makes use of criminous elements. "No Room at the Inn" is one such melding of genres; it features John Quincannon, a former U.S. Treasury agent turned private investigator, in a tale of pursuit and puzzlement set in a High Sierra snowstorm on Christmas Eve, 1894. Among Pronzini's Western novels are Quincannon *(1985), which also features the hero of "No Room at the Inn";* Starvation Camp *(1984),* The Last Days of Horse-Shy Halloran *(1987), and* The Hangings *(1989). A collection of his short fiction,* The Best Western Stories of Bill Pronzini, *was published by Swallow Press in 1990. He has also edited or coedited more than twenty-five Western anthologies.*

When the snowstorm started, Quincannon was high up in a sparsely populated section of the Sierra Nevada—alone except for his rented horse, with not much idea of where he was and no idea at all of where Slick Henry Garber was.

And as if all of that wasn't enough, it was almost nightfall on Christmas Eve.

The storm had caught him by surprise. The winter sky had been clear when he'd set out from Big Creek in mid-morning, and it had stayed clear until two hours ago; then the clouds had commenced piling up rapidly, the way they sometimes did in this high-mountain country, getting thicker and darker-veined until the whole sky was the color of moiling coal smoke. The wind had sharpened to an icy breath that buffeted both him and the ewe-necked strawberry roan. And now, at dusk, the snow flurries had begun—thick flakes driven and agitated by the wind so that the pine and spruce forests through which the trail climbed were a misty blur and he could see no more than forty or fifty feet ahead.

He rode huddled inside his fleece-lined long coat and rabbit-fur mittens and cap, feeling sorry for himself and at the same time cursing himself for a rattlepate. If he had paid more mind to that buildup of clouds, he would have realized the need to find shelter much sooner than he had. As it was, he had begun looking too late. So far no cabin or mine shaft or cave or suitable geographical configuration had presented itself—not one place in all this vast wooded emptiness where he and the roan could escape the snapping teeth of the storm.

A man had no sense wandering around an unfamiliar mountain wilderness on the night before Christmas, even if he *was* a manhunter by trade and a greedy gloryhound by inclination. He ought to be home in front of a blazing fire, roasting chestnuts in the company of a good woman. Sabina, for instance. Dear, sweet Sabina, waiting for him back in San Francisco. Not by his hearth or in his bed, curse the luck, but at least in the Market Street offices of Carpenter and Quincannon, Professional Detective Services.

Well, it was his own fault that he was alone up here, freezing to death in a snowstorm. In the first place he could have refused the job of tracking down Slick Henry Garber when it was offered to him by the West Coast Banking Association two weeks ago. In the second place he could have decided not to come to Big Creek to investigate a report that Slick Henry and his satchel full of counterfeit mining stock were in the vicinity. And in the third place he could have remained in Big Creek this morning when Slick Henry managed to elude his clutches and flee even higher into these blasted mountains.

But no, Rattlepate John Quincannon had done none of those sensible things. Instead he had accepted the Banking Association's fat fee, thinking only of that *and* of the additional $5000 reward for Slick Henry's apprehension or demise being offered by a mining coalition in Colorado *and* of the glory of nabbing the most notorious—and the most dangerous—confidence trickster operating west of the Rockies in this year of 1894. Then, after tracing his quarry to Big Creek, he had not only bungled the arrest but made a second mistake in setting out on Slick Henry's trail with the sublime confidence of an unrepentant sinner looking for the Promised Land—only to lose that trail two hours ago, at a road fork, just before he made his *third* mistake of the day by underestimating the weather.

Christmas, he thought. 'Tis the season to be jolly. Bah. Humbug.

Ice particles now clung to his beard, his eyebrows; kept trying to freeze his eyelids shut. He had to continually rub his eyes clear in order to see where he was going. Which, now, in full darkness, was along the rim of a snow-skinned meadow that had opened up on his left. The wind was even fiercer here, without one wall of trees to deflect some of its force. Quincannon shivered and huddled and cursed and felt sorrier for himself by the minute.

He should never have decided to join forces with Sabina and open a detective agency. She had been happy with her position as a female operative with the Pinkerton Agency's Denver office; he had been more or less content working in the San Francisco office of the United States Secret Service. What had possessed him to suggest, not long after their first professional meeting, that they pool their talents? Well, he knew the answer to that well enough. *Sabina* had possessed him. Dear, sweet, unseducible, infuriating Sabina—

Was that light ahead?

He scrubbed at his eyes and leaned forward in the saddle, squinting. Yes, light—lamplight. He had just come around a jog in the trail, away from the open meadow, and there it was, ahead on his right: a faint glowing rectangle in the night's churning white-and-black. He could just make out the shapes of buildings, too, in what appeared to be a clearing before a sheer rock face.

The lamplight and the buildings changed Quincannon's bleak remonstrations into murmurs of thanksgiving. He urged the stiff-legged and balky roan into a quicker pace. The buildings took on shape and definition as he approached. There were three of them, grouped in a loose triangle; two appeared to be cabins, fashioned of rough-hewn logs and planks, each with a sloping roof, while the bulkiest structure had the look of a barn. The larger cabin, the one with the lighted window, was set between the other two and farther back near the base of the rock wall.

A lane led off the trail to the buildings. Quincannon couldn't see it under its covering of snow, but he knew it was there by a painted board sign nailed to one of the trees at the intersection. *TRAVELER'S REST,* the sign said, and below that, in smaller letters, *Meals and Lodging.* One of the tiny roadhouses, then, that dotted the Sierras and catered to prospectors, hunters, and foolish wilderness wayfarers such as himself.

It was possible, he thought as he turned past the sign, that Slick Henry Garber had come this way and likewise been drawn to the Traveler's Rest. Which would allow Quincannon to make amends today, after all, for his earlier bungling, and perhaps even permit him to spend Christmas Day in the relative comfort of the Big Creek Hotel. Given his recent run of foul luck, however, such a serendipitous turnabout was as likely to happen as Sabina presenting him, on his return to San Francisco, with the holiday gift he most desired.

Nevertheless, caution here was indicated. So despite the warmth promised by the lamplit window, he rode at an off-angle toward the barn. There was also the roan's welfare to consider. He would have to pay for the animal if it froze to death while in his charge.

If he was being observed from within the lighted cabin, it was covertly: no one came out and no one showed himself in the window. At the barn he dismounted, took himself and the roan inside, struggled to reshut the doors against the howling thrust of the wind. Blackness surrounded him, heavy with the smells of animals and hay and oiled leather. He stripped off both mittens, found a lucifer in one of his pockets and scraped it alight. The barn lantern hung from a hook near the doors; he reached up to light the wick. Now he could see that there were eight stalls, half of which were occupied: three saddle horses and one work horse, each nibbling a pile of hay. He didn't bother to examine the saddle horses because he had no idea what type of animal Slick Henry had been riding. He hadn't got close enough to his quarry all day to get a look at him or his transportation.

He led the roan into an empty stall, unsaddled it, left it there munching a hay supper of its own. Later, he would ask the owner of Traveler's Rest to come out and give the beast a proper rubdown. With his hands mittened again he braved the storm on foot, slogging through calf-deep snow to the lighted cabin.

Still no one came out or appeared at the window. He moved along the front wall, stopped to peer through the rimmed window glass.

What he could see of the big parlor inside was uninhabited. He plowed ahead to the door.

It was against his nature to walk unannounced into the home of a stranger, mainly because it was a fine way to get shot, but in this case he had no choice. He could have shouted himself hoarse in competition with the storm before anyone heard him. Thumping on the door would be just as futile; the wind was already doing that. Again he stripped off his right mitten, opened his coat for easy access to the Remington Navy revolver he carried at his waist, unlatched the door with his left hand, and cautiously let the wind push him inside.

The entire parlor was deserted. He leaned back hard against the door to get it closed again and then called out, "Hello the house! Company!" No one answered.

He stood scraping snowcake off his face, slapping it off his clothing. The room was warm: a log fire crackled merrily on the hearth, banking somewhat because it hadn't been fed in a while. Two lamps were lit in here, another in what looked to be a dining room adjacent. Near the hearth, a cut spruce reached almost to the raftered ceiling; it was festooned with Christmas decorations—strung popcorn and bright-colored beads, stubs of tallow candles in bent can tops, snippets of fleece from some old garment sprinkled on the branches to resemble snow, a five-pointed star atop the uppermost branch.

All very cozy and inviting, but where were the occupants? He called out again, and again received no response. He cocked his head to listen. Heard only the plaint of the storm and the snicking of flung snow against the windowpane—no sound at all within the cabin.

He crossed the parlor, entered the dining room. The puncheon table was set for two, and in fact two people had been eating there not so long ago. A clay pot of venison stew sat in the center of the table; when he touched it he found it and its contents still slightly warm. Ladlings of stew and slices of bread were on each of the two plates.

The hair began to pull along the nape of his neck, as it always did when he sensed a wrongness to things. Slick Henry? Or something else? With his hand now gripping the butt of his Navy, he eased his way through a doorway at the rear of the dining room.

Kitchen and larder. Stove still warm, a kettle atop it blackening smokily because all the water it had contained had boiled away. Quincannon transferred the kettle to the sink drainboard. Moved then to another closed door that must lead to a bedroom, the last of the cabin's rooms. He depressed the latch and pushed the door wide.

Bedroom, indeed. And as empty as the other three rooms. But there were two odd things here: The sash of a window in the far wall was raised a few inches; and on the floor was the base of a lamp that had been dropped or knocked off the bedside table. Snow coated the window sill and there was a sifting of it on the floor and on the lamp base.

Quincannon stood puzzled and scowling in the icy draft. No room at the inn? he thought ironically. On the contrary, there was plenty of room at this inn on Christmas Eve. It didn't seem to have *any* people in it.

On a table near the bed he spied a well-worn family Bible. Impulse took him to it; he opened it at the front, where such vital statistics as marriages, births, and deaths were customarily recorded. Two names were written there in a fine woman's hand: Martha and Adam Keene. And a wedding date: July 17, 1893. That was all.

Well, now he knew the identity of the missing occupants. But what had happened to them? He hadn't seen them in the barn. And the other, smaller cabin—guest accommodations, he judged—had also been in darkness upon his arrival. It made no sense that a man and his wife would suddenly quit the warmth of their home in the middle of a Christmas Eve supper, to lurk about in a darkened outbuilding. It also made no sense that they would voluntarily decide to rush off into a snowstorm on foot or on horseback. Forced out of here, then? By Slick Henry Garber or someone else? If so, *why?*

Quincannon returned to the parlor. He had no desire to go out again into the wind and swirling snow, but he was not the sort of man who could allow a confounding mystery to go uninvestigated—particularly a mystery that might involve a criminal with a handsome price on his head. So, grumbling a little, his unmittened hands deep in the pockets of his coat, he bent his body into what was swiftly becoming a full-scale blizzard.

He fought his way to the barn first, because it was closer and to satisfy himself that it really *was* occupied only by horses. The wind had blown out the lantern when he'd left earlier; he relighted it, but not until he had first drawn his revolver. One of the animals—not the rented roan—moved restlessly in its stall as he walked toward the far end. There were good-sized piles of hay in each of the empty stalls as well, he noticed. He leaned into those stalls with the lantern. If anyone were hiding in a haypile it would have to be close to the surface to avoid the risk of suffocation; he poked at each pile in turn with the Navy's barrel. Hay and nothing but hay.

In one corner of the back wall was an enclosure that he took to be a harness room. Carefully he opened the door with his gun hand. Buckles and bit chains gleamed in the narrow space within; he saw the shapes of saddles, bridles, hackamores. Something made a scurrying noise among the floor shadows and he lowered the lantern in time to see the tail end of a packrat disappear behind a loose board. Dust was the only other thing on the floor.

He went back toward the front, stopped again when he was abreast of the loft ladder. He climbed it with the lantern lifted above his head. But the loft contained nothing more than several tightly stacked bales of hay and a thin scattering of straw that wouldn't have concealed the packrat, much less a man or a woman.

No one in the main cabin, no one in the barn. That left only the guest cabin. And if that, too, was deserted? Well, then, he thought irascibly, he would sit down in the main cabin and gorge himself on venison stew while he waited for somebody—the Keenes, Slick Henry, the Ghost of Christmas Past—to put in an appearance. He was cold and tired and hungry, and mystery or no mystery he was not about to wander around in a blizzard hunting for clues.

Out once more into the white fury. By the time he worked his way through what were now thigh-deep drifts to the door of the guest cabin, his legs and arms were stiff and his beard was caked with frozen snow. He wasted no time getting the door open, but he didn't enter right away. Instead he let the wind hurl the door inward, so that it cracked audibly against the wall, while he hung back and to one side with his revolver drawn.

Nothing happened inside.

He waited another few seconds, but already the icebound night was beginning to numb his bare hand; another minute or two of exposure and the skin would freeze to the gunmetal. He entered the cabin in a sideways crouch, caught hold of the door and crowded it shut until it latched. Chill, clotted black encased him now, so thick that he was virtually blind. Should he risk lighting a match? Well, if he wanted to see who or what this cabin might contain, he would *have* to risk it. Floundering around in the dark would no doubt mean a broken limb, his luck being what it was these days.

He fumbled in his pocket for another lucifer, struck it on his left thumbnail, ducked down and away from the flare of light. Still nothing happened. But the light revealed that this cabin was divided into two sparsely furnished bedrooms with an open door in the dividing wall; and it also revealed some sort of huddled mass on the floor of the rear bedroom.

In slow strides, holding the match up and away from his body, he moved toward the doorway. The flame died just as he reached it—just as he recognized the huddled mass as the motionless body of a man. He thumbed another match alight, went through the doorway, leaned down for a closer look. The man lay drawn up on his back, and on one temple blood from a bullet furrow glistened blackly in the wavering flame. Young man, sandy-haired, wearing an old vicuna cloth suit and a clean white shirt now spotted with blood. A man Quincannon had never seen before—

Something moved behind him.

Something else slashed the air, grazed the side of Quincannon's head as he started to turn and dodge, drove him sideways to the floor.

The lucifer went out as he was struck; he lost his grip on the Navy and it went clattering away into blackness as thick as the inside of Old Scratch's fundament. The blow had been sharp enough to set up a ringing in his ears, but the thick rabbit-fur cap had cushioned it enough so that he wasn't stunned. He pulled around onto his knees, lunged back toward the doorway with both hands reaching. Above him he heard again that slashing of the air, only this time the swung object missed him entirely. Which threw the man who had swung off balance, at the same instant Quincannon's right hand found a grip on sheepskin material not unlike that of his own coat. He yanked hard, heard a grunt, and then the heavy weight of his assailant came squirming and cursing down on top of him.

The floor of an unfamiliar, black-dark room was the last place Quincannon would have chosen for hand-to-hand combat. But he was a veteran of any number of skirmishes, and had learned ways to do grievous damage to an opponent that would have shocked the Marquis of Queensbury. (Sabina, too, no doubt.) Besides which, this particular opponent, whoever he was, was laboring under the same disadvantages as he was.

There were a few seconds of scrambling and bumping about, some close-quarters pummeling on both sides, a blow that split Quincannon's lip and made his Scot's blood boil even more furiously, a brief and violent struggle for possession of what felt like a long-barreled revolver, and then, finally, an opportunity for Quincannon to use a mean and scurrilous trick he had learned in a free-for-all on the Baltimore docks. His assailant screamed, quit fighting, began to twitch instead; and to groan and wail and curse feebly. This vocal combination made Quincannon's head hurt all the more, and led him, since he now had possession of the long-barreled revolver, to thump the man on top of the head with the weapon. The groaning and wailing and cursing ceased abruptly. So did the twitching.

Quincannon got to his feet, stood shakily wiping blood from his torn lip. He made the mistake then of taking a blind step and almost fell over one or the other of the two men now lying motionless on the floor. He produced another lucifer from his dwindling supply. In its flare he spied a lamp, and managed to get to it in time to light the wick before the flame died. He located his Navy, holstered it, then carried the lamp to where the men lay and peered at the face of the one who had tried to brain him.

"Well, well," he said aloud, with considerable relish. "A serendipitous turnabout after all. Just what I wanted for Christmas—Slick Henry Garber."

Slick Henry Garber said nothing, nor would he be able to for a good while.

The young, sandy-haired lad—Adam Keene, no doubt—was also unconscious. The bullet wound on his head didn't seem to be serious, but he would need attention. *He* wouldn't be saying anything, either, for a good while. Quincannon would just have to wait for the full story of what had happened here before his arrival. Unless, of course, he got it from Adam Keene's wife . . .

Where *was* Adam Keene's wife?

Carrying the lamp, he searched the two bedrooms. No sign of Martha Keene. He did find Slick Henry's leather satchel, in a corner of the rear room; it contained several thousand shares of bogus mining stock and nine thousand dollars in greenbacks. He also found evidence of a struggle, and not one but two bullet holes in the back wall.

These things, plus a few others, plus a belated application of imagination and logic, allowed him to make a reasonably accurate guess as to tonight's sequence of events. Slick Henry had arrived just before the snowstorm and just as the Keenes were sitting down to supper. He had either put his horse in the barn himself or Adam Keene had done it; that explained why there had been *three* saddle horses present when only *two* people lived at Traveler's Rest. Most likely Slick Henry had then thrown down on the Keenes: he must have been aware that Quincannon was still close behind him, even if Quincannon hadn't known it, and must have realized that with the impending storm it was a good bet his pursuer would also stop at Traveler's Rest. And what better place for an ambush than one of these three buildings? Perhaps he'd chosen the guest cabin on the theory that Quincannon would be less on his guard there than at the other two. To ensure that, Slick Henry had taken Adam Keene with him at gunpoint, leaving Mrs. Keene in the main cabin with instructions to tell Quincannon that no other travelers had appeared today and to then send him to the guest cabin.

But while the two men were in that cabin Adam Keene had hero-ically attempted to disarm Slick Henry, there had been a struggle, and Keene had unheroically received a bullet wound for his efforts. Martha Keene must have heard at least one of the shots, and fearing the worst she had left the main cabin through the bedroom window and hidden herself somewhere. Had Slick Henry found her? Not likely. But it seemed reasonable to suppose he had been out hunting for her when Quincannon came. The violence of the storm had kept him from springing his trap at that point; he had decided instead to return to the guest cabin as per his original plan. And this was where he had been ever since, waiting in the dark for his nemesis to walk in like a damned fool—which was just what Quincannon had done.

This day's business, Quincannon thought ruefully, had been one long, grim comedy of errors on all sides. Slick Henry's actions were at least half doltish and so were his own. Especially his own—blundering in half a dozen different ways, including not even once considering the possibility of a planned ambush. Relentless manhunter, intrepid detective. Bah. It was a wonder he hadn't been shot dead. Sabina would chide him mercilessly if he told her the entire story of his capture of Slick Henry Garber. Which, of course, he had no intention of doing.

Well, he could redeem himself somewhat by finding Martha Keene. Almost certainly she had to be in one of the three buildings. She wouldn't have remained in the open, exposed, in a raging mountain storm. She would not have come anywhere near the guest cabin because of Slick Henry. And she hadn't stayed in the main cabin; the open bedroom window proved that. Ergo, she was in the barn. But he had searched the barn, even gone up into the hayloft. No place to hide up there, or in the harness enclosure, or in one of the stalls, or—

The lamp base on the bedroom floor, he thought.

No room at the inn, he thought.

"Well, of course, you blasted rattlepate," he said aloud. "It's the only place she *can* be."

Out once more into the whipping snow and freezing wind (after first taking the precaution of binding Slick Henry's hands with the man's own belt). Slog, slog, slog, and finally into the darkened barn. He lighted the lantern, took it to the approximate middle of the building, and then called out, "Mrs. Keene! My name is John Quincannon, I am a detective from San Francisco, and I have just cracked the skull of the man who terrorized you and your husband tonight. You have nothing more to fear."

No response.

"I know you're here, and approximately where. Won't you save both of us the embarrassment of my poking around with a pitchfork?"

Silence.

"Mrs. Keene, your husband is unconscious with a head wound and he needs you. Please believe me."

More silence. Then, just as he was about to issue another plea, there was a rustling and stirring in one of the empty stalls to his left. He moved over that way in time to see Martha Keene rise up slowly from her hiding place deep under the pile of hay.

She was young, attractive, as fair-haired as her husband, and wrapped warmly in a heavy fleece-lined coat. She was also, Quincannon noted with surprise, quite obviously with child.

What didn't surprise him was the length of round, hollow glass she held in one hand—the chimney that belonged to the lamp base on the bedroom floor. She had had the presence of mind to snatch it up before climbing out of the window, in her haste dislodging the base from the bedside table. The chimney was the reason neither he nor Slick Henry had found her; by using it as a breathing tube, she had been able to burrow deep enough into the haypile to escape a superficial search.

For a space she stared at Quincannon out of wide, anxious eyes. What she saw seemed to reassure her. She released a thin, sighing breath and said tremulously, "My husband . . . you're sure he's not—?"

"No, no. Wounded I said and wounded I meant. He'll soon be good as new."

"Thank God!"

"And you, my dear? Are you all right?"

"Yes, I . . . yes. Just frightened. I've been lying here imagining all sorts of dreadful things." Mrs. Keene sighed again, plucked clinging straw from her face and hair. "I didn't *want* to run and hide, but I thought Adam must be dead and I was afraid for my baby . . . oh!" She winced as if with a sudden sharp pain, dropped the lamp chimney and placed both hands over the swell of her abdomen. "All the excitement . . . I believe the baby will arrive sooner than expected."

Quincannon gave her a horrified look. "Right here? *Now?*"

"No, not that soon." A wan smile. "Tomorrow . . ."

It was his turn to put forth a relieved sigh as he moved into the stall to help her up. Tomorrow. Christmas Day. Appropriate that she should have her baby then. But it wasn't the only thing about this situation that was appropriate to the season. This was a stable, and what was the stall where she had lain with her unborn child but a manger? There were animals in attendance, too. And at least one wise man (wise in *some* things, surely) who had come bearing a gift without even knowing it, a gift of a third—no, a half—of the $5000 reward for the capture of Slick Henry Garber.

Peace on earth, good will to men.

Quincannon smiled; of a sudden he felt very jolly and very much in a holiday spirit. This was, he thought, going to be a very fine Christmas after all.

Gunman's Christmas

Caddo Cameron

Before turning his hand to fiction writing, Caddo Cameron led an adventurous and nomadic life as a cowhand, windmill grease monkey, hay baler, seaman, and railroad engineer in the tropics. In the thirties and forties he was a prolific contributor of action Western and adventure fiction to such pulp magazines as Short Stories. *His series featuring a pair of rowdy, humorous, and fast-shooting undercover operatives for the Texas Rangers, Private Badger Coe and Sergeant Blizzard Wilson, was so popular in its day that each Coe and Wilson magazine serial was later published in book form; these include* It's Hell to Be a Ranger *(1937),* At the End of a Texas Rope *(1938), and* Ghosts on the Range Tonight *(1941). A second popular series by Cameron ran in* Short Stories *and was narrated by an unnamed outlaw who lived by his wits while dodging the law in the backwaters of Texas and The Nations (Oklahoma). "Gunman's Christmas," in which an oddly assorted foursome come together to share Christmas dinner, is among the best of his "anonymous gunman" stories—and has the added virtue of sharing with the reader a couple of mouth-watering rangeland recipes.*

Christmas is just four days away on my range and for all I know, the guns of the law are even closer than that. Far and wide, marshals with posses at their backs are combing The Nations and boys with bounties on their scalps are a-huntin' their holes. They say there's five thousand wanted men in the Indian Territory this winter. Maybe so, but I'm interested in just one of 'em—me, *myself*—so I hit for my hideout in the breaks of the North Canadian and I don't throw off none until I get there. Why am I on the dodge? That's not a fair question in this country, mister, and besides—I ain't never been no hand to talk about my personal virtues and shortcomin's.

I located and built this here sanctuary myself. It's a half-dugout-and-log backed into the high side of a draw under tall trees and heavy brush so that my smoke can lose itself in the trees and my horses can take cover in the brush. Five ways out of the place if you know how to find 'em, and I do. There's an everlastin' spring in the draw and good feed for any horseflesh that I happen to be holdin' while it gets over its homesickness. Got plenty privacy here, too, and I like that for I always trail alone. Company sorta spooks me, makes my gunhand plumb skittish. I'll admit that I ain't got much of a spread here on the Canadian, but it's home to a man who don't want a home until he gets to needin' a home powerful bad, a quiet place to rest up or patch up in; and sometimes a fella has to cache a bankroll until it cools down to where it ain't too hot to handle. Fact is, I seen the time when— But I ain't no hand to talk much.

Pretty soon day-after-tomorrow is Christmas—not that Christmas means anything to a man like me, but a fella will get to thinkin' about company and such round Christmas time—and I'm up on the bluff in a clump of dead jimson weeds about the color of my clothes where I spend more or less time when the law is on the loose, and I've got my spyglass. I'm a-lookin' for company. I don't want no company. After a while I spot a band of riders a-joggin' up my side of the river and before long my glass tells me that the man a-pointin' that bunch is Marshal Heck Henderson. He knows me, Heck does, knows the taste of my gunsmoke and the feel of my lead. He don't like me much. But Heck carries his posse right on by me and I watch 'em until they're out of sight upriver and then I breathe easy like. Reckon he ain't lookin' for me in this part of the country. So I go to figgerin' that this ought to be a right quiet and peaceable Christmas for me. No company.

I'm fixin' to climb down and go and mix me a batch of bread when I swing my glass around for a last look. Yonder comes another rider! He's a-trailin' the posse, or I miss my guess, and he's mighty careful to stay out of sight of 'em. When he comes close enough I see that I don't know him and from his looks I don't want to know the cuss nohow; but there *is somethin'* about him that makes me think I'd ought to know him. Imagination I reckon. He keeps on a-ramblin' until I lose sight of him at the bend, so I'm kind of easy in my mind again. Probably no company.

On the way down the bluff I think maybe I'd ought to go to the turkey roost this evenin' and knock over a fat gobbler for my Christmas dinner. After all, Christmas is—well, it's Christmas. Or maybe I'd better fetch in *two* fat gobblers. With the country gettin' crowded thisaways, I *might* have company for Christmas.

Marshal Heck Henderson says that the devil gave me cat eyes and wolf ears, but he's wrong about that. Of course, most any man can train himself to pick up and recognize, without thinkin', all the every-day sounds and movements around him and if he's a hair-trigger cuss any sound or motion that don't belong there will touch him off. I'm thataway, but I don't see and hear everything regardless of what Heck says. Like now—it's comin' dusk and I'm back in camp, out by the woodpile a-drawin' my turkeys, and the breeze is a-whisperin' through the naked trees and brush and a-rustlin' dead leaves and grass and an old coyote is a-tunin' up over on the bluff and I hear my horses feedin' down on the spring branch, and a fool cottontail goes a-skitterin' past and a twig pops like they do when it's frosty, then in the back of my brain somewhere I realize that *it ain't that cold now*—

And when I come to I'm facin' the other way with a turkey in my left hand and a gun in my right, and it's a-pointin' dead center at a man's belly! My thumb is slippin' the hammer. I barely catch it in time.

He folds his arms slow and cautious-like. His mouth is wide and his teeth look white in his thin, dark face. He ain't makin' a sound, but he's laughin' at me!

I'm mad and I'm ashamed because he caught me nappin' thisaway, maybe more ashamed than mad, but I don't let on.

"You're a damned fool, stranger," I tell him.

He nods. "I know it. But when I got close enough to get a good look at you I knew who you were. I've heard of you. I wanted to see your draw. I'm interested in gunplay. I'll give you ten dollars to do it again."

"Go to hell." I put away my Colt. "Gunslingin' ain't my business."

"But it *is* mine, or rather my hobby." He grins and unfolds his arms plumb careful. "Hate to admit it, but I think I can learn something from you. I'll make it twenty if you'll do that again."

"As I was sayin', stranger, you can go clean to hell and I hope you have to walk every foot of the way."

He looks sorta hurt, if a face as mean as his can show hurt. Knowin' that he could have made a sieve out of my hide before I heard him, maybe I ain't got no call to be so cussed; but by now I've figured out who he is and what I mean, I'd rather wake up and find a rattler in my blankets than to turn around and find that breed killer in my camp. He's half Indian—which nobody holds against him, of course—and he goes by the name of Choctaw. I've heard many a story about his doin's and I never hear a man say a good word for him. Far as I know, he ain't got a friend in the world. Men who would stand up and shoot it out with the devil himself are afraid of Choctaw, or at least they cut a circle around him rather than to face him because you never can tell when he'll burn a man down just to add another notch to his gun. Law officers are his favorite game and he cuts bigger notches for them, tallyin' twelve of 'em I hear. Choctaw is more or less a mystery. They say he don't drink or carouse none, he's got education and talks language and he reads books when he ain't too busy dodgin' the law or a-huntin' it down.

For a short spell now he don't say nothin'. Just stands there tall and wiry in his moccasins, sorta on the balls of his feet like a man fixed to jump in any direction, meanwhile lookin' me and my camp over good. I've had *my* say. I keep my mouth shut and my eyes open and he can't so much as bat a winker without me catchin' him at it. I've done picked the spot where I'll let him have it—about twelve inches above where his gunbelts cross.

Pretty soon, he says, "I like this place."

"Too bad. I'm here first. How did you ever find it."

He grins. Puts me in mind of a mad dog tryin' to be friendly. "I'm half Indian, half white. The Indian's eyes found your cleverly hidden trail and the white man's hunger for the society of his breed brought me here. Christmas, you know, and white men need company at Christmas."

I'll gamble he's a liar, but I don't say so. I tell him, "You were trailin' Heck Henderson's posse. Were you a-huntin' company then, or layin' for a chance to earn another credit?"

He's the damndest fella to laugh without makin' a sound. "Won't deny that I'd like to notch my gun for Henderson, but I didn't know that was his posse until I trailed them to their camp northwest of here. Picked up the tracks this morning. I knew they were white men's horses and white men riding them. I followed them because I wanted the company of white men. Christmas, you know."

Comin' out of a face like his, Choctaw's voice is plumb surprisin'—low, soft and easy listenin'. And I'm a-talkin' to him more than I usually talk. Before today I ain't spoke to a man for close onto a month and then I didn't have much to say. Just "Stick 'em up!" as I recollect it.

So I tell this breed killer, "Christmas, hell! Who wants company for Christmas?"

He don't turn a hair. He says right out, "You do. You were a boy not *too* long ago. You've remembered that today. You've been thinking of Christmas today. You want company for Christmas, but you won't admit it even to yourself. I'm here. Do I stay?"

"Go and fetch up your horse."

Choctaw is a right handy man around camp and he does his share of the chores outside. He talks a blue streak all the time about this and that and everything like a fella will when he's a bustin' to talk. I never let him get behind me. To be fair and square about it though, he don't try to. In fact, he seems to be takin' care not to, as if he thought my back was more dangerous than the front of me. He's a plumb peculiar cuss, Choctaw is. When we're goin' into the dugout, I hold back the buffalo robe door and nod for him to go ahead.

Carryin' his blanket-roll, saddle-bags and rifle scabbard, he grins and makes a move to put 'em down. "It isn't polite for a guest to go armed into his host's house. Want me to take off my belts?"

"Hell, no, man! If I ain't got no better sense than to sleep with a rattler, damned if I'll make him shed his fangs."

Choctaw laughed at that, laughed out loud for the first time since he come. Then he sobers up, and tells me right serious, "I've got a confession to make before I accept your hospitality. There was—"

"No need to confess your sins to me, mister. Go and hunt you up a parson."

He grins, and goes on, "Got to do it. There was a man spying on Henderson's camp while I was there. He must have seen me, too, because he followed me when I left. I made no effort to foul my trail.

He may show up down here, then you'll have more company. Thought I'd ought to tell you."

I'll never know why I didn't get mad about that. I just ask him, "Why did you make sign right into my place thataway?"

"Didn't know whether I'd find anybody down here and I wanted to make sure of company for Christmas."

I motion for him to go in. "Drop your beddin' on a bunk. Got four of 'em. Don't know why I ever put 'em in."

"You knew that you'd get lonesome, that's why."

By now I think I've figured this gunslinger out. He's got a twist in his head. He really does want to be with folks at Christmas and he's a fightin' down the temptation to kill. If it wasn't for Christmas, I'll gamble that he'd have made a play against me before this. Men like Choctaw will ride miles to test their gunplay with a man if he's got a bigger reputation as a gunsharp, or if they're nursin' a suspicion that he's faster than they are. They'll risk their lives to prove that he ain't. They're plumb loco thataway. I never did believe in such foolishness.

My six-shooters are tools that I use in my work and the least I have to use the things, the better I'm satisfied.

Me and Choctaw have finished our supper and we're a-playin' the coffee pot. All of a sudden he stops with a tincup halfway to his mouth and I'm a-standin' there pourin' coffee onto the table instead of into my cup. We hear a man singin'. He's down the draw a-piece and he ain't a-singin' very loud, but his voice carries high, clear and sharp on the frosty air. I blow out the light, set down the pot and we both head for the door.

The moon is up full and it's good shootin' light.

We hunker down in a shadow and listen to the singin' as it comes closer and closer, slow-like up the draw.

Pretty soon, I allow, "That there pilgrim ain't as big a fool as you are."

Choctaw laughs a little. "But he can sing and I can't." He cocks an ear for a minute. "If he's the man I think he is, he's an even bigger fool than I am."

"Can't hardly believe it."

Far's I'm concerned, I can listen to that brand of singin' from now on. It's a new song that everybody is hummin' and whistlin' up and down the range and I hear that a crazy buffalo hunter made it up a short time back. It starts off like this:

> I love these wild flowers, in this fair land of ours,
> I love to hear the wild curlew scream
> On the cliffs of white rock, where the antelope flock,
> To graze on the herbage so green.
> O, give me a home, where the buffalo roam,
> Where the deer and the antelope play,
> Where seldom is heard a discouragin' word
> And the sky is not cloudy all day.

After a little while, Choctaw says, "He's the man, all right."

With this the breed stands up, stretches himself and tries his guns in their leather. I don't like the set of his head, sorta stickin' out at the end of his neck like a wolf a-testin' the air, and I don't like anything about him right now. Temptation is fixin' to get the best of him, Christmas regardless.

So I tell him quiet-like, "Looky here, mister. Start trouble and you make yourself short in this here camp."

That woke him up. He grins quick, and says right gentle, "Mighty sorry. I once saw that man in action and ever since then I've been wanting to meet up with him. Sorry I almost forgot."

"Forgot what?"

"Christmas, you know."

The stranger sings his way right up to the door. There he stops, folds his hands on his saddle-horn and grins down at us. His hat is a-ridin' the back of his head and the moon holds his face up for us to see plain as day, and right off I like that face. Shore, it's reckless and full of the devil to boot, but it ain't a bad face as faces go in this country. Looks so doggoned young, I betcha the fellas call him "Baby Face" when they know him well enough.

There's a laughter in his voice, "Merry Christmas, folks!"

"Christmas ain't hit these parts yet, stranger," I tell him, "but light and cool the seat of your britches until it does."

I ain't hardly got the words out of my mouth before he leaves the saddle as if he's afraid I'll change my mind a split second later and he wants to beat me to it. He's plumb cat on his feet and his eyes don't miss nothin' either. They sorta stumble when they brush against

Choctaw, but the stranger don't say anything and he's quick to put out his hand to me.

"Mighty glad to take you at your word, mister," he says, happy-like. "I've been huntin' company for Christmas, wantin' it bad. Call me— call me Kansas and let it go at that."

Kansas don't offer to shed his belts when he has put up his horse and goes to pack his trunk inside, and I see that he don't ever show his back to Choctaw. But that don't seem to spoil his fun, though. He eats like a man that's hungry for food and he talks like a man that's starved for talk, and he eats and talks and laughs and carries on until he has me and Choctaw a laughin' too. I can see that Kansas is one of them salty young devils that is likely to make any kind of a fool play when-ever the notion strikes him, but right now he swears he's a-fixin' to celebrate Christmas and I believe him. The breed is a-behavin' himself decent now. Funny what Christmas does to some men.

Time slides past at a high trot with Kansas a-whoopin' it up thataway and I don't know how long it is before I hear somethin' outside. Like always, I been keepin' one ear inside and the other ear outside. With the outside ear I'm a listenin' to Henry Clay and his woman makin' sweet talk in that tall maple over the woodpile, Old Henry bein' a barred owl mighty nigh as big as a turkey, and when their talk stops sudden-like I know somethin' or other is a-snoopin' round the draw.

So I says cautious to the boys, "Keep up the racket. I'm goin' to scout the camp."

Choctaw holds up a blanket to cut down the light and I slip through the door. I Injun down in the brush by the trail and listen, and shore enough—somethin' is a-movin' my way and I'll swear it's a-walkin' on its hind legs. It ain't long before he shows up and stops ten feet away, lookin' hard at the dugout and a-listenin' just as hard I reckon. I don't show myself first off because if he's got set triggers and explodes at sight of me, I might have to gun the cuss.

So I lay low in the brush, and tell him pleasant-like, "Stranger, if you're lookin' for somebody and want to live to find 'em, better stick your fingers in your ears and keep 'em stuck."

He does, quick. He don't so much as twitch his hide either, so I figure he's been ridin' his feelin's with a powerful tight rein for a long time, or he's made out of stuff that ain't got no feelin's. I walk out while he's standin' there thataway.

He says, "Howdy, mister. Have I drifted into some place where I ain't got no business to be?"

"That all depends," I tell him. "All depends on who you are and what you want. Drop your hands if you're a mind to."

"Much obliged," he sorta drawls, humorous-like. "Comin' from a man past thirty years old I know it sounds plumb childish to say that I'm huntin' a good place to spend my Christmas, but I am."

What the hell? I think. Another one!

He goes on, "I ran smack onto a posse up yonder a ways, but they didn't see me. I ain't hankerin' to Christmas with a posse, but I did take time to look 'em over and kind of wonder whether any of 'em would know me if I moseyed into their camp. While I'm watchin' 'em I see two other fellas doin' the same thing. After a while they left, one followin' the other, so I lit out and trailed 'em to this draw before it got too dark to read sign. I've been hidin' down below until I figured it was safe to go up to your house and see if I could hear somethin'. In times like these a man has to make shore, don't he?"

I nod.

He grins sheepish. His face is like a brown sandstone rock, but he can grin. He winds up, "I hate like blazes to spend my Christmas alone on the prairie with coyotes and wolves and buffalo and the Spanish pony I'm ridin'. They're mighty poor company."

"Maybe so," I tell him, "but they're a damned sight gentler than the company you'll find here, Mister—er—"

"Off hand, Arkansaw is the best name I can think of."

"It'll do."

"Do to hang with, you mean," he says, chucklin' down low somewheres.

"Go and fetch your pony."

He nods a "Thank you," pleased as a pig in a punkin patch, and moves off—big, but light on his feet like a bear.

I keep a eye on him and I'm thinkin', yonder goes a *good* man who'd be a *bad* man to monkey with.

Arkansaw fits into my Christmas company all right. He's a good feeder, likes his coffee hot and black and he talks fit to kill same as the other fellas do when they first come. Kansas and him warm up to each other right from the start. He's plumb sociable to me and Choctaw too, but I can see that he ain't lettin' the breed out of his sight none to speak of. Fact is, all three of us are thataway about Choctaw. It ain't because he isn't all white, either. Men like us who are damned by society and hunted by the law don't ever get uppity about color. We don't judge a man by the blood he was borned with. We measure him by the blood he's got in his veins *now*, 'cause we figure he made it whatever it is—good or bad. The trouble with Choctaw is, he don't use his guns to save his own hide like most of us long riders do. He kills for the fun of it and he's proud to notch credits on his gun. Far as we're concerned, *that's* what makes his blood smell of sulphur.

But, aside from keepin' a sharp eye on the cuss, we treat Choctaw as if he'd never done anything more than to stick up a bank or a stage or a army paymaster or lift a band of horses or clean out a gamblin' joint and swap lead with the law while makin' his getaway. In other words, we treat him like he's one of us. I'll say this for him, too: he's a-fightin' that old temptation to show the world and himself how good he is, and to earn credits. Christmas, I reckon. Time and again I see him a-studyin' how Kansas and Arkansaw pack their weapons and handle theirselves generally, and more'n once I feel his eyes on me. I can stand big cold, but when I feel Choctaw's eyes on me thataway my backbone freezes solid.

My pillows are stuffed with buffalo hair and my bunks are filled with soft buffalo grass and everybody has plenty of blankets, but I betcha nobody gets much sleep that night unless maybe Kansas does. I know I don't. Every time a man moves or even draws a long breath that dead grass whispers a warnin' that sounds mighty loud in a dug-out full of hair-trigger men who don't trust nobody. Kansas might have done some sleepin', though, 'cause he's the take-it-as-it-comes kind. Anyhow, he's the first man in his boots in the mornin' and he choruses the balance of us out of our blankets at the break of day, a-raisin' hell like a frisky colt, and he stirs up the fire and puts on a chunk and takes the coffee pot out of the ashes and fills our cups, and he reminds us that it's Christmas Eve and Santa Claus is no doubt a-whackin' his eight-deer hitch down the Northern Trail already.

"I figure he'll hit The Nations about two minutes before midnight," allows Kansas, "unless he gets caught up in a Nebraska blizzard."

"Huh!" I grunt. "He'd better stay clean away from The Nations. Betcha there's a warrant out for him and a posse on his tail before he's been in this country a hour."

"And you ain't talkin'," declared Arkansaw. "The marshals will corral him and they'll feed his deer to reservation Indians and they'll take him to Fort Smith, and Judge Parker will hang Old Santa there."

Choctaw spins the cylinder of his right-hand gun, maybe to make certain that nobody ain't unloaded it during the night. He grins across at us, and says, "Maybe Old Santa will give Judge Parker the slip. I have, twice. That hanging murderer has been trying to get his bloody paws on me for years. Some day I'll file a notch for him, a big notch."

Ordinarily men like us could talk all day about the Hangin' Judge and what we'd like to do to him, but somehow or other he ain't interestin' subject on Christmas Eve. Nobody taken up where Choctaw left off. Kansas allows that we'd ought to have a big feed tomorrow, Christmas, so right after breakfast I set the boys off to do some work while I go up the bluff with my spyglass to look the scenery over. With a posse a-nosin' round it don't pay to get careless. The guns of the law don't take Christmas off.

Everything looks natural, not a soul in sight from the bluff. All of a sudden it comes to me that Old Heck and his deputies are probably huntin' the trail of the fella that stuck up that English lord and his guide and two flunkies a short time back. That happened more than fifty mile northwest of here. The Englishman was a-headin' for the buffalo range to show the American boys how to kill 'em in style, and he had five thousand in cash on him and a lot of fancy grub in his wagon and him and his men were set afoot out there—their saddle stock and wagon taken a likin' to the stick-up man and followed him off, and— But I ain't no hand to talk much.

When I get back to camp, Arkansaw has dug a good pit for turkey cookin' and Kansas has gone to the claybank where I sent him and fetched down plenty clay for mortar and Choctaw has gone to the thicket where I told him he'd find a nice young buck—good eatin' size. He's huntin' with a bow and war arrows that I taken off one of Peta Nocona's warriors who wouldn't need 'em no more. I hunt with that bow when gunfire ain't smart. Arkansaw and Kansas are gatherin' dry blackjack oak to make coals without much smoke, and they're laughin' and carryin' on like a brace of boys a-campin' out. I watch 'em for a minute and I'm listenin' to 'em and I'm a-thinkin', company for Christmas ain't so bad at that.

Pretty soon Choctaw comes in with the buck over his shoulder and

I can see that the hunt has done him good 'cause that there temptation ain't a-workin' on him so hard now.

He looks at other men like they were men instead of marks to shoot at. So I send him up onto the bluff with my spyglass and we take turns a-standin' guard up there until sundown with never a sight of a human: just buffalo, antelope, deer, mustangs and such.

Meanwhile we're all busy as prairie dogs. I take the liver, heart, sweetbreads and a slice of tenderloin from the buck and make us a larrupin' son-of-a-gun stew for supper, and Arkansaw he fixes a dried peach cobbler that's big enough for two meals, and Kansas goes to a pool downriver that I tell him about and comes back with a dozen big catfish for breakfast Christmas mornin', and Choctaw sees a cottontail and right away decides he wants a rabbit stew for eatin' sometime today—he ain't particular when—so he takes the bow and arrows again and comes back with six rabbits, and durned if I ain't makin' another stew before I know it. I reckon men on the dodge eat more than other men when they get a chance. With the law sniffin' and a-growlin' at your hocks, if you stop to eat you won't live to eat.

Watchin' me and Arkansaw a-mixin' this and that, Choctaw wants to know, "Where did you ever get all this fancy stuff away out here? White flour, long sweetening (sorghum), short sweetening (white sugar), canned milk, spices, onions, sweet potatoes, lard, and all kinds of dried fruit. Where did you ever get it?"

I look at him. "Personal question, Choctaw, and nobody but a durned fool ever answers a personal question."

Choctaw allows he's plumb sorry and Arkansaw says he'd ought to be, and then everybody laughs fit to kill, and I'm thinkin', company for Christmas ain't a bad idea.

The big event of the day, as a fella says, comes when I put the turkeys down to cook. It's full dark and everybody is there and I reckon nobody is thinkin' about gunfightin' and killin' and the law and hangin's and such, 'cause all we're talkin' about is this here turkey bake. We've got a big bed of redhot coals in the pit. I mix me a clay mortar and plaster the gobblers, feathers and all, about three inches thick with the sticky stuff and lay 'em down there on the coals, then we cover 'em with dirt and build a slow fire on top of 'em and we stretch buffalo robes around it and the green deer skin over it to hide the glow.

When we're finished, I tell the boys, "Them turks ought to be about right for eatin' by tomorrow, and that's Christmas."

Kansas is a-starin' into the fire sorta dreamy-like, and he says, "A Christmas dinner with all the fixin's."

Regardless of the fact that we play four-handed Seven Up until midnight and don't sleep much after that, this fool Kansas rousts us out when it's comin' day on Christmas mornin'. Ain't he got a brain in his head, that kid. He swears he heard Santa Claus on the room last night and I tell him that all he heard was Old Henry Clay a-crunchin' a packrat's bones, and Choctaw declares I lit in the middle of the floor with a six-shooter when the first bone popped and I tell him he's a liar, but Arkansaw swears it's so and dadblame me if they don't mighty nigh convince me that it *is*.

Then Choctaw says, "As I told you, I'll give you twenty dollars to show us that draw of yours."

I shake my head, pourin' him some coffee.

"I'll make it fifty, cash, if you'll do it slow."

"Go to hell," I tell Choctaw.

That old temptation must have been workin' on him in his sleep, and I'm thinkin', Christmas don't look none too promisin'.

But a wallopin' breakfast of corn pone and fried catfish topped off with a middlin' big helpin' of left-over rabbit stew sorta smothers the temptation and Choctaw behaves right human for a while. He pitches in and helps Arkansaw and Kansas fry a stack of venison steaks to be warmed up in their gravy and go with the turkey, and I say I'll mix a bakin' of cush to go with both of 'em.

"What's cush?" asks Kansas.

"Cush? Ain't you never heard of cush? It's outlaw cake and I was brung up on it."

So I take some stale wheat bread and crumble it and mix it with corn meal and soak 'em in hot water, then I put in hog fat—bear fat will do—and some raisins 'cause I got 'em, and salt and plenty pepper, and I cook my cush in a skillet until it's nice and brown and fit to go with any fat gobbler.

Meanwhile the boys are so wrapped up in fixin' our Christmas dinner, nobody ain't offered to stand guard on the bluff and I don't say anything about it. Damned careless, I know. But, to tell the truth, I reckon all of us are burnt out on eternally standin' guard, asleep and awake, and we're mighty glad to sorta forget the law and The Hangin'

Judge for one day at least. Now that I think of it—one of the best night's sleep I ever got, I got in jail. Next day I busted out and didn't get no sleep for a week.

It ain't noways time for dinner, but the boys keep a-wonderin' out loud whether them turks ain't burnt to a crisp and such talk—I'll swear they're like kids—until I can't put up with it no longer, so I tell Kansas and Choctaw to go and dig them gobblers up. There ain't a sign of a leak in their clay shells, which makes me right proud. When we crack 'em open feathers and skin come away with the shell and there's our turk, plumb juicy like Nature made him. Nothin' gets away, not even the gobble, and his meat is a-fallin' from his bones. I mighty nigh have to hold the boys off with a six-shooter.

We set the table inside right stylish and the boys' eyes pop out when I go to puttin' on a linen tablecloth and silver eatin' tools and English jams and jellies, but nobody asks me where I got the stuff.

Choctaw goes to his saddle-bags and finds two quarts of champagne. He gives 'em to me, sayin', "I've been saving these for Christmas. They've taken up room that I really needed for ammunition."

Arkansaw has been diggin' in his towsack morral. Up he comes with a pint of Old Crow, and hands it over. " 'Tain't much, but it'll give us a taste of Christmas cheer."

Kansas fetches somethin' from his warbag. He looks sheepish and he talks thataway, too. "Here's a jar of wild plum jelly. A week or so back a squatter's old lady gave it to me for my Christmas dinner wherever I happened to be. Said she lost her own boy this time last year. Killed in a gunfight at Pond Creek."

Liquor and Old Temptation work in double harness and I'm afraid of what this team will do to Choctaw. I watch him close.

But he just sips a little champagne and stops at that and nobody else drinks much, which sets me thinkin' that if every man in the country was a gunsharp the anti-saloon preachers wouldn't have much to preach about. No gunfighter with a lick of sense will slow himself down by drinkin' when he's in fast company like this here Christmas gatherin' of mine.

I know we're a-celebratin' Christmas in a hole in the ground and the guns of the law may be linin' their sights on us for all we know, but we eat and talk and laugh and eat some more just like other folks do and I betcha we're havin' more fun than they do 'cause we ain't had a chance to celebrate thisaway since we were boys, maybe some of us never before. Kansas is havin' the time of his life. This sorrel-topped kid raises more Cain than any of us, and when it's gettin' dark and we build up a big fire in the chimney and shove the table out of the way and get our tobacco to goin' good, he starts to sing in that fine voice of his. Nobody talks then. Everybody listens—listens and thinks, I reckon.

Kansas sings about Christmas and happy folks who can show a light without fear of the law, and he sings of pretty things until my dingy old dugout commences to show spots of cheerful color, like bright curtains in place of a slab shutter on its window, and holly berries and mistletoe a-hangin' here and there, and a yellow tomcat a-sleepin' in front of the fire—his name was Slug—and over in the corner a little old cedar saplin' is all dressed up with red paper and cotton and red candles, and there's three pair of black stockin's a-hangin' on the tree, all of 'em darned a-plenty, and the longest stockin's are mine, and—

Hell! I'm a-seein' things that I thought I'd done forgot. I go and pour me some coffee. Choctaw holds out his cup. He's got a faraway look in his eye. I wonder, maybe he's a-seein' things, too.

Arkansaw is just a-settin' there on his bunk. He's watchin' Kansas and a-listenin' with his eyes half shut part of the time, and he ain't a-talkin'. In the light from the fire and the oil lamp his face looks more than ever like a sandstone rock that's weathered and chipped, and I'm wonderin' what serious thing he's got on his mind. So I ask him if he can't spin us a yarn that will make good listenin' on Christmas night.

Arkansaw grins, mostly with his eyes, and says, "Yes, boys, I reckon I've got a story I can tell." He looks at his watch. "It's gettin' along. My story is a Christmas story, so I'd better get goin' on it 'cause Christmas will soon be over.

We settle down to listen—Choctaw tilted back on a stool in the corner by the fireplace, Kansas on his bunk straight across the room and me on my bunk same side as Arkansaw.

"If this should happen to be my last Christmas, boys, I want you-all to know that it's the best I ever had." That's the way Arkansaw started out. "And it has set me to thinkin' hard about a boy who never had a Christmas. I'll call him Bud for short. Early on the mornin' of the first Christmas that Bud can remember good, a noise woke him up and he figured it was Santa Claus a-climbin' down the cabin chimney. It was Comanches. They killed his maw and paw and carried Bud off."

Arkansaw keeps still for a minute, a-drawin' on a cold pipe like he sorta hates to go on with his story. Pretty soon he does, though.

"Bud missed five Christmases while the Indians had him. Then the Rangers got him away from the Comanches and an old bachelor down in Texas adopted the boy. This ornery old skinflint didn't believe in Christmas any more than the Indians did. All he believed in was makin' money and hangin' onto it and he worked Bud from mornin' to night, winter and summer. The boy would hear other kids carryin' on about Christmas and sometimes he'd catch sight of a Christmas tree through a window or in somebody's yard, but he never had a Christmas of his own. That went on until he was comin' fourteen. Then the day before Christmas he took the old man's rifle and six-shooters and lifted a horse and lit out. Of course, they had the law on his trail that very day. Bud celebrated *that* Christmas a-straddle of his pony, cold and hungry and a-ridin' hard."

Arkansaw stops for a long breath, then he says, "The posse cornered Bud on the Brazos. He fit 'em like a wildcat and got clean away. Nobody was killed, but he did wing a few of the lawmen and that made the boy an outlaw with a bounty on his scalp."

Arkansaw stops to load his pipe. Kansas is settin' back against the wall with his arms folded and his long legs crossed, a-takin' in every word. Choctaw sits up on his stool soon as ever talk about gunfightin' and shootin' lawmen commences. Me—I'm a-thinkin' about a heap of things that happened when I was a boy.

"From then on it's the old story," says Arkansaw when his pipe is goin' good. "The law hounded Bud from pillar to post, tacked crimes onto him that he never committed, and before long folks were callin' him the Boy Bandit and the Daring Desperado and such foolishness until there came a time when he had to shoot or bluff his way out of any town he stopped in. His gunplay had made a reputation big enough to stir up the jealousy of badmen who could not stand for anybody to be faster with a six-shooter than they were, and they went lookin' for Bud. He downed several of 'em in fair fights."

I can see that his line of talk ain't doin' Choctaw a particle of good. It's playin' right into the hand of Old Temptation. The breed is a-settin' there like he's fixed to dive for cover or slap leather any second, and I ain't never seen hotter eyes in a meaner face than his'n. I'm wishin' to hell that I hadn't asked Arkansaw for a story.

"In all those years Bud never had a chance to celebrate a peaceable Christmas," he's sayin', " 'cause the law and gunsharps keep him on the move. In a shootin' scrape some time back he saved the life of a young fool who had no business to be where he was and Bud had taken this Young Wild West home to his dad, then rode off in a mile-high cloud of dust before the old man hardly had a chance to thank him. This old jasper is rich and he thinks a heap of his boy. When he finally got the whole story out of the kid he hired detectives to learn all they could about Bud's history, and to find him. They got the history all right, but they never got Bud. The old man never gave up, though. He swears he'll find Bud and fight his case through all the courts in the country if need be to clear him. This old cattle king fired the detectives and hired a Deputy United States Marshal who was on leave and told him to go and find Bud, if the outlaw was still above ground, no matter how long the trail or where it took him."

Arkansaw looks at his watch, puts it back in his pocket slow and careful-like. "Doggoned if it ain't two minutes after midnight and Christmas is over."

Then he grins, and says, "Well, Bud, you've had your Christmas at last."

He's lookin' straight at Kansas!

Kansas disappears behind a cloud of smoke. So does Choctaw. Arkansaw's smoke slaps me in the face. Dishes rattle and the log roof bounces and the lamp goes out. Arkansaw jerks back. Choctaw is slammed against the wall, then he topples onto the stool and hangs there like a dead wolf.

I grab a holt of Arkansaw. So does Kansas.

With a hand inside his shirt, the Deputy grins, and whispers, "Ain't hurt bad. He peeled a rib for me, that's all. Fast work, boys, mighty fast. Much obliged."

I blow the smoke from my gun and put it away.

And I'm thinkin', company for Christmas is a powerful fine idea.

The Death
of Dutch Creel

Loren D. Estleman

*One of today's foremost writers of Western (and detective) fiction, Loren
D. Estleman has earned two Spur Awards from the Western Writers of
America, including one for Best Novel of 1981* (Aces and Eights), *and
has also received numerous other awards, as well as nominations for both
the National Book Award and the Pulitzer Prize. Outstanding among his
other frontier novels are* The Hider *(1978),* Mister St. John *(1983),*
This Old Bill *(1984), and* Bloody Season *(1988). Equally noteworthy is
his collection* The Best Western Stories of Loren D. Estleman *(1989).
In this wry and witty story of the life—and death on Christmas Eve, 1899
—of the outlaw Dutch Creel, he shows that there is often a vast difference
between historical fact and what fiction writers and Hollywood film-
makers would have us believe.*

When they went and made a moving picture about Dutch, I swore I'd
never go see it. They didn't ask me to help, for one thing, and the only
way I found out they done it at all, I read it was coming to the old
Ladybird Theater in Absaroka. But saying you'll do or not do a thing is
easier to make good on when you're not married, and still twice as easy
when you're married to anyone but Addie.

She got on me about how was I to know it was no good if I didn't go
look at it, and how even if it *was* no good, it still beat sitting home

night after night the way we usually done, and how she never took no vow to spend all her evenings sewing samplers and reading *The Oklahoma Farmer,* and all, and finally just to shut her up I took her in the flivver to the Ladybird and we went and seen it. These moving pictures are the end of married peace.

It was some show. This curly-headed fellow that was made out to be Dutch Creel wore a tall black hat and two guns low and used them both at the same time, never just the one and then border-shifting when it run out of cartridges, which was the way they done it in the wild days. He stuck up banks and stagecoaches and jumped on trains and swapped lead with the laws and occasionally dropped one, and there was so much dust and smoke you swore you heard gunshots and hoofbeats, though of course there wasn't no sound, just this skinny tenderheel banging a piano up by the screen like he was slapping hornets.

Addie, she loved it. She had fried a chicken and packed it in a wicker basket, and every time one of them bullets went home, she bit into a leg or a wing till there wasn't nothing left but the bones, and I begun to worry if she'd leave even *them* for the hogs. I never got none of it.

After twenty minutes or so, the laws cornered old Dutch in a shack in a box canyon and this big good-looking jasper that was supposed to be Sheriff Rube Belford went in alone and outdrawed him and that there was the end. It was some show all right. Everybody that was in that theater that night went home happy as a bitch dog.

Everybody but me.

It didn't none of it happen that way, you see; especially the last part. I'm fixing to put the whole kit down here just as it was, and I will swear on a wagonload of King James Bibles it's the goods. I was there.

Kind of.

You already know about the guns. They come dear in them days. If you had a pistol at all—shotguns and squirrel rifles was like hoes to a granger and common as outhouses—well, you was right royal. *Two* pistols was gilding the lily, and if you still had the wherewithal to buy cartridges for to practice with and get good with both hands, I don't know why you'd feel the need to stick up even one bank. Which was as many as Dutch ever stuck up before deciding whilst he was healing that bank-robbing weren't his specialty. Stopping trains wasn't, neither; and since even then stagecoaches was as scarce as river ferries are now, they was plenty safe from him too. Dutch stole livestock.

Not that he was your everyday horse thief or rustler, riding off on another man's transportation while the man was indoors bellying up to some fancy. Dutch and his gang could slip an entire herd out from under the nighthawks' noses slick as spit outside El Paso on Wednesday and sell it to some fat Spanish grandee in Chihuahua on Friday, then run that same grandee's remuda across the river on their way back north and sell it on Sunday to the cattleman whose beef they stole in the first place. Done it, too, on more than one occasion, and likely still would be, if not for that thing in El Paso in '99. But that's taking a dally before the lariat is throwed, and I'll come to it.

The curly hair was wrong too. Dutch was Cherokee on his ma's side and his hair hung straight as a stovepipe and just as black. He was born in the Nations, what's called Oklahoma now, where the Five Civilized Tribes lived under the protection of Judge Parker's court in Fort Smith, over the border in Arkansas. Leastwise they did when bad white men wanted for crimes in other places wasn't hiding out there, stirring up six kinds of hell and bringing the laws in after them. Ford Harper, he was one.

Ford was around twenty when he come, nobody knew where from, though most said Missouri, and lost no time taking up with a Creek widow near twice his age, baptized Mary Elizabeth Treefall, whose first husband had left her a section over by McAlester. White men was not let own property in the Nations unless they was married to Indians.

In the spring of '96, Ford hired Dutch, who was then eighteen, to help him work the spread, which Ford had took it in his head was tailor-made for raising horses. Well, Dutch and Ford got on right handy, being so close in age and temperament, and with them two out mending fence all day and cutting the wolf loose in McAlester nights I don't reckon poor old Mary Treefall seen much of her new man after Dutch come on. I don't know if she found that satisfactory, but she hadn't no complaints to make about the way the ranch was run, because inside of six months they had twice as many horses as they started with.

One night, five of Parker's marshals and two trackers rode onto the Treefall spread when everyone was in bed and called upon Ford to surrender himself for the crime of rustling in the Nations. They had the house surrounded and enough weapons between them to take Canada away from Queen Victoria. But Canada didn't have Dutch Creel.

He slept up in the hayloft of the barn with a new Model 1894 Winchester he bought on his rustler's wages. When the bellering woke him up, he crawled over to the opening and drawed a bead on one of the riders and plucked him clean out of his saddle. It was a lucky shot by moonlight, but it made him his reputation from then on as a gun-man and someone to walk around. The fact that he never duplicated it is a matter of no consequence to the legend.

Right away those marshals changed their minds about the house and opened up on the barn. Dutch shot back and they returned fire, and pretty soon that barn had enough holes in it to stand for a corn-crib, though the only casualty turned out to be a plug mare in a stall on the ground that picked up a slug in its right haunch and a predisposi-tion against lawmen for the rest of its days. They wasn't much better marksmen than Dutch, you see.

But the odds were poor and Dutch knowed it. When the marshals set fire to a hay wagon and started it toward the barn to burn him out, he clumb down and surrendered. Ford Harper meanwhile had shin-nied down the rainpipe from the upstairs bedroom he shared with Mary Treefall and lit out.

The laws took Dutch in irons to Fort Smith, where as it turned out he had been lucky in his choice of targets, as the man he shot was not a marshal but a Choctaw tracker and hit only in the leg, though he did finally have to have it cut off. When the jury handed in the guilty verdict, Parker put the lie to that Hanging Judge tag the Eastern papers hung on him and sentenced Dutch to fourteen years in the Detroit House of Corrections.

Accounts vary on just how the prisoner busted loose of his armed escort on the way to the train station. Some say Ford went and got up a gang and shot him out. The Fort Smith paper said Dutch overpow-ered a marshal still under the influence from a birthday celebration the night before and got his pistol. More than likely, Ford paid some-one in the escort to slip Dutch a weapon; some of them marshals wasn't no better than bandits theirselves, and Ford always was the kind to let his poke do his talking for him, it being the one thing he had managed to rescue along with his hide when he left the Treefall spread in such a hurry. However it happened, Dutch got away in a hail of lead that didn't hit much of anyone or anything, and Ford Harper was seen driving the buckboard he was riding in.

I reckon that's where the legend got its start. Rustlers in those parts was thicker than mosquito wigglers, but desperadoes that bucked Judge Parker's justice come few and far between. It didn't hurt, neither, that a New York journalist happened to be in Fort Smith to interview the Judge at the time of the escape and wrote a nickel novel called *The Border Bandit, or For the Love of a Creek Princess,* in which he lopped twenty years off Mary Treefall's true age and transferred her affections from Ford to Dutch. There would be a dozen more before Dutch was through, with not enough truth in the whole batch of them to sink a cement boat.

Meanwhile Dutch and Ford was on the run with a hundred dollars reward on each of their heads. They stopped at the ranch for horses and rode down to Texas, where Ford had a married sister raising cattle and tumbleweeds on a little spread north of Dallas. They made theirselves useful there and might have had permanent positions in the cow trade if Ford's brother-in-law that owned the spread hadn't lost it one night in a poker game in Dallas and then got himself killed when he tried to draw a hideout gun on the winner.

Dutch and Ford had a falling-out then. Ford wanted to go down to Old Mexico, but Dutch was all for heading back to the Nations and taking up where they left off, wanted men or no. So they split up. Ford's sister Henrietta went with Dutch.

A word about Henrietta. She was a tough little redhead brought up by a widowed father in a family of boys and had been doing a man's work since she was ten. She was pretty, too, with a direct way of speaking that appealed to a man of Dutch's temperament. I'm not saying they done anything before Henrietta's husband drawed to an inside straight and a bellyful of lead, but they become right friendly after the fact.

With a woman to support, Dutch got right to work doing the thing he done best. He put her up with Mary Treefall, who had been running the horse ranch alone in Ford's absence, and got together a gang in McAlester. His reputation was well along by then and finding recruits wasn't the problem it might have been a year or so earlier. Two of them, Bob Stonemason and Dick Leaping Deer, deserve mention here because they went on to greater fame with their own outfits after Dutch's death.

It was with this bunch that Dutch got most of his glory. When they was about, there wasn't a string of horses or a herd of cattle safe between Little Rock and Chihuahua. The law looked hard, but the law didn't have many friends in the Nations. News of posses spread like telegraph. Dutch was always gone from the ranch when they come to call, and Mary and Henrietta always swore they hadn't seen him in weeks. The reward for his capture went up to a thousand dollars.

When you're that good at what you do, the thing you most got to watch out for is yourself. Dutch didn't. He got to believing what the papers said about him, how he had a second sight that made him invincible, and he got to thinking how a gift like his was wasted on livestock. He had his heart set on robbing a bank.

The one he chose was the Cattleman's Trust in El Paso. He'd read about it in the *Police Gazette,* which reported the bank's assets at a million and a half dollars and announced that its security was the best in the West, with a newfangled time lock on the vault and six armed Pinkerton guards on duty around the clock. It seemed a proper challenge for the Bandit of the Border.

I personally think Dutch's decision not to ever rob another bank had less to do with how the raid come off than the amount of time he put into planning it. That was work, which if he'd been willing to do in the first place he wouldn't have took up the outlaw trail. It was a good plan that had a lot to do with timing. It might even have been a *great* plan, but we'll never know, because the law in El Paso got wind of it somehow and was waiting for the gang when they rode up.

It wasn't no day for plans. The one the law thought up was to let Dutch and the rest get inside the bank and then open fire on them when they come out with the cash, but one of the amateurs in the posse didn't think much of that plan and started the ball by shooting the hat off Dick Leaping Deer's head as he was dismounting in front of the hitching rail.

At that point the fighting become general. The laws poured lead into the gang of horsemen and the outlaws fired back from the porch and from behind the cover of watering troughs and their own mounts. Two of Dutch's men, Harvey Narr and Alkali Ed McGrath, was killed outright, and a third, Sam Cutnose, died of his wounds the next day in the city jail. The law lost four men and a Swede named Lindstrom got his head blowed clean off by a shotgun when he come running around the corner to see what all the noise was about. They laid that to the

Creel gang, but Bob Stonemason maintained until the day they hung him that nobody in Dutch's outfit was carrying a scattergun that day.

The laws, figuring they had a sure thing, hadn't bothered to close off the street, and in all the smoke and shouting, Dutch and Bob managed to get mounted and took off in two directions. Dick got his horse shot out from under him when he had one foot in the stirrup and Dutch, seeing his predicament, wheeled around and galloped back through all that hell and pulled him up behind his own saddle. He was shot twice for his trouble, once in the left thigh and once through the right lung.

The posse caught up with Bob, himself suffering with a slug in his back, north of El Paso, where he'd ridden under the notion that he was heading south toward the Mexican border, and arrested him without a fight. They dug the slug out of him and patched him up and sent him to the Huntsville penitentiary for life. Two years later he escaped, assembled a bunch of his own, and raised six kinds of hell throughout Texas until the Rangers pulled him out of a whorehouse in Austin and put a rope around his neck.

Dick Leaping Deer doctored Dutch's wounds as best he could and took him to a nothing ranch outside Juárez. It took an Indian to find the place, following directions provided by Dutch during his semi-lucid periods. Now, the last thing Ford Harper expected, having taken up with a woman named Juanita Flores on a tenant basis in the northwest corner of a spread the size of California, was to have his past come smack to his doorstep this way. But being Ford and therefore soft on his old *compadres,* he took them both in, and between him and Dick and Juanita they brung Dutch through a bad patch of pneumonia back to health. After a few weeks, in answer to a coded telegram sent to a trusted friend in McAlester, Henrietta come all the way from the Nations to help with the nursing.

She also brung news that I like to think helped the healing process along: She was expecting Dutch's child.

By and by, frisky with the knowledge that he was going to be a pa, Dutch made plans to go back home. Mary Treefall had sent word with Henrietta that the outlaw life was no life for a family man and that she wouldn't mind taking Dutch on as a partner in the horse-raising business, provided he held the stolen stock down to a respectable minimum. The lesson he had had in the matter of his invincibility had not been lost on him during his long convalescence. He was all fired up to give the straight life a whirl.

Dick and Henrietta wasn't so sure. For one thing, the reward for his capture since El Paso now came to twenty-five hundred dollars dead or alive, which made him a more valuable property than ever to certain of his friends and neighbors, most of whom didn't have a penny to pitch or a place to pitch it. For another, he was in no condition to travel. Dick had been able to pry the slug out of Dutch's thigh on the way from Texas, but nobody knew nothing about removing the one that had passed through his lung, so it was still inside him. Also, he was just over the pneumonia, a tricky complaint that has a sidewindy habit of bending back around and biting you just when you think it's had enough. They asked him to wait another month.

Dutch wouldn't listen, no sir. What he wanted was home. So the three of them said good-bye to Ford and Juanita and left in the buckboard Henrietta had come in on.

It wasn't no trip for a man without his strength. They had to keep to the back roads to avoid Rangers, and that made it near twice as long, especially it being December and pumphandle cold. Pretty soon Dutch took with fever. He was out of his head when they put into Nacogdoches and rented a bed in a rooming house for Dutch and Henrietta while Dick fetched a doctor. The landlady she recognized the sick man from a wanted dodger and soaked them for most of the cash they had, on account of the risk. That didn't leave them but just enough to pay the doctor, who listened to Dutch's chest and pried back his eyelids and told them they oughtn't to be wasting a medical man's time when any fool could see what they needed was a priest.

Dutch Creel fooled him, though. He lived into the next day and past sundown that evening, with Henrietta not budging from his side the whole time except to find water for to bathe his forehead when he was burning up and an extra blanket to cover him with when his teeth chattered. It was all just marking time. Dick, he poked his head in finally to see if she needed anything and found her sitting next to the bed holding Dutch's hand, and he knowed by the stillness in the room that there was a dead man in it. It was Christmas Eve, 1899.

A quiet passing, you say, for such an unquiet soul. But the story ain't finished, not by a long shot. Because right then was when Henrietta told Dick Leaping Deer about Dutch's last request.

It seemed that he had come out of his fog just long enough to make it, then shut his eyes and never said another word until Henrietta noticed he had stopped breathing. Dick, he listened, not sure at first if she was telling it true or if the tragic situation had unhinged her. By the end of it he was grinning in spite of his loss.

"Dutch," he said, "you son of a bitch."

Henrietta, who was level-headed for a woman and not one to waste time blubbering when work needed doing, agreed with Dick's assessment of the dead man's character in all its good-natured spirit. She had already made up her mind to do the thing. Dick wanted to help, but being on the run himself was forced to lie low while Henrietta went alone to the sheriff's office.

Now, Rube Belford was a good old boy to be pinned to a star. Twice a widower, he was coming up on sixty and was a deacon in the Presbyterian church who'd run a harness shop in town for twenty years before retiring to the job of peace officer. The moving picture my Addie and me seen made him out tall and rangy and kind of handsome, but he was built more along the lines of a parlor stove and ugly as a mud fence. You'd have to have made his acquaintance for at least five minutes to realize he had a heart as big as his big bald head.

But he was a businessman, and after a little haggling, he agreed to "Miz Creel's" proposition. Before locking up the office to escort her back to the rooming house, he selected a Stephens ten-gauge from among the shotguns and rifles in the rack and loaded it with double-ought buck; I seen the gun once in this little museum in Absaroka before it burned to the ground with everything inside, including an Old Sharps pistol I donated myself that Dutch used to carry around for potting rattlers with when he mended fence.

The rooming house landlady had retired for the evening. Henrietta let the sheriff in the front door quiet as a preacher's daughter saying good night to a beau and led him to the little hall bedroom where Dutch lay. Dick wasn't nowhere about, but before he left, he had got Dutch into his clothes and propped him up against the headboard of the bed with his Colt in his lap. Rube Belford, he looked over the situation and told Henrietta to take the air. Commands weren't much good with her since she was a tomboy on her daddy's farm, but she didn't want to be around for what the sheriff was fixing to do and so she obeyed. She wasn't gone two minutes when she heard the roar of that big Stephens.

Belford had never before shot a man, but he weren't nobody's fool.

He put nine double-ought slugs into the middle of Dutch's dead body, avoiding the face so no one could claim mistaken identity and cause the ranchers that put up that bounty to keep the twenty-five hundred for theirselves. Just to be sure there was no cheating done, he wired the Pinkerton office in Houston on Christmas morning, and they sent out a man to take pictures of Dutch strapped to a door for Bertillon measurements, which was a scientific process to guard against ringers.

In due course the reward was paid. Sheriff Belford gave half to Henrietta as agreed, and that money come in right handy when she went back to the Treefall spread and hired a foreman and crew and stock to run. She held a little aside for Dick Leaping Deer, but he never come to collect. You can read in your history texts what he done with a gang of his own in Texas before he went down to South America or someplace and just got swallowed up.

A month or so after the papers carried Rube Belford's hair-raising account of his shoot-out with the great desperado, he told it again to a book writer, who published it as *The True and Authentic Life of "Dutch" Creel, By His Slayer*. It went into seven printings, and Rube, who never forgot a partnership, split his share with Henrietta. I reckon that's the reason, when Dutch's son was born six months after his pa's death, she named the boy Reuben.

They're all of them gone now. The influenza took Henrietta in 1917, seven years to the day after Mary Elizabeth Treefall passed to her reward in the same house. I heard Ford Harper got himself stomped to death by a chestnut stallion on his little tenant place the day before the century turned. Nobody knows what become of Dick Leaping Deer, but it's a fair bet cannibals et him if he wasn't hung or shot by some greaser lawman down there below the Equator. And in 1905 they found Rube Belford slumped over a ledger in his office, his big old heart bust. They tell me half of Texas come out for the burying in the same cemetery where they planted the man who made him famous after the man was dead.

That there's the real story behind the death of Dutch Creel on Christmas Eve, 1899. Don't look for it in no moving picture house anytime soon.

REUBEN CREEL
Treefall Ranch, Oklahoma
March 12, 1924

Stubby Pringle's Christmas

Jack Schaefer

With the publication of his short novel, Shane, *in 1949, Jack Schaefer immediately established himself as a preeminent talent among writers of Western fiction. The books which followed—*First Blood *(1953),* The Canyon *(1953),* Company of Cowards *(1957),* Monte Walsh *(1963), and such collections as* The Big Range *(1953),* The Pioneers *(1954), and* The Kean Land *(1959)—firmly solidified his reputation. Humor both subtle and broad and a fine sense of nostalgia are prevalent in Schaefer's fiction, and in no story are these elements better combined than "Stubby Pringle's Christmas," a Yuletide farce (or is it?) that is widely regarded as one of the best of his shorter works and the best Western Christmas story yet penned.*

High on the mountainside by the little line cabin in the crisp clean dusk of evening Stubby Pringle swings into saddle. He has shape of bear in the dimness, bundled thick against cold. Double socks crowd scarred boots. Leather chaps with hair out cover patched corduroy pants. Fleece-lined jacket with wear of winters on it bulges body and heavy gloves blunt fingers. Two gay red bandannas folded together fatten throat under chin. Battered hat is pulled down to sit on ears and in side pocket of jacket are rabbit-skin earmuffs he can put to use if he needs them.

Stubby Pringle swings up into saddle. He looks out and down over worlds of snow and ice and tree and rock. He spreads arms wide and they embrace whole ranges of hills. He stretches tall and hat brushes stars in sky. He is Stubby Pringle, cowhand of the Triple X, and this is his night to howl. He is Stubby Pringle, son of the wild jackass, and he is heading for the Christmas dance at the schoolhouse in the valley.

Stubby Pringle swings up and his horse stands like rock. This is the pride of his string, flop-eared ewe-necked cat-hipped strawberry roan that looks like it should have died weeks ago but has iron rods for bones and nitroglycerin for blood and can go from here to doomsday with nothing more than mouthfuls of snow for water and tufts of winter-cured bunch-grass snatched between drifts for food. It stands like rock. It knows the folly of trying to unseat Stubby. It wastes no energy in futile explosions. It knows that twenty-seven miles of hard winter going are foreordained for this evening and twenty-seven more of harder uphill return by morning. It has done this before. It is saving the dynamite under its hide for the destiny of a true cow pony which is to take its rider where he wants to go—and bring him back again.

Stubby Pringle sits his saddle and he grins into cold and distance and future full of festivity. Join me in a look at what can be seen of him despite the bundling and frosty breath vapor that soon will hang icicles on his nose. Those are careless haphazard scrambled features under the low hat brim, about as handsome as a blue boar's snout. Not much fuzz yet on his chin. Why, shucks, is he just a boy? Don't make the mistake, though his twentieth birthday is still six weeks away. Don't make the mistake Hutch Handley made last summer when he thought this was young unseasoned stuff and took to ragging Stubby and wound up with ears pinned back and upper lip split and nose mashed flat and the whole of him dumped in a rainbarrel. Stubby has been taking care of himself since he was orphaned at thirteen. Stubby has been doing man's work since he was fifteen. Do you think Hardrock Harper of the Triple X would have anything but an all-around hard-proved hand up here at his farthest winter line camp siding Old Jake Hanlon, toughest hard-bitten old cowman ever to ride range?

Stubby Pringle slips gloved hand under rump to wipe frost off the saddle. No sense letting it melt into patches of corduroy pants. He slaps rightside saddlebag. It contains a burlap bag wrapped around a two-pound box of candy, of fancy chocolates with variegated interiors he acquired two months ago and has kept hidden from Old Jake. He slaps leftside saddlebag. It holds a burlap bag wrapped around a paper parcel that contains a close-folded piece of dress goods and a roll of pink ribbon. Interesting items, yes. They are ammunition for the campaign he has in mind to soften the affections of whichever female of the right vintage among those at the schoolhouse appeals to him most and seems most susceptible.

Stubby Pringle settles himself firmly into the saddle. He is just another of far-scattered poorly-paid patched-clothes cowhands that inhabit these parts and likely marks and smells of his calling have not all been scrubbed away. He knows that. But this is his night to howl. He is Stubby Pringle, true-begotten son of the wildest jackass, and he has been riding line through hell and high water and winter storms for two months without a break and he has done his share of the work and more than his share because Old Jake is getting along and slowing some and this is his night to stomp floorboards till schoolhouse shakes and kick heels up to lanterns above and whirl a willing female till she is dizzy enough to see past patched clothes to the man inside them. He wriggles toes deep into stirrups and settles himself firmly in the saddle.

"I could of et them choc'lates," says Old Jake from the cabin doorway. "They wasn't hid good," he says. "No good at all."

"An' be beat like a drum," says Stubby. "An' wrung out like a dirty dishrag."

"By who?" says Old Jake. "By a young un like you? Why, I'd of tied you in knots afore you knew what's what iffen you tried it. You're a dang-blatted young fool," he says. "A ding-busted dang-blatted fool. Riding out a night like this iffen it is Chris'mas eve. A dong-bonging ding-busted dang-blatted fool," he says. "But iffen I was your age again, I reckon I'd be doing it too." He cackles like an old rooster. "Squeeze one of 'em for me," he says and he steps back inside and he closes the door.

Stubby Pringle is alone out there in the darkening dusk, alone with flop-eared ewe-necked cat-hipped roan that can go to the last trumpet call under him and with cold of wicked winter wind around him and with twenty-seven miles of snow-dumped distance ahead of him. "Wahoo!" he yells. "Skip to my Loo!" he shouts. "Do-si-do and round about!"

He lifts reins and the roan sighs and lifts feet. At easy warming-up amble they drop over the edge of benchland where the cabin snugs into tall pines and on down the great bleak expanse of mountainside.

Stubby Pringle, spurs a jingle, jogs upslope through crusted snow. The roan, warmed through, moves strong and steady under him. Line cabin and line work are far forgotten things back and back and up and up the mighty mass of mountain. He is Stubby Pringle, rooting tooting hard-working hard-playing cowhand of the Triple X, heading for the Christmas dance at the schoolhouse in the valley.

He tops out on one of the lower ridges. He pulls rein to give the roan a breather. He brushes an icicle off his nose. He leans forward and reaches to brush several more off sidebars of old bit in the bridle. He straightens tall. Far ahead, over top of last and lowest ridge, on into the valley, he can see tiny specks of glowing allure that are school-house windows. Light and gaiety and good liquor and fluttering skirts are there. "Wahoo!" he yells. "Gals an' women an' grandmothers!" he shouts. "Raise your skirts and start askipping! I'm acoming!"

He slaps spurs to roan. It leaps like mountain lion, out and down, full into hard gallop downslope, rushing, reckless of crusted drifts and ice-coated bush-branches slapping at them. He is Stubby Pringle, born with spurs on, nursed on tarantula juice, weaned on rawhide, at home in the saddle of a hurricane in shape of horse that can race to outer edge of eternity and back, heading now for high-jinks two months overdue. He is ten feet tall and the horse is gigantic, with wings, iron-boned and dynamite-fueled, soaring in forty-foot leaps down the flank of the whitened wonder of a winter world.

They slow at the bottom. They stop. They look up the rise of the last low ridge ahead. The roan paws frozen ground and snorts twin plumes of frosty vapor. Stubby reaches around to pull down fleece-lined jacket that has worked a bit up back. He pats rightside saddle-bag. He pats leftside saddlebag. He lifts reins to soar up and over last low ridge.

Hold it, Stubby. What is that? Off to the right.

He listens. He has ears that can catch snitch of mouse chewing on chunk of bacon rind beyond the log wall by his bunk. He hears. Sound of ax striking wood.

What kind of dong-bonging ding-busted dang-blatted fool would be chopping wood on a night like this and on Christmas Eve and with a dance underway at the schoolhouse in the valley? What kind of chopping is this anyway? Uneven in rhythm, feeble in stroke. Trust Stubby Pringle, who has chopped wood enough for cook stove and fireplace to fill a long freight train, to know how an ax should be handled.

There. That does it. That whopping sound can only mean that the blade has hit at an angle and bounced away without biting. Some dong-bonged ding-busted dang-blatted fool is going to be cutting off some of his own toes.

He pulls the roan around to the right. He is Stubby Pringle, born to tune of bawling bulls and blatting calves, branded at birth, cowman raised and cowman to the marrow, and no true cowman rides on without stopping to check anything strange on range. Roan chomps on bit, annoyed at interruption. It remembers who is in saddle. It sighs and obeys. They move quietly in dark of night past boles of trees jet black against dim grayness of crusted snow on ground. Light shows faintly ahead. Lantern light through a small oiled-paper window.

Yes. Of course. Just where it has been for eight months now. The Henderson place. Man and woman and small girl and waist-high boy. Homesteaders. Not even fools, homesteaders. Worse than that. Out of their minds altogether. All of them. Out here anyway. Betting the government they can stave off starving for five years in exchange for one hundred sixty acres of land. Land that just might be able to support seven jackrabbits and two coyotes and nine rattlesnakes and maybe all of four thin steers to a whole section. In a good year. Homesteaders. Always out of almost everything, money and food and tools and smiles and joy of living. Everything. Except maybe hope and stubborn endurance.

Stubby Pringle nudges the reluctant roan along. In patch-light from the window by a tangled pile of dead tree branches he sees a woman. Her face is gray and pinched and tired. An old stocking-cap is pulled down on her head. Ragged man's jacket bumps over long woolsey dress and clogs arms as she tries to wing an ax into a good-sized branch on the ground.

Whopping sound and ax bounces and barely misses an ankle.

"Quit that!" says Stubby, sharp. He swings the roan in close. He looks down at her. She drops ax and backs away, frightened. She is ready to bolt into two-room bark-slab shack. She looks up. She sees that haphazard scrambled features under low hat brim are crinkled in what could be a grin. She relaxes some, hand on door latch.

"Ma'am," says Stubby. "You trying to cripple yourself?" She just stares at him. "Man's work," he says. "Where's your man?"

"Inside," she says; then, quick, "he's sick."

"Bad?" says Stubby.

"Was," she says. "Doctor that was here this morning thinks he'll be all right now. Only he's almighty weak. All wobbly. Sleeps most of the time."

"Sleeps," says Stubby, indignant. "When there's wood to be chopped."

"He's been almighty tired," she says, quick, defensive. "Even afore he was took sick. Wore out." She is rubbing cold hands together, trying to warm them. "He tried," she says, proud. "Only a while ago. Couldn't even get his pants on. Just fell flat on the floor."

Stubby looks down at her. "An' you ain't tired?" he says.

"I ain't got time to be tired," she says. "Not with all I got to do."

Stubby Pringle looks off past dark boles of trees at last row ridge-top that hides valley and schoolhouse. "I reckon I could spare a bit of time," he says. "Likely they ain't much more'n started yet," he says. He looks again at the woman. He sees gray pinched face. He sees cold-shivering under bumpy jacket, "Ma'am," he says. "Get on in there an' warm your gizzard some. I'll just chop you a bit of wood."

Roan stands with dropping reins, ground-tied, disgusted. It shakes head to send icicles tinkling from bit and bridle. Stopped in midst of epic run, wind-eating, mile-gobbling, iron-boned and dynamite-fueled, and for what? For silly chore of chopping.

Fifteen feet away Stubby Pringle chops wood. Moon is rising over last low ridgetop and its light, filtered through trees, shines on leaping blade. He is Stubby Pringle, moonstruck maverick of the Triple X, born with ax in hands, with strength of stroke in muscles, weaned on whetstone, fed on cordwood, raised to fell whole forests. He is ten feet tall and ax is enormous in moonlight and chips fly like stormflakes of snow and blade slices through branches thick as his arm, through logs thick as his thigh.

He leans ax against a stump and he spreads arms wide and he scoops up whole cords at a time and strides to door and kicks it open. . . .

Both corners of front room by fireplace are piled full now, floor to ceiling, good wood, stout wood, seasoned wood, wood enough for a whole wicked winter week. Chore done and done right, Stubby looks around him. Fire is burning bright and well-fed, working on warmth. Man lies on big old bed along opposite wall, blanket over, eyes closed, face gray-pale, snoring long and slow. Woman fusses with something at old woodstove. Stubby steps to doorway to backroom. He pulls aside hanging cloth. Faint in dimness inside he sees two low bunks and in one, under an old quilt, a curly-headed small girl and in the other, under the old quilt, a boy who would be waist-high awake and standing. He sees them still and quiet, sleeping sound. "Cute little devils," he says.

He turns back and the woman is coming toward him, cup of coffee in hand, strong and hot and steaming. Coffee the kind to warm the throat and gizzard of chore-doing hard-chopping cowhand on a cold cold night. He takes the cup and raises it to his lips. Drains it in two gulps. "Thank you, ma'am," he says. "That was right kindly of you." He sets cup on table. "I got to be getting along," he says. He starts toward outer door.

He stops, hands on door latch. Something is missing in two-room shack. Trust Stubby Pringle to know what. "Where's your tree?" he says. "Kids got to have a Christmas tree."

He sees the woman sink down on chair. He hears a sigh come from her. "I ain't had time to cut one," she says.

"I reckon not," says Stubby. "Man's job anyway," he says. "I'll get it for you. Won't take a minute. Then I got to be going."

He strides out. He scoops up ax and strides off, upslope some where small pines climb. He stretches tall and his legs lengthen and he towers huge among trees swinging with ten-foot steps. He is Stubby Pringle, born an expert on Christmas trees, nursed on pine needles, weaned on pine cones, raised with an eye for size and shape and symmetry. There. A beauty. Perfect. Grown for this and for nothing else. Ax blade slices keen and swift. Tree topples. He strides back with tree on shoulder. He rips leather whangs from his saddle and lashes two pieces of wood to tree bottom, crosswise, so tree can stand upright again.

Stubby Pringle strides into shack, carrying tree. He sets it up, center of front-room floor, and it stands straight, trim and straight, perky and proud and pointed. "There you are, ma'am," he says. "Get your things out an' start decorating. I got to be going." He moves toward outer door.

He stops in outer doorway. He hears the sigh behind him. "We got no things," she says. "I was figuring to buy some but sickness took the money."

Stubby Pringle looks off at last low ridge-top hiding valley and schoolhouse. "Reckon I still got a bit of time," he says. "They'll be whooping it mighty late." He turns back, closing door. He sheds hat and gloves and bandannas and jacket. He moves about checking every-thing in the sparse front room. He asks for things and the woman jumps to get those few of them she has. He tells her what to do and she does. He does plenty himself. With this and with that magic wonders arrive. He is Stubby Pringle, born to poverty and hard work, weaned on nothing, fed on less, raised to make do with least possible and make the most of that. Pinto beans strung on thread brighten tree in firelight and lantern light like strings of store-bought beads. Strips of one bandanna, cut with shears from sewing-box, bob in bows on branch-ends like gray red flowers. Snippets of fleece from jacket-lining sprinkled over tree glisten like fresh fall of snow. Miracles flow from strong blunt fingers through bits of old paper-bags and dabs of flour paste into link chains and twisted small streamers and two jaunty little hats and two smart little boats with sails.

"Got to finish it right," says Stubby Pringle. From strong blunt fin-gers comes five-pointed star, triple-thickness to make it stiff, twisted bit of old wire to hold it upright. He fastens this to topmost tip of topmost bough. He wraps lone bandanna left around throat and jams battered hat on head and shrug into now-skimpy-lined jacket. "A right nice little tree," he says. "All you got to do now is get out what you got for the kids and put it under. I really got to be going." He starts toward outer door.

He stops in open doorway. He hears the sigh behind him. He knows without looking around the woman has slumped into old rocking chair. "We ain't got anything for them," she says. "Only now this tree. Which I don't mean it isn't a fine grand tree. It's more'n we'd of had 'cept for you."

Stubby Pringle stands in open doorway looking out into cold clean moonlit night. Somehow he knows without turning head two tears are sliding down thin pinched cheeks. "You go on along," she says. "They're good young uns. They know how it is. They ain't expecting a thing."

Stubby Pringle stands in doorway looking out at last ridge-top that hides valley and schoolhouse. "All the more reason," he says soft to himself. "All the more reason something should be there when they wake." He sighs too. "I'm a dong-bonging ding-busted dang-blatted fool," he says. "But I reckon I still got a mite more time. Likely they'll be sashaying around till it's most morning."

Stubby Pringle strides on out, leaving door open. He strides back, closing door with heel behind him. In one hand he has burlap bag wrapped around paper parcel. In other hand he has squarish chunk of good pine wood. He tosses bag-parcel into lap-folds of woman's apron.

"Unwrap it," he says. "There's the makings for a right cute dress for the girl. Needle-and-threader like you can whip it up in no time. I'll just whittle me out a little something for the boy."

Moon is high in cold cold sky. Frosty clouds drift up there with it. Tiny flakes of snow float through upper air. Down below by a two-room shack droops a disgusted cow pony roan, ground-tied, drooping like statue snow-crusted. It is accepting the inescapable destiny of its kind which is to wait for its rider, to conserve deep-bottomed dyna-mite energy, to be ready to race to the last margin of motion when waiting is done.

Inside the shack fire in fireplace cheerily gobbles wood, good wood, stout wood, seasoned wood, warming two-rooms well. Man lies on bed, turned on side, curled up some, snoring slow and steady. Woman sits in rocking chair, sewing. Her head nods slow and drowsy and her eyelids sag weary but her fingers fly, stitch-stitch-stitch. A dress has shaped under her hands, small and flounced and with little puff-sleeves, fine dress, fancy dress, dress for smiles and joy of living. She is sewing pink ribbon around collar and down front and into fluffy bow on back.

On a stool nearby sits Stubby Pringle, piece of good pine wood in one hand, knife in other hand, fine knife, splendid knife, all-around-accomplished knife, knife he always has with him, seven-bladed knife with four for cutting from little to big and corkscrew and can opener and screwdriver. Big cutting blade has done its work. Little cutting blade is in use now. He is Stubby Pringle, born with feel for knives in hand, weaned on emery wheel, fed on shavings, raised to whittle his way through the world. Tiny chips fly and shavings flutter. There in his hands, out of good pine wood, something is shaping. A horse. Yes. Flop-eared ewe-necked cat-hipped horse. Flop-eared head is high on ewe neck, stretched out, sniffing wind, snorting into distance. Cat-hips are hunched forward, caught in crouch for forward leap. It is a horse fit to carry a waist-high boy to uttermost edge of eternity and back.

Stubby Pringle carves swift and sure. Little cutting blade makes final little cutting snitches. Yes. Tiny mottlings and markings make no mistaking. It is a strawberry roan. He closes knife and puts it in pocket. He looks up. Dress is finished in woman's lap. But woman's head has dropped down in exhaustion. She sits slumped deep in rocking chair and she too snores slow and steady.

Stubby Pringle stands up. He takes dress and puts it under tree, fine dress, fancy dress, dress waiting now for small girl to wake and wear it with smiles and joy of living. He sets wooden horse beside it, fine horse, proud horse, snorting-into-distance horse, cat-hips crouched, waiting now for waist-high boy to wake and ride it around the world.

Quietly he piles wood on fire and banks ashes around to hold it for morning. Quietly he pulls on hat and wraps bandanna around and shrugs into skimpy-lined jacket. He looks at old rocking chair and tired woman slumped in it. He strides to outer door and out, leaving door open. He strides back, closing door with heel behind. He carries other burlap bag wrapped around box of candy, of fine chocolates, fancy chocolates with variegated interiors. Gently he lays this in lap of woman. Gently he takes big old shawl from wall nail and lays this over her. He stands by big old bed and looks down at snoring man. "Poor devil," he says. "Ain't fair to forget him." He takes knife from pocket, fine knife, seven-bladed knife, and lays this on blanket on bed. He picks up gloves and blows out lantern and swift as sliding moon shadow he is gone.

High high up frosty clouds scuttle across face of moon. Wind whips through topmost tips of tall pines. What is it that hurtles like hurricane far down there on upslope of last low ridge, scattering drifts, smashing through brush, snorting defiance at distance? It is flop-eared ewe-necked cat-hipped roan, iron-boned and dynamite-fueled, ramming full gallop through the dark of night. Firm in saddle is Stubby Pringle, spurs ajingle, toes atingle, out on prowl, ready to howl, heading for the dance at the schoolhouse in the valley. He is ten feet tall, great as a grizzly, and the roan is gigantic, with wings, soaring upward in thirty-foot leaps. They top out and roan rears high, pawing stars out of sky, and drops down, cat-hip hunched for fresh leap out and down.

Hold it, Stubby. Hold hard on reins. Do you see what is happening on out there in the valley?

Tiny lights that are schoolhouse windows are winking out. Tiny dark shapes moving about are horsemen riding off, are wagons pulling away.

Moon is dropping down the sky, haloed in frosty mist. Dark gray clouds dip and swoop around sweep of horizon. Cold winds weave rustling through ice-coated bushes and trees. What is that moving slow and lonesome up snow-covered mountainside? It is a flop-eared ewe-necked cat-hipped roan, just that, nothing more, small cow pony, worn and weary, taking its rider back to clammy bunk in cold line cabin. Slumped in saddle is Stubby Pringle, head down, shoulders sagged. He is just another of far-scattered poorly paid patched-clothes cowhands who inhabit these parts. Just that. And something more. He is the biggest thing there is in the whole wide roster of the human race. He is a man who has given of himself, of what little he has and is, to bring smiles and joy of living to others along his way.

He jogs along, slump-sagged in saddle, thinking of none of this. He is thinking of dances undanced, of floorboards unstomped, of willing women left unwhirled.

He jogs along, half-asleep in saddle, and he is thinking now of bygone Christmas seasons and of a boy born to poverty and hard work and made-do poring in flicker of firelight over ragged old Christmas picturebook. And suddenly he hears something. The tinkle of sleigh bells.

Sleigh bells?

Yes. I am telling this straight. He and roan are weaving through thick-clumped brush. Winds are sighing high overhead and on up the mountainside and lower down here they are whipping mists and snow flurries all around him. He can see nothing in mystic moving dimness. But he can hear. The tinkle of sleigh bells, faint but clear, ghostly but unmistakable. And suddenly he sees something. Movement off to the left. Swift as wind, glimmers only through brush and mist and whirling snow, but unmistakable again. Antlered heads high, frosty breath streaming, bodies rushing swift and silent, floating in flash of movement past, seeming to leap in air alone needing no touch of ground beneath. Reindeer? Yes. Reindeer strong and silent and fleet out of some far frozen northland marked on no map. Reindeer swooping down and leaping past and rising again and away, strong and effortless and fleeting. And with them, hard on their heels, almost lost in swirling snow mist of their passing, vague and formless but there, something big and bulky with runners like sleigh and flash of white beard whipping in wind and crack of long whip snapping.

Startled roan has seen something too. It stands rigid, head up, staring left and forward. Stubby Pringle, body atingle, stares too. Out of dark of night ahead, mingle with moan of wind, comes a long-drawn chuckle, deep deep chuckle, jolly and cheery and full of smiles and joy of living. And with it long-drawn words.

We-e-e-l-l-l do-o-o-ne . . . pa-a-a-artner!

Stubby Pringle shakes his head. He brushes an icicle from his nose. "An' I didn't have a single drink," he says. "Only coffee an' can't count that. Reckon I'm getting soft in the head." But he is cowman through and through, cowman through to the marrow. He can't ride on without stopping to check anything strange on his range. He swings down and leads off to the left. He fumbles in jacket pocket and finds a match. Strikes it. Holds it cupped and bends down. There they are. Unmistakable. Reindeer tracks.

Stubby Pringle stretches up tall. Stubby Pringle swings into saddle. Roan needs no slap of spurs to unleash strength in upward surge, up up up steep mountainside. It knows. There in saddle once more is Stubby Pringle, moonstruck maverick of the Triple X, all-around hard-proved hard-honed cowhand, ten feet tall, needing horse gigantic, with wings, iron-boned and dynamite-fueled, to take him home to little line cabin and some few winks of sleep before another day's hard work. . . .

Stubby Pringle slips into cold clammy bunk. He wriggles vigorous to warm blanket under and blanket over.

"Was it worth all that riding?" comes voice of Old Jake Hanlon from other bunk on other wall.

"Why, sure," says Stubby. "I had me a right good time."

All right, now. Say anything you want. I know, you know, any dong-bonged ding-busted dang-blatted fool ought to know, that icicles breaking off branches can sound to drowsy ears something like sleigh bells. That blurry eyes half-asleep can see strange things. That deer and elk make tracks like those of reindeer. That wind sighing and soughing and moaning and maundering down mountains and through piny treetops can sound like someone shaping words. But we could talk and talk and it would mean nothing to Stubby Pringle.

Stubby is wiser than we are. He knows, he will always know, who it was, plump and jolly and belly-bouncing, that spoke to him that night out on wind-whipped winter-worn mountainside.

We-e-e-l-l-l do-o-o-ne . . . pa-a-a-rt-ner!

ACKNOWLEDGMENTS

"Three Yuletide Poems" by S. Omar Barker. "Draggin' In the Tree": Copyright © 1945 by Street & Smith Publications, Inc. First published in *Western Story.* "Bunkhouse Christmas": Copyright © 1967 by Grosset & Dunlap. First published in *The Cattleman's Steak Book* by Carol Truax and S. Omar Barker. "A Cowboy's Christmas Prayer": Copyright © 1968 by S. Omar Barker. From *Rawhide Rhymes* by S. Omar Barker. Reprinted by permission of the estate of S. Omar Barker.

"Standing Alone in the Darkness" by Arthur Winfield Knight. Copyright © 1990 by Arthur Winfield Knight. An original story published by permission of the author.

"Winter Harvest" by John Prescott. Copyright © 1965 by The Western Writers of America. Revised version copyright © 1990 by John Prescott. Reprinted by permission of the author and Scott Meredith Literary Agency, Inc., 845 Third Avenue, New York, N.Y. 10022.

"Mainwaring's Gift" by Ed Gorman. Copyright © 1990 by Ed Gorman. An original story published by permission of the author.

"Christmas Eve in San Augustine" by Edward D. Hoch. Copyright © 1990 by Edward D. Hoch. An original story published by permission of the author.

"No Room at the Inn" by Bill Pronzini. Copyright © 1988 by Bill Pronzini. Reprinted by permission of the author.

"The Death of Dutch Creel" by Loren D. Estleman. Copyright © 1990 by Loren D. Estleman. An original story published by permission of the author.

"Stubby Pringle's Christmas" by Jack Schaefer. Copyright © 1966 by Jack Schaefer. From *The Collected Stories of Jack Schaefer.* Reprinted by permission of Houghton Mifflin Company.